THE ROOM IN THE TOWER

That dream or variations upon it occurred to me intermittently for fifteen years. Most often it came in exactly this form: the arrival, the tea laid out on the lawn, the deadly silence succeeded by that one deadly sentence, the mounting with Jack Stone up to the room in the tower where horror dwelt . . . A young man is plagued by a recurring nightmare — though the characters within it gradually age and disappear over the years, the vision invariably culminates in a moment of unspeakable terror. And when he visits the home of his friend John, he is confronted with the house from his dream . . .

E. F. BENSON

THE ROOM IN THE TOWER
and Other Stories

Complete and Unabridged

ULVERSCROFT
Leicester

First published in Great Britain in 1912

This Large Print Edition
published 2018

A catalogue record for this book is available
from the British Library.

ISBN 978–1–4448–3626–4

Published by
F. A. Thorpe (Publishing)
Anstey, Leicestershire

Set by Words & Graphics Ltd.
Anstey, Leicestershire
Printed and bound in Great Britain by
T. J. International Ltd., Padstow, Cornwall

This book is printed on acid-free paper

Contents

Contents

The Room in the Tower

It is probable that everybody who is at all a constant dreamer has had at least one experience of an event or a sequence of circumstances which have come to his mind in sleep being subsequently realized in the material world. But, in my opinion, so far from this being a strange thing, it would be far odder if this fulfilment did not occasionally happen, since our dreams are, as a rule, concerned with people whom we know and places with which we are familiar, such as might very naturally occur in the awake and daylit world. True, these dreams are often broken into by some absurd and fantastic incident, which puts them out of court in regard to their subsequent fulfilment, but on the mere calculation of chances, it does not appear in the least unlikely that a dream imagined by anyone who dreams constantly should occasionally come true. Not long ago, for instance, I experienced such a fulfilment of a dream which seems to me in no way remarkable and to have no kind of psychical significance. The manner of it was as follows.

A certain friend of mine, living abroad, is

amiable enough to write to me about once in a fortnight. Thus, when fourteen days or thereabouts have elapsed since I last heard from him, my mind, probably, either consciously or subconsciously, is expectant of a letter from him. One night last week I dreamed that as I was going upstairs to dress for dinner I heard, as I often heard, the sound of the postman's knock on my front door, and diverted my direction downstairs instead. There, among other correspondence, was a letter from him. Thereafter the fantastic entered, for on opening it I found inside the ace of diamonds, and scribbled across it in his well-known handwriting, 'I am sending you this for safe custody, as you know it is running an unreasonable risk to keep aces in Italy.' The next evening I was just preparing to go upstairs to dress when I heard the postman's knock, and did precisely as I had done in my dream. There, among other letters, was one from my friend. Only it did not contain the ace of diamonds. Had it done so, I should have attached more weight to the matter, which, as it stands, seems to me a perfectly ordinary coincidence. No doubt I consciously or subconsciously expected a letter from him, and this suggested to me my dream. Similarly, the fact that my friend had not written to me for a fortnight suggested to

4

him that he should do so. But occasionally it is not so easy to find such an explanation, and for the following story I can find no explanation at all. It came out of the dark, and into the dark it has gone again.

All my life I have been a habitual dreamer: the nights are few, that is to say, when I do not find on awaking in the morning that some mental experience has been mine, and sometimes, all night long, apparently, a series of the most dazzling adventures befall me. Almost without exception these adventures are pleasant, though often merely trivial. It is of an exception that I am going to speak.

It was when I was about sixteen that a certain dream first came to me, and this is how it befell. It opened with my being set down at the door of a big red-brick house, where, I understood, I was going to stay. The servant who opened the door told me that tea was being served in the garden, and led me through a low dark-panelled hall, with a large open fireplace, on to a cheerful green lawn set round with flower beds. There were grouped about the tea-table a small party of people, but they were all strangers to me except one, who was a schoolfellow called Jack Stone, clearly the son of the house, and he introduced me to his mother and father and a couple of sisters. I was, I remember,

5

somewhat astonished to find myself here, for the boy in question was scarcely known to me, and I rather disliked what I knew of him; moreover, he had left school nearly a year before. The afternoon was very hot, and an intolerable oppression reigned. On the far side of the lawn ran a red-brick wall, with an iron gate in its centre, outside which stood a walnut tree. We sat in the shadow of the house opposite a row of long windows, inside which I could see a table with cloth laid, glimmering with glass and silver. This garden front of the house was very long, and at one end of it stood a tower of three stories, which looked to me much older than the rest of the building.

Before long, Mrs. Stone, who, like the rest of the party, had sat in absolute silence, said to me, 'Jack will show you your room: I have given you the room in the tower.'

Quite inexplicably my heart sank at her words. I felt as if I had known that I should have the room in the tower, and that it contained something dreadful and significant. Jack instantly got up, and I understood that I had to follow him. In silence we passed through the hall, and mounted a great oak staircase with many corners, and arrived at a small landing with two doors set in it. He pushed one of these open for me to enter, and without coming in himself, closed it after me. Then I knew that my conjecture had been right: there was something awful in the room, and with the terror of nightmare growing swiftly and enveloping me, I awoke in a spasm of terror.

Now that dream or variations on it occurred to me intermittently for fifteen years. Most often it came in exactly this form: the arrival, the tea laid out on the lawn, the deadly silence succeeded by that one deadly sentence, the mounting with Jack Stone up to the room in the tower where horror dwelt, and it always came to a close in the nightmare of terror at that which was in the room, though I never saw what it was. At other times I experienced variations on this same theme. Occasionally, for instance, we would be sitting at dinner in the dining-room, into the windows of which I had looked on the first night when the dream of this house visited me, but wherever we were, there was the same silence, the same sense of dreadful oppression and foreboding. And the silence I knew would always be broken by Mrs. Stone saying to me, 'Jack will show you your room: I have given you the room in the tower.' Upon which (this was invariable) I had to follow him up the oak staircase with many corners, and enter the place that I dreaded more and more each time that I visited it in sleep. Or, again, I would find myself playing cards still in silence in a drawing-room lit with immense chandeliers, that gave a blinding illumination. What the game was I have no idea; what I remember, with a sense of miserable anticipation, was that soon Mrs. Stone would get up and say to me, 'Jack will show you your room: I have given you the room in the tower.' This drawing-room where we played cards was next to the dining-room, and, as I have said, was always brilliantly illuminated, whereas the rest of the house was full of dusk and shadows. And yet, how often, in spite of those bouquets of lights, have I not pored over the cards that were dealt me, scarcely able for some reason to see them. Their designs, too, were strange: there were no red suits, but all were black, and among them there were certain cards which were black all over. I hated and dreaded those.

As this dream continued to recur, I got to know the greater part of the house. There was a smoking-room beyond the drawing-room, at the end of a passage with a green baize door. It was always very dark there, and as often as I went there I passed somebody whom I could not see in the doorway coming out. Curious developments, too, took place in the characters that peopled the dream as

8

might happen to living persons. Mrs. Stone, for instance, who, when I first saw her, had been black-haired, became grey, and instead of rising briskly, as she had done at first when she said, 'Jack will show you your room: I have given you the room in the tower,' got up very feebly, as if the strength was leaving her limbs. Jack also grew up, and became a rather ill-looking young man, with a brown moustache, while one of the sisters ceased to appear, and I understood she was married.

Then it so happened that I was not visited by this dream for six months or more, and I began to hope, in such inexplicable dread did I hold it, that it had passed away for good. But one night after this interval I again found myself being shown out onto the lawn for tea, and Mrs. Stone was not there, while the others were all dressed in black. At once I guessed the reason, and my heart leaped at the thought that perhaps this time I should not have to sleep in the room in the tower, and though we usually all sat in silence, on this occasion the sense of relief made me talk and laugh as I had never yet done. But even then matters were not altogether comfortable, for no one else spoke, but they all looked secretly at each other. And soon the foolish stream of my talk ran dry, and gradually an apprehension worse than anything I had previously known gained on me as the light slowly faded.

Suddenly a voice which I knew well broke the stillness, the voice of Mrs. Stone, saying, 'Jack will show you your room: I have given you the room in the tower.' It seemed to come from near the gate in the red-brick wall that bounded the lawn, and looking up, I saw that the grass outside was sown thick with gravestones. A curious greyish light shone from them, and I could read the lettering on the grave nearest me, and it was, 'In evil memory of Julia Stone.' And as usual Jack got up, and again I followed him through the hall and up the staircase with many corners. On this occasion it was darker than usual, and when I passed into the room in the tower I could only just see the furniture, the position of which was already familiar to me. Also there was a dreadful odour of decay in the room, and I woke screaming.

The dream, with such variations and developments as I have mentioned, went on at intervals for fifteen years. Sometimes I would dream it two or three nights in succession; once, as I have said, there was an intermission of six months, but taking a reasonable average, I should say that I dreamed it quite as often as once in a month. It had, as is plain, something of nightmare about it, since it always ended in the same appalling terror, which so far from getting less, seemed to me to gather fresh fear every time that I experienced it. There was, too, a strange and dreadful consistency about it. The characters in it, as I have mentioned, got regularly older, death and marriage visited this silent family, and I never in the dream, after Mrs. Stone had died, set eyes on her again. But it was always her voice that told me that the room in the tower was prepared for me, and whether we had tea out on the lawn, or the scene was laid in one of the rooms overlooking it, I could always see her gravestone standing just outside the iron gate. It was the same, too, with the married daughter; usually she was not present, but once or twice she returned again, in company with a man, whom I took to be her husband. He, too, like the rest of them, was always silent. But, owing to the constant repetition of the dream, I had ceased to attach, in my waking hours, any significance to it. I never met Jack Stone again during all those years, nor did I ever see a house that resembled this dark house of my dream. And then something happened.

I had been in London in this year, up till the end of the July, and during the first week in August went down to stay with a friend in a house he had taken for the summer months, in the Ashdown Forest district of Sussex. I left London early, for John Clinton was to meet me at Forest Row Station, and we were going to spend the day golfing, and go to his house in the evening. He had his motor with him, and we set off, about five of the afternoon, after a thoroughly delightful day, for the drive, the distance being some ten miles. As it was still so early we did not have tea at the club house, but waited till we should get home. As we drove, the weather, which up till then had been, though hot, deliciously fresh, seemed to me to alter in quality, and become very stagnant and oppressive, and I felt that indefinable sense of ominous apprehension that I am accustomed to before thunder. John, however, did not share my views, attributing my loss of lightness to the fact that I had lost both my matches. Events proved, however, that I was right, though I do not think that the thunderstorm that broke that night was the sole cause of my depression.

Our way lay through deep high-banked lanes, and before we had gone very far I fell asleep, and was only awakened by the stopping of the motor. And with a sudden thrill, partly of fear but chiefly of curiosity, I found myself standing in the doorway of my house of dream. We went, I half wondering whether or not I was dreaming still, through a low oak-panelled hall, and out onto the lawn, where tea was laid in the shadow of the house. It was set in flower beds, a red-brick wall, with a gate in it, bounded one side, and out beyond that was a space of rough grass with a walnut tree. The facade of the house was very long, and at one end stood a three-storied tower, markedly older than the rest.

Here for the moment all resemblance to the repeated dream ceased. There was no silent and somehow terrible family, but a large assembly of exceedingly cheerful persons, all of whom were known to me. And in spite of the horror with which the dream itself had always filled me, I felt nothing of it now that the scene of it was thus reproduced before me. But I felt intensest curiosity as to what was going to happen.

Tea pursued its cheerful course, and before long Mrs. Clinton got up. And at that moment I think I knew what she was going to say. She spoke to me, and what she said was:

'Jack will show you your room: I have given you the room in the tower.'

At that, for half a second, the horror of the dream took hold of me again. But it quickly passed, and again I felt nothing more than the most intense curiosity. It was not very long before it was amply satisfied.

John turned to me.

'Right up at the top of the house,' he said, 'but I think you'll be comfortable. We're absolutely full up. Would you like to go and see it now? By Jove, I believe that you are right, and that we are going to have a thunderstorm. How dark it has become.'

I got up and followed him. We passed through the hall, and up the perfectly familiar staircase. Then he opened the door, and I went in. And at that moment sheer unreasoning terror again possessed me. I did not know what I feared: I simply feared. Then like a sudden recollection, when one remembers a name which has long escaped the memory, I knew what I feared. I feared Mrs. Stone, whose grave with the sinister inscription, 'In evil memory,' I had so often seen in my dream, just beyond the lawn which lay below my window. And then once more the fear passed so completely that I wondered what there was to fear, and I found myself, sober and quiet and sane, in the room in the tower, the name of which I had so often heard in my dream, and the scene of which was so familiar.

I looked around it with a certain sense of proprietorship, and found that nothing had been changed from the dreaming nights in which I knew it so well. Just to the left of the door was the bed, lengthways along the wall, with the head of it in the angle. In a line with it was the fireplace and a small bookcase; opposite the door the outer wall was pierced by two lattice-paned windows, between which stood the dressing-table, while ranged along the fourth wall was the washing-stand and a big cupboard. My luggage had already been unpacked, for the furniture of dressing and undressing lay orderly on the wash-stand and toilet-table, while my dinner clothes were spread out on the coverlet of the bed. And then, with a sudden start of unexplained dismay, I saw that there were two rather conspicuous objects which I had not seen before in my dreams: one a life-sized oil painting of Mrs. Stone, the other a black-and-white sketch of Jack Stone, representing him as he had appeared to me only a week before in the last of the series of these repeated dreams, a rather secret and evil-looking man of about thirty. His picture hung between the windows, looking straight across the room to the other portrait, which hung at the side of the bed. At that I looked next, and as I looked I felt once more the horror of nightmare seize me.

It represented Mrs. Stone as I had seen her

last in my dreams: old and withered and white-haired. But in spite of the evident feebleness of body, a dreadful exuberance and vitality shone through the envelope of flesh, an exuberance wholly malign, a vitality that foamed and frothed with unimaginable evil. Evil beamed from the narrow, leering eyes; it laughed in the demon-like mouth. The whole face was instinct with some secret and appalling mirth; the hands, clasped together on the knee, seemed shaking with suppressed and nameless glee. Then I saw also that it was signed in the left-hand bottom corner, and wondering who the artist could be, I looked more closely, and read the inscription, 'Julia Stone by Julia Stone.'

There came a tap at the door, and John Clinton entered.

'Got everything you want?' he asked.

'Rather more than I want,' said I, pointing to the picture.

He laughed.

'Hard-featured old lady,' he said. 'By herself, too, I remember. Anyhow she can't have flattered herself much.'

'But don't you see?' said I. 'It's scarcely a human face at all. It's the face of some witch, of some devil.'

He looked at it more closely.

'Yes; it isn't very pleasant,' he said.

16

'Scarcely a bedside manner, eh? Yes; I can imagine getting the nightmare if I went to sleep with that close by my bed. I'll have it taken down if you like.'

'I really wish you would,' I said. He rang the bell, and with the help of a servant we detached the picture and carried it out onto the landing, and put it with its face to the wall.

'By Jove, the old lady is a weight,' said John, mopping his forehead. 'I wonder if she had something on her mind.'

The extraordinary weight of the picture had struck me too. I was about to reply, when I caught sight of my own hand. There was blood on it, in considerable quantities, covering the whole palm.

'I've cut myself somehow,' said I.

John gave a little startled exclamation.

'Why, I have too,' he said.

Simultaneously the footman took out his handkerchief and wiped his hand with it. I saw that there was blood also on his handkerchief.

John and I went back into the tower room and washed the blood off; but neither on his hand nor on mine was there the slightest trace of a scratch or cut. It seemed to me that, having ascertained this, we both, by a sort of tacit consent, did not allude to it again. Something in my case had dimly occurred to me that I did not wish to think about. It was but a conjecture, but I fancied that I knew the same thing had occurred to him.

The heat and oppression of the air, for the storm we had expected was still undischarged, increased very much after dinner, and for some time most of the party, among whom were John Clinton and myself, sat outside on the path bounding the lawn, where we had had tea. The night was absolutely dark, and no twinkle of star or moon ray could penetrate the pall of cloud that overset the sky. By degrees our assembly thinned, the women went up to bed, men dispersed to the smoking or billiard room, and by eleven o'clock my host and I were the only two left. All the evening I thought that he had something on his mind, and as soon as we were alone he spoke.

'The man who helped us with the picture had blood on his hand, too, did you notice?' he said.

'I asked him just now if he had cut himself, and he said he supposed he had, but that he could find no mark of it. Now where did that blood come from?'

By dint of telling myself that I was not going to think about it, I had succeeded in not doing so, and I did not want, especially just at bedtime, to be reminded of it.

'I don't know,' said I, 'and I don't really care so long as the picture of Mrs. Stone is not by my bed.'

He got up.

'But it's odd,' he said. 'Ha! Now you'll see another odd thing.'

A dog of his, an Irish terrier by breed, had come out of the house as we talked. The door behind us into the hall was open, and a bright oblong of light shone across the lawn to the iron gate which led on to the rough grass outside, where the walnut tree stood. I saw that the dog had all his hackles up, bristling with rage and fright; his lips were curled back from his teeth, as if he was ready to spring at something, and he was growling to himself. He took not the slightest notice of his master or me, but stiffly and tensely walked across the grass to the iron gate. There he stood for a moment, looking through the bars and still growling. Then of a sudden his courage seemed to desert him: he gave one long howl, and scuttled back to the house with a curious crouching sort of movement.

'He does that half-a-dozen times a day.' said John. 'He sees something which he both hates and fears.'

I walked to the gate and looked over it.

Something was moving on the grass outside, and soon a sound which I could not instantly identify came to my ears. Then I remembered what it was: it was the purring of a cat. I lit a match, and saw the purrer, a big blue Persian, walking round and round in a little circle just outside the gate, stepping high and ecstatically, with tail carried aloft like a banner. Its eyes were bright and shining, and every now and then it put its head down and sniffed at the grass.

I laughed.

'The end of that mystery, I am afraid.' I said. 'Here's a large cat having Walpurgis night all alone.'

'Yes, that's Darius,' said John. 'He spends half the day and all night there. But that's not the end of the dog mystery, for Toby and he are the best of friends, but the beginning of the cat mystery. What's the cat doing there? And why is Darius pleased, while Toby is terror-stricken?'

At that moment I remembered the rather horrible detail of my dreams when I saw through the gate, just where the cat was now, the white tombstone with the sinister inscription. But before I could answer the rain began, as suddenly and heavily as if a tap had been turned on, and simultaneously the big cat squeezed through the bars of the gate, and came leaping across the lawn to the house for shelter. Then it sat in the doorway, looking out eagerly into the dark. It spat and struck at John with its paw, as he pushed it in, in order to close the door.

Somehow, with the portrait of Julia Stone in the passage outside, the room in the tower had absolutely no alarm for me, and as I went to bed, feeling very sleepy and heavy, I had nothing more than interest for the curious incident about our bleeding hands, and the conduct of the cat and dog. The last thing I looked at before I put out my light was the square empty space by my bed where the portrait had been. Here the paper was of its original full tint of dark red: over the rest of the walls it had faded. Then I blew out my candle and instantly fell asleep.

My awaking was equally instantaneous, and I sat bolt upright in bed under the impression that some bright light had been flashed in my face, though it was now absolutely pitch dark. I knew exactly where I was, in the room which I had dreaded in dreams, but no horror that I ever felt when asleep approached the fear that now invaded and froze my brain. Immediately after a peal of thunder crackled just above the house, but the probability that it was only a flash of lightning which awoke me gave no reassurance to my galloping heart. Something I knew was in the room with me, and instinctively I put out my right hand, which was nearest the wall, to keep it away. And my hand touched the edge of a picture-frame hanging close to me.

I sprang out of bed, upsetting the small table that stood by it, and I heard my watch, candle, and matches clatter onto the floor. But for the moment there was no need of light, for a blinding flash leaped out of the clouds, and showed me that by my bed again hung the picture of Mrs. Stone. And instantly the room went into blackness again. But in that flash I saw another thing also, namely a figure that leaned over the end of my bed, watching me. It was dressed in some close-clinging white garment, spotted and stained with mould, and the face was that of the portrait.

Overhead the thunder cracked and roared, and when it ceased and the deathly stillness succeeded, I heard the rustle of movement coming nearer me, and, more horrible yet, perceived an odour of corruption and decay. And then a hand was laid on the side of my neck, and close beside my ear I heard quick-taken, eager breathing. Yet I knew that this thing, though it could be perceived by touch, by smell, by eye and by ear, was still not of this earth, but something that had passed out of the body and had power to make itself manifest. Then a voice, already familiar to me, spoke.

'I knew you would come to the room in the tower,' it said. 'I have been long waiting for you. At last you have come. Tonight I shall feast; before long we will feast together.'

And the quick breathing came closer to me; I could feel it on my neck.

At that the terror, which I think had paralyzed me for the moment, gave way to the wild instinct of self-preservation. I hit wildly with both arms, kicking out at the same moment, and heard a little animal-squeal, and something soft dropped with a thud beside me. I took a couple of steps forward, nearly tripping up over whatever it was that lay there, and by the merest good-luck found the handle of the door. In another second I ran out on the landing, and had banged the door behind me. Almost at the same moment I heard a door open somewhere below, and John Clinton, candle in hand, came running upstairs.

'What is it?' he said. 'I sleep just below you, and heard a noise as if — Good heavens, there's blood on your shoulder.'

I stood there, so he told me afterwards, swaying from side to side, white as a sheet, with the mark on my shoulder as if a hand covered with blood had been laid there.

'It's in there,' I said, pointing. 'She, you know. The portrait is in there, too, hanging up on the place we took it from.'

At that he laughed.

'My dear fellow, this is mere nightmare,' he said.

He pushed by me, and opened the door, I standing there simply inert with terror, unable to stop him, unable to move.

'Phew! What an awful smell,' he said.

Then there was silence; he had passed out of my sight behind the open door. Next moment he came out again, as white as myself, and instantly shut it.

'Yes, the portrait's there,' he said, 'and on the floor is a thing — a thing spotted with earth, like what they bury people in. Come away, quick, come away.'

How I got downstairs I hardly know. An awful shuddering and nausea of the spirit rather than of the flesh had seized me, and more than once he had to place my feet upon the steps, while every now and then he cast glances of terror and apprehension up the stairs. But in time we came to his dressing-room on the floor below, and there I told him what I have here described.

The sequel can be made short; indeed, some of my readers have perhaps already guessed what it was, if they remember that inexplicable affair of the churchyard at West Fawley, some eight years ago, where an attempt was made three times to bury the body of a certain woman who had committed suicide. On each occasion the coffin was found in the course of a few days again protruding from the ground. After the third attempt, in order that the thing should not be talked about, the body was buried elsewhere in unconsecrated ground. Where it was buried was just outside the iron gate of the garden belonging to the house where this woman had lived. She had committed suicide in a room at the top of the tower in that house. Her name was Julia Stone.

Subsequently the body was again secretly dug up, and the coffin was found to be full of blood.

Gavon's Eve

It is only the largest kind of ordnance map that records the existence of the village of Gavon, in the shire of Sutherland, and it is perhaps surprising that any map on whatever scale should mark so small and huddled a group of huts, set on a bare, bleak headland between moor and sea, and, so one would have thought, of no import at all to any who did not happen to live there. But the river Gavon, on the right bank of which stand this half-dozen of chimneyless and wind-swept habitations, is a geographical fact of far greater interest to outsiders, for the salmon there are heavy fish, the mouth of the river is clear of nets, and all the way up to Gavon Loch, some six miles inland, the coffee-coloured water lies in pool after deep pool, which verge, if the river is in order and the angler moderately sanguine, on a fishing probability amounting almost to a certainty. In any case, during the first fortnight of September last I had no blank day on those delectable waters, and up till the 15th of that month there was no day on which some one at the lodge in which I was stopping did not land a fish out of the famous Picts' pool. But after the 15th that pool was not fished again. The reason why is here set forward.

The river at this point, after some hundred yards of rapid, makes a sudden turn round a rocky angle, and plunges madly into the pool itself. Very deep water lies at the head of it, but deeper still further down on the east side, where a portion of the stream flicks back again in a swift dark backwater towards the top of the pool again. It is fishable only from the western bank, for to the east, above this backwater, a great wall of black and basaltic rock, heaved up no doubt by some fault in strata, rises sheer from the river to the height of some sixty feet. It is in fact nearly precipitous on both sides, heavily serrated at the top, and of so curious a thinness, that at about the middle of it where a fissure breaks its topmost edge, and some twenty feet from the top, there exists a long hole, a sort of lancet window, one would say, right through the rock, so that a slit of daylight can be seen through it. Since, therefore, no one would care to cast his line standing perched on that razor-edged eminence, the pool must needs be fished from the western bank. A decent fly, however, will cover it all.

It is on the western bank that there stand the remains of that which gave its title to the pool, namely, the ruins of a Pict castle, built out of rough and scarcely hewn masonry, unmortared but on a certain large and impressive scale, and in a very well-preserved condition considering its extreme antiquity. It is circular in shape and measures some twenty yards of diameter in its internal span. A staircase of large blocks with a rise of at least a foot leads up to the main gate, and opposite this on the side towards the river is another smaller postern through which down a rather hazardously steep slope a scrambling path, where progress demands both caution and activity, conducts to the head of the pool which lies immediately beneath it. A gate-chamber still roofed over exists in the solid wall: inside there are foundation indications of three rooms, and in the centre of all a very deep hole, probably a well. Finally, just outside the postern leading to the river is a small artificially levelled platform, some twenty feet across, as if made to support some super-incumbent edifice. Certain stone slabs and blocks are dispersed over it.

Brora, the post-town of Gavon, lies some six miles to the south-west, and from it a track over the moor leads to the rapids immediately above the Picts' pool, across which by somewhat extravagant striding from boulder to boulder a man can pass dry-foot when the river is low, and make his way up a steep path to the north of the basaltic rock, and so to the village. But this transit demands a steady head, and at the best is a somewhat giddy passage. Otherwise the road between it and Brora lies in a long detour higher up the moor, passing by the gates of Gavon Lodge, where I was stopping. For some vague and ill-defined reason the pool itself and the Picts' Castle had an uneasy reputation on the countryside, and several times trudging back from a day's fishing I have known my gillie take a longish circuit, though heavy with fish, rather than make this short cut in the dusk by the castle. On the first occasion when Sandy, a strapping yellow-bearded viking of twenty-five, did this he gave as a reason that the ground round about the castle was 'mossy,' though as a God-fearing man he must have known he lied. But on another occasion he was more frank, and said that the Picts' pool was 'no canny' after sunset. I am now inclined to agree with him, though, when he lied about it, I think it was because as a God-fearing man he feared the devil also.

It was on the evening of September 14 that I was walking back with my host, Hugh Graham, from the forest beyond the lodge. It had been a day unseasonably hot for the time of year, and the hills were blanketed with soft, furry clouds. Sandy, the gillie of whom I have spoken, was behind with the ponies, and, idly enough, I told Hugh about his strange distaste for the Picts' pool after sunset. He listened, frowning a little.

'That's curious,' he said. 'I know there is some dim local superstition about the place, but last year certainly Sandy used to laugh at it. I remember asking him what ailed the place, and he said he thought nothing about the rubbish folk talked. But this year you say he avoids it.'

'On several occasions with me he has done so.'

Hugh smoked a while in silence, striding noiselessly over the dusky fragrant heather.

'Poor chap,' he said, 'I don't know what to do about him. He's becoming useless.'

'Drink?' I asked.

'Yes, drink in a secondary manner. But trouble led to drink, and trouble, I am afraid, is leading him to worse than drink.'

'The only thing worse than drink is the devil,' I remarked.

'Precisely. That's where he is going. He goes there often.'

'What on earth do you mean?' I asked.

'Well, it's rather curious,' said Hugh. 'You know I dabble a bit in folklore and local superstition, and I believe I am on the track of something odder than odd. Just wait a moment.'

We stood there in the gathering dusk till the ponies laboured up the hillside to us, Sandy with his six feet of lithe strength strolling easily beside them up the steep brae, as if his long day's trudging had but served to half awaken his dormant powers of limb.

'Going to see Mistress Macpherson again tonight?' asked Hugh.

'Aye, puir body,' said Sandy. 'She's auld, and she's lone.'

'Very kind of you, Sandy,' said Hugh, and we walked on.

'What then?' I asked when the ponies had fallen behind again.

'Why, superstition lingers here,' said Hugh, 'and it's supposed she's a witch. To be quite candid with you, the thing interests me a good deal. Supposing you asked me, on oath, whether I believed in witches, I should say 'No.' But if you asked me again, on oath, whether I suspected I believed in them, I should, I think, say 'Yes.' And the fifteenth of this month — tomorrow — is Gavon's Eve.'

'And what in Heaven's name is that?' I asked. 'And who is Gavon? And what's the trouble?'

'Well, Gavon is the person, I suppose, not saint, who is what we should call the eponymous hero of this district. And the trouble is Sandy's trouble. Rather a long story. But there's a long mile in front of us yet, if you care to be told.'

During that mile I heard Sandy had been engaged a year ago to a girl of Gavon who was in service at Inverness. In March last he had gone, without giving notice, to see her, and as he walked up the street in which her mistress's house stood, had met her suddenly face to face, in company with a man whose clipped speech betrayed him English, whose manner a kind of gentleman. He had a flourish of his hat for Sandy, pleasure to see him, and scarcely any need of explanation as to how he came to be walking with Catrine. It was the most natural thing possible, for a city like Inverness boasted its innocent urbanities, and a girl could stroll with a man. And for the time, since also Catrine was so frankly pleased to see him, Sandy was satisfied. But after his return to Gavon, suspicion, fungus-like, grew rank in his mind, with the result that a month ago he had, with infinite pains and blottings, written a letter to Catrine, urging her return and immediate marriage. Thereafter it was known that she had left Inverness; it was known that she had arrived by train at Brora. From Brora she had started to walked across the moor by the path leading just above the Picts' Castle, crossing the rapids to Gavon, leaving her box to be sent by the carrier. But at Gavon she had never arrived. Also it was said that, although it was a hot afternoon, she wore a big cloak.

By this time we had come to the lodge, the lights of which showed dim and blurred through the thick hill-mists that had streamed sullenly down from the higher ground.

'And the rest,' said Hugh, 'which is as fantastic as this is sober fact, I will tell you later.'

Now, a fruit-bearing determination to go to bed is, to my mind, as difficult to ripen as a fruit-bearing determination to get up, and in spite of our long day, I was glad when Hugh (the rest of the men having yawned themselves out of the smoking-room) came back from the hospitable dispensing of bedroom candlesticks with a briskness that denoted that, as far as he was concerned, the distressing determination was not imminent.

'As regards Sandy,' I suggested.

'Ah, I also was thinking of that,' he said. 'Well, Catrine Gordon left Brora, and never arrived here. That is fact. Now for what remains. Have you any remembrance of a woman always alone walking about the moor by the loch? I think I once called your attention to her.'

'Yes, I remember,' I said. 'Not Catrine, surely; a very old woman, awful to look at.

'Moustache, whiskers, and muttering to herself. Always looking at the ground, too.'

'Yes, that is she — not Catrine. Catrine! My word, a May morning! But the other — it is Mrs. Macpherson, reputed witch. Well, Sandy trudges there, a mile and more away, every night to see her. You know Sandy: Adonis of the north. Now, can you account by any natural explanation for that fact? That he goes off after a long day to see an old hag in the hills?'

'It would seem unlikely,' said I.

'Unlikely! Well, yes, unlikely.'

Hugh got up from his chair and crossed the room to where a bookcase of rather fusty-looking volumes stood between windows. He took a small morocco-backed book from a top shelf.

'Superstitions of Sutherlandshire,' he said, as he handed it to me. 'Turn to page 128, and read.'

'September 15 appears to have been the date of what we may call this devil festival. On the night of that day the powers of darkness held pre-eminent dominion, and over-rode for any who were abroad that night and invoked their aid, the protective Providence of Almighty God.

'Witches, therefore, above all, were peculiarly potent. On this night any witch could entice to herself the heart and the love of any young man who consulted her on matters of philtre or love charm, with the result that on any night in succeeding years of the same date, he, though he was lawfully affianced and wedded, would for that night be hers. If, however, he should call on the name of God through any sudden grace of the Spirit, her charm would be of no avail. On this night, too, all witches had the power by certain dreadful incantations and indescribable profanities, to raise from the dead those who had committed suicide.'

'Top of the next page,' said Hugh. 'Leave out this next paragraph; it does not bear on this last.'

'Near a small village in this country,' I read, 'called Gavon, the moon at midnight is said to shine through a certain gap or fissure in a wall of rock close beside the river on to the ruins of a Pict castle, so that the light of its beams falls on to a large flat stone erected there near the gate, and supposed by some to be an ancient and pagan altar. At that moment, so the superstition still lingers in the countryside, the evil and malignant spirits which hold sway on Gavon's Eve, are at the zenith of their powers, and those who invoke their aid at this moment and in this place, will, though with infinite peril to their immortal souls, get all that they desire of them.'

The paragraph on the subject ended here, and I shut the book.

'Well?' I asked.

'Under favourable circumstances two and two make four,' said Hugh.

'And four means — '

'This. Sandy is certainly in consultation with a woman who is supposed to be a witch, whose path no crofter will cross after nightfall. He wants to learn, at whatever cost, poor devil, what happened to Catrine. Thus I think it more than possible that to-morrow, at midnight, there will be folk by the Picts' pool. There is another curious thing. I was fishing yesterday, and just opposite the river gate of the castle, someone has set up a great flat stone, which has been dragged (for I noticed the crushed grass) from the debris at the bottom of the slope.'

'You mean that the old hag is going to try to raise the body of Catrine, if she is dead?'

'Yes, and I mean to see myself what happens. Come too.'

The next day Hugh and I fished down the river from the lodge, taking with us not Sandy, but another gillie, and ate our lunch on the slope of the Picts' Castle after landing a couple of fish there. Even as Hugh had said, a great flat slab of stone had been dragged on to the platform outside the river gate of the castle, where it rested on certain rude supports, which, now that it was in place, seemed certainly designed to receive it. It was also exactly opposite that lancet window in the basaltic rock across the pool, so that if the moon at midnight did shine through it, the light would fall on the stone. This, then, was the almost certain scene of the incantations.

Below the platform, as I have said, the ground fell rapidly away to the level of the pool, which owing to rain on the hills was running very high, and, streaked with lines of greyish bubbles, poured down in amazing and ear-filling volume. But directly underneath the steep escarpment of rock on the far side of the pool it lay foamless and black, a still backwater of great depth. Above the altar-like erection again the ground rose up seven rough-hewn steps to the gate itself, on each side of which, to the height of about four feet, ran the circular wall of the castle. Inside again were the remains of partition walls between the three chambers, and it was in the one nearest to the river gate that we determined to conceal ourselves that night. From there, should the witch and Sandy keep tryst at the altar, any sound of movement would reach us, and through the aperture of the gate itself we could see, concealed in the shadow of the wall, whatever took place at the altar or down below at the pool. The lodge, finally, was but a short ten minutes away, if one went in the direct line, so that by starting at a quarter to twelve that night, we could enter the Picts' Castle by the gate away from the river, thus not betraying our presence to those who might be waiting for the moment when the moon should shine through the lancet window in the wall of rock on to the altar in front of the river gate.

Night fell very still and windless, and when not long before midnight we let ourselves silently out of the lodge, though to the east the sky was clear, a black continent of cloud was creeping up from the west, and had now nearly reached the zenith. Out of the remote fringes of it occasional lightning winked, and the growl of very distant thunder sounded drowsily at long intervals after.

But it seemed to me as if another storm hung over our heads, ready every moment to burst, for the oppression in the air was of a far heavier quality than so distant a disturbance could have accounted for.

To the east, however, the sky was still luminously clear; the curiously hard edges of the western cloud were star-embroidered, and by the dove-coloured light in the east it was evident that the moonrise over the moor was imminent. And though I did not in my heart believe that our expedition would end in anything but yawns, I was conscious of an extreme tension and rawness of nerves, which I set down to the thunder-charged air.

For noiselessness of footstep we had both put on india-rubber-soled shoes, and all the way down to the pool we heard nothing but the distant thunder and our own padded tread. Very silently and cautiously we ascended the steps of the gate away from the river, and keeping close to the wall inside, sidled round to the river gate and peered out. For the first moment I could see nothing, so black lay the shadow of the rock-wall opposite across the pool, but by degrees I made out the lumps and line of the glimmering foam which streaked the water. High as the river was running this morning it was infinitely more voluminous and turbulent now, and the sound of it filled and bewildered the ear with its sonorous roaring. Only under the very base of the rock opposite it ran quite black and unflecked by foam: there lay the deep still surface of the backwater. Then suddenly I saw something black move in the dimness in front of me, and against the grey

foam rose up first the head, then the
shoulders, and finally the whole figure of a
woman coming towards us up the bank.
Behind her walked another, a man, and the
two came to where the altar of stone had
been newly erected and stood there side by
side silhouetted against the churned white of
the stream. Hugh had seen too, and touched
me on the arm to call my attention. So far
then he was right: there was no mistaking the
stalwart proportions of Sandy.

Suddenly across the gloom shot a tiny spear
of light, and momentarily as we watched, it
grew larger and longer, till a tall beam, as
from some window cut in the rock opposite,
was shed on the bank below us. It moved
slowly, imperceptibly to the left till it struck
full between the two black figures standing
there, and shone with a curious bluish gleam
on the flat stone in front of them.

Then the roar of the river was suddenly
overscored by a dreadful screaming voice, the
voice of a woman, and from her side her arms
shot up and out as if in invocation of some
power.

At first I could catch none of the words,
but soon from repetition they began to
convey an intelligible message to my brain,
and I was listening as in paralytic horror of
nightmare to a bellowing of the most hideous

and un-nameable profanity. What I heard I cannot bring myself to record; suffice it to say that Satan was invoked by every adoring and reverent name, that cursing and unspeakable malediction was poured forth on Him whom we hold most holy. Then the yelling voice ceased as suddenly as it had began, and for a moment there was silence again, but for the reverberating river.

Then once more that horror of sound was uplifted.

'So, Catrine Gordon,' it cried, 'I bid ye in the name of my master and yours to rise from where ye lie. Up with ye — up!'

Once more there was silence; then I heard Hugh at my elbow draw a quick sobbing breath, and his finger pointed unsteadily to the dead black water below the rock. And I too looked and saw.

Right under the rock there appeared a pale subaqueous light, which waved and quivered in the stream. At first it was very small and dim, but as we looked it seemed to swim upwards from remote depths and grew larger till I suppose the space of some square yard was illuminated by it.

Then the surface of the water was broken, and a head, the head of a girl, dead-white and with long, flowing hair, appeared above the stream. Her eyes were shut, the corners of her mouth drooped as in sleep, and the moving water stood in a frill round her neck. Higher and higher rose the figure out of the tide, till at last it stood, luminous in itself, so it appeared, up to the middle.

The head was bent down over the breast, and the hands clasped together. As it emerged from the water it seemed to get nearer, and was by now half-way across the pool, moving quietly and steadily against the great flood of the hurrying river.

Then I heard a man's voice crying out in a sort of strangled agony.

'Catrine!' it cried; 'Catrine! In God's name; in God's name!'

In two strides Sandy had rushed down the steep bank, and hurled himself out into that mad swirl of waters. For one moment I saw his arms flung up into the sky, the next he had altogether gone. And on the utterance of that name the unholy vision had vanished too, while simultaneously there burst in front of us a light so blinding, followed by a crack of thunder so appalling to the senses, that I know I just hid my face in my hands. At once, as if the floodgates of the sky had been opened, the deluge was on us, not like rain, but like one sheet of solid water, so that we cowered under it. Any hope or attempt to rescue Sandy was out of the question; to dive into that whirlpool of mad water meant instant death, and even had it been possible for any swimmer to live there, in the blackness of the night there was absolutely no chance of finding him. Besides, even if it had been possible to save him, I doubt whether I was sufficiently master of my flesh and blood as to endure to plunge where that apparition had risen.

Then, as we lay there, another horror filled and possessed my mind. Somewhere close to us in the darkness was that woman whose yelling voice just now had made my blood run ice-cold, while it brought the streaming sweat to my forehead. At that moment I turned to Hugh.

'I cannot stop here,' I said. 'I must run, run right away. Where is she?'

'Did you not see?' he asked.

'No. What happened?'

'The lightning struck the stone within a few inches of where she was standing. We — we must go and look for her.'

I followed him down the slope, shaking as if I had the palsy, and groping with my hands on the ground in front of me, in deadly terror of encountering something human. The thunderclouds had in the last few minutes spread over the moon, so that no ray from the window in the rock guided our search. But up and down the bank from the stone that lay shattered there to the edge of the pool we groped and stumbled, but found nothing. At length we gave it up: it seemed morally certain that she, too, had rolled down the bank after the lightning stroke, and lay somewhere deep in the pool from which she had called the dead.

None fished the pool next day, but men with drag-nets came from Brora. Right under the rock in the backwater lay two bodies, close together, Sandy and the dead girl. Of the other they found nothing.

It would seem, then, that Catrine Gordon, in answer to Sandy's letter, left Inverness in heavy trouble. What happened afterwards can only be conjectured, but it seems likely she took the short cut to Gavon, meaning to cross the river on the boulders above the Picts' pool. But whether she slipped accidentally in her passage, and so was drawn down by the hungry water, or whether unable to face the future, she had thrown herself into the pool, we can only guess. In any case they sleep together now in the bleak, wind-swept graveyard at Brora, in obedience to the inscrutable designs of God.

The Dust-Cloud

The big French windows were open on to the lawn, and, dinner being over, two or three of the party who were staying for the week at the end of August with the Combe-Martins had strolled out on to the terrace to look at the sea, over which the moon, large and low, was just rising and tracing a path of pale gold from horizon to shore, while others, less lunar of inclination, had gone in search of bridge or billiards. Coffee had come round immediately after dessert, and the end of dinner, according to the delectable custom of the house, was as informal as the end of breakfast.

Every one, that is to say, remained or went away, smoked, drank port or abstained, according to his personal tastes. Thus, on this particular evening it so happened that Harry Combe-Martin and I were very soon left alone in the dining-room, because we were talking unmitigated motor 'shop,' and the rest of the party (small wonder) were bored with it, and had left us. The shop was home-shop, so to speak, for it was almost entirely concerned with the manifold perfections of the new six-cylinder Napier which my host in a moment of extravagance, which he did not in the least regret, had just purchased; in which, too, he proposed to take me over to lunch at a friend's house near Hunstanton on the following day. He observed with legitimate pride that an early start would not be necessary, as the distance was only eighty miles and there were no police traps.

'Queer things these big motors are,' he said, relapsing into generalities as we rose to go.

'Often I can scarcely believe that my new car is merely a machine. It seems to me to possess an independent life of its own. It is really much more like a thoroughbred with a wonderfully fine mouth.'

'And the moods of a thoroughbred?' I asked.

'No; it's got an excellent temper, I'm glad to say. It doesn't mind being checked, or even stopped, when it's going its best. Some of these big cars can't stand that. They get sulky — I assure you it is literally true — if they are checked too often.'

He paused on his way to ring the bell. 'Guy Elphinstone's car, for instance,' he said: 'it was a bad-tempered brute, a violent, vicious beast of a car.'

'What make?' I asked.

'Twenty-five horse-power Amédée. They are a fretful strain of car; too thin, not enough bone — and bone is very good for the nerves. The brute liked running over a chicken or a rabbit, though perhaps it was less the car's ill-temper than Guy's, poor chap. Well, he paid for it — he paid to the uttermost farthing. Did you know him?'

'No; but surely I have heard the name. Ah, yes, he ran over a child, did he not?'

'Yes,' said Harry, 'and then smashed up against his own park gates.'

'Killed, wasn't he?'

'Oh, yes, killed instantly, and the car just a heap of splinters. There's an old story about it, I'm told, in the village: rather in your line.'

'Ghosts?' I asked.

'Yes, the ghost of his motor-car. Seems almost too up-to-date, doesn't it?'

'And what's the story?' I demanded.

'Why, just this. His place was outside the village of Bircham, ten miles out from Norwich; and there's a long straight bit of road there — that's where he ran over the child — and a couple of hundred yards further on, a rather awkward turn into the park gates. Well, a month or two ago, soon after the accident, one old gaffer in the village swore he had seen a motor there coming full tilt along the road, but without a sound, and it disappeared at the lodge gates of the park, which were shut. Soon after another said he had heard a motor whirl by him at the same place, followed by a hideous scream, but he saw nothing.'

'The scream is rather horrible,' said I.

'Ah, I see what you mean! I only thought of his syren. Guy had a syren on his exhaust, same as I have. His had a dreadful frightened sort of wail, and always made me feel creepy.'

'And is that all the story?' I asked: 'that one old man thought he saw a noiseless motor, and another thought he heard an invisible one?'

Harry flicked the ash off his cigarette into the grate. 'Oh dear no!' he said. 'Half a dozen of them have seen something or heard something. It is quite a heavily authenticated yarn.'

'Yes, and talked over and edited in the public-house,' I said.

'Well, not a man of them will go there after dark. Also the lodge-keeper gave notice a week or two after the accident. He said he was always hearing a motor stop and hoot outside the lodge, and he was kept running out at all hours of the night to see what it was.'

'And what was it?'

'It wasn't anything. Simply nothing there. He thought it rather uncanny, anyhow, and threw up a good post. Besides, his wife was always hearing a child scream, and while her man toddled out to the gate she would go and see whether the kids were all right. And the kids themselves — '

'Ah, what of them?' I asked.

'They kept coming to their mother, asking who the little girl was who walked up and down the road and would not speak to them or play with them.'

'It's a many-sided story,' I said. 'All the witnesses seem to have heard and seen different things.'

'Yes, that is just what to my mind makes the yarn so good,' he said. 'Personally I don't take much stock in spooks at all. But given that there are such things as spooks, and given that the death of the child and the death of Guy have caused spooks to play about there, it seems to me a very good point that different people should be aware of different phenomena. One hears the car, another sees it, one hears the child scream, another sees the child. How does that strike you?'

This, I am bound to say, was a new view to me, and the more I thought of it the more reasonable it appeared. For the vast majority of mankind have all those occult senses by which is perceived the spiritual world (which, I hold, is thick and populous around us), sealed up, as it were; in other words, the majority of mankind never hear or see a ghost at all. Is it not, then, very probable that of the remainder — those, in fact, to whom occult experiences have happened or can happen — few should have every sense unsealed, but that some should have the unsealed ear, others the unsealed eye — that some should be clairaudient, others clairvoyant?

'Yes, it strikes me as reasonable,' I said. 'Can't you take me over there?'

'Certainly! If you will stop till Friday I'll take you over on Thursday. The others all go that day, so that we can get there after dark.'

I shook my head. 'I can't stop till Friday, I'm afraid,' I said. 'I must leave on Thursday. But how about to-morrow? Can't we take it on the way to or from Hunstanton?'

'No; it's thirty miles out of our way. Besides, to be at Bircham after dark means that we shouldn't get back here till midnight. And as host to my guests — '

'Ah! things are only heard and seen after dark, are they?' I asked. 'That makes it so much less interesting. It is like a séance where all lights are put out.'

'Well, the accident happened at night,' he said. 'I don't know the rules, but that may have some bearing on it, I should think.'

I had one question more in the back of my mind, but I did not like to ask it. At least, I wanted information on this subject without appearing to ask for it.

'Neither do I know the rules of motors,' I said; 'and I don't understand you when you say that Guy Elphinstone's machine was an irritable, cross-grained brute, that liked running over chickens and rabbits. But I think you subsequently said that the irritability may have been the irritability of its owner. Did he mind being checked?'

'It made him blind-mad if it happened often,' said Harry. 'I shall never forget a drive I had with him once: there were hay-carts and perambulators every hundred yards. It was perfectly ghastly; it was like being with a madman. And when we got inside his gate, his dog came running out to meet him. He did not go an inch out of his course: it was worse than that — he went for it, just grinding his teeth with rage. I never drove with him again.'

He stopped a moment, guessing what might be in my mind. 'I say, you mustn't think — you mustn't think — ' he began.

'No, of course not,' said I.

Harry Combe-Martin's house stood close to the weather-eaten, sandy cliffs of the Suffolk shore, which are being incessantly gnawed away by the hunger of the insatiable sea. Fathoms deep below it, and now any hundred yards out, lies what was once the second port in England; but now of the ancient town of Dunwich, and of its seven great churches, nothing remains but one, and that ruinous and already half destroyed by the falling cliff and the encroachments of the sea. Foot by foot, it too is disappearing, and of the graveyard which surrounded it more than half is gone, so that from the face of the sandy cliff on which it stands there stick out like straws in glass, as Dante says, the bones of those who were once committed there to the kindly and stable earth.

Whether it was the remembrance of this rather grim spectacle as I had seen it that afternoon, or whether Harry's story had caused some trouble in my brain, or whether it was merely that the keen bracing air of this place, to one who had just come from the sleepy languor of the Norfolk Broads, kept me sleepless, I do not know; but, anyhow, the moment I put out my light that night and got into bed, I felt that all the footlights and gas-jets in the internal theatre of my mind sprang into flame, and that I was very vividly and alertly awake. It was in vain that I counted a hundred forwards and a hundred backwards, that I pictured to myself a flock of visionary sheep coming singly through a gap in an imaginary hedge, and tried to number their monotonous and uniform countenances, that I played noughts and crosses with myself, that I marked out scores of double lawn-tennis courts, — for with each repetition of these supposedly soporific exercises I only became more intensely wakeful. It was not in remote hope of sleep that I continued to repeat these weary performances long after their inefficacy was proved to the hilt, but because I was strangely unwilling in this timeless hour of the night to think about those protruding relics of humanity; also I quite distinctly did not desire to think about that subject with regard to which I had, a few hours ago, promised Harry that I would not make it the subject of reflection. For these reasons I continued during the black hours to practise these narcotic exercises of the mind, knowing well that if I paused on the tedious treadmill my thoughts, like some released spring, would fly back to rather gruesome subjects. I kept my mind, in fact, talking loud to itself, so that it should not hear what other voices were saying.

Then by degrees these absurd mental occupations became impossible; my mind simply refused to occupy itself with them any longer; and next moment I was thinking intently and eagerly, not about the bones protruding from the gnawed section of sandcliff, but about the subject I had said I would not dwell upon.

And like a flash it came upon me why Harry had bidden me not think about it. Surely in order that I should not come to the same conclusion as he had come to.

Now the whole question of 'haunt' — haunted spots, haunted houses, and so forth — has always seemed to me to be utterly unsolved, and to be neither proved nor disproved to a satisfactory degree. From the earliest times, certainly from the earliest known Egyptian records, there has been a belief that the scene of a crime is often revisited, sometimes by the spirit of him who has committed it — seeking rest, we must suppose, and finding none; sometimes, and more inexplicably, by the spirit of his victim, crying perhaps, like the blood of Abel, for vengeance.

And though the stories of these village gossips in the alehouse about noiseless visions and invisible noises were all as yet unsifted and unreliable, yet I could not help wondering if they (such as they were) pointed to something authentic and to be classed under this head of appearances. But more striking than the yarns of the gaffers seemed to me the questions of the lodge-keeper's children. How should children have imagined the figure of a child that would not speak to them or play with them? Perhaps it was a real child, a sulky child. Yes — perhaps. But perhaps not. Then after this preliminary skirmish I found myself settling down to the question that I had said I would not think about; in other words, the possible origin of these phenomena interested me more than the phenomena themselves. For what exactly had Guy Elphinstone, that savage driver, done? Had or had not the death of the child been entirely an accident, a thing (given he drove a motor at all) outside his own control? Or had he, irritated beyond endurance at the checks and delays of the day, not pulled up when it was just possible he might have, but had run over the child as he would have run over a rabbit or a hen, or even his own dog? And what, in any case, poor wretched brute, must have been his thoughts in that terrible instant that intervened between the child's death and his own, when a moment later he smashed into the closed gates of his own lodge? Was remorse his — bitter, despairing contrition? That could hardly have been so; or else surely, knowing only for certain that he had knocked a child down, he would have stopped; he would have done his best, whatever that might be, to repair the irreparable harm. But he had not stopped: he had gone on, it seemed, at full speed, for on the collision the car had been smashed into matchwood and steel shavings. Again, with double force, had this dreadful thing been a complete accident, he would have stopped. So then — most terrible question of all — had he, after making murder, rushed on to what proved to be his own death, filled with some hellish glee at what he had done? Indeed, as in the church-yard on the cliff, bones of the buried stuck starkly out into the night.

The pale tired light of earliest morning had turned the window-blinds into glimmering squares before I slept; and when I woke, the servant who called me was already rattling them briskly up on their rollers, and letting the calm serenity of the August day stream into the room. Through the open windows poured in sunlight and sea-wind, the scent of flowers and the song of birds; and each and all were wonderfully reassuring, banishing the hooded forms that had haunted the night, and I thought of the disquietude of the dark hours as a traveller may think of the billows and tempests of the ocean over which he has safely journeyed, unable, now that they belong to the limbo of the past, to recall his qualms and tossings with any vivid uneasiness. Not without a feeling of relief, too, did I dwell on the knowledge that I was definitely not going to visit this equivocal spot. Our drive to-day, as Harry had said, would not take us within thirty miles of it, and to-morrow I but went to the station and away.

Though a thorough-paced seeker after truth might, no doubt, have regretted that the laws of time and space did not permit him to visit Bircham after the sinister dark had fallen, and test whether for him there was visible or audible truth in the tales of the village gossips, I was conscious of no such regret. Bircham and its fables had given me a very bad night, and I was perfectly aware that I did not in the least want to go near it, though yesterday I had quite truthfully said I should like to do so. In this brightness, too, of sun and sea-wind I felt none of the malaise at my waking moments which a sleepless night usually gives me; I felt particularly well, particularly pleased to be alive, and also, as I have said, particularly content not to be going to Bircham. I was quite satisfied to leave my curiosity unsatisfied.

The motor came round about eleven, and we started at once, Harry and Mrs. Morrison, a cousin of his, sitting behind in the big back seat, large enough to hold a comfortable three, and I on the left of the driver, in a sort of trance — I am not ashamed to confess it — of expectancy and delight. For this was in the early days of motors, when there was still the sense of romance and adventure round them. I did not want to drive, any more than Harry wanted to; for driving, so I hold, is too absorbing; it takes the attention in too firm a grip: the mania of the true motorist is not consciously enjoyed. For the passion for motors is a taste — I had almost said a gift — as distinct and as keenly individual as the passion for music or mathematics. Those who use motors most (merely as a means of getting rapidly from one place to another) are often entirely without it, while those whom adverse circumstances (over which they have no control) compel to use them least may have it to a supreme degree. To those who have it, analysis of their passion is perhaps superfluous; to those who have it not, explanation is almost unintelligible. Pace, however, and the control of pace, and above all the sensuous consciousness of pace, is at the root of it; and pleasure in pace is common to most people, whether it be in the form of a galloping horse, or the pace of the skate hissing over smooth ice, or the pace of a free-wheel bicycle humming down-hill, or, more impersonally, the pace of the smashed ball at lawn-tennis, the driven ball at golf, or the low boundary hit at cricket. But the sensuous consciousness of pace, as I have said, is needful: one might experience it seated in front of the engine of an express train, though not in a wadded, shut-windowed carriage, where the wind of movement is not felt. Then add to this rapture of the rush through riven air the knowledge that huge relentless force is controlled by a little lever, and directed by a little wheel on which the hands of the driver seem to lie so negligently. A great untamed devil has there his bridle, and he answers to it, as Harry had said, like a horse with a fine mouth. He has hunger and thirst, too, unslakeable, and greedily he laps of his soup of petrol which turns to fire in his mouth; electricity, the force that rends clouds asunder, and causes towers to totter, is the spoon with which he feeds himself; and as he eats he races onward, and the road opens like torn linen in front of him. Yet how obedient, how amenable is he! — for with a touch on his snaffle his speed is redoubled, or melts into thin air, so that before you know you have touched the rein he has exchanged his swallow-flight for a mere saunter through the lanes. But he ever loves to run; and knowing this, you will bid him lift up his voice and tell those who are in his path that he is coming, so that he will not need the touch that checks. Hoarse and jovial is his voice, hooting to the wayfarer; and if his hooting be not heard he has a great guttural falsetto scream that leaps from octave to octave, and echoes from the hedges that are passing in blurred lines of hanging green. And, as you go, the romantic isolation of divers in deep seas is yours; masked and hooded companions may be near you also, in their driving-dress for this plunge through the swift tides of air; but you, like them, are alone and isolated, conscious only of the ripped riband of road, the two great lantern-eyes of the wonderful monster that look through drooped eyelids by day, but gleam with fire by night, the two ear-laps of splash-boards, and the long lean bonnet in front which is the skull and brain-case of that swift untiring energy that feeds on fire, and whirls its two tons of weight up hill and down dale, as if some new law as ever-lasting as gravity, and like gravity making it go ever swifter, was its sole control.

For the first hour the essence of these joys, any description of which compared to the real thing is but as a stagnant pond compared to the bright rushing of a mountain stream, was mine. A straight switchback road lay in front of us, and the monster plunged silently down hill, and said below his breath, 'Ha-ha — ha-ha — ha-ha,' as, without diminution of speed, he breasted the opposing slope. In my control were his great vocal cords (for in those days hooter and syren were on the driver's left, and lay convenient to the hand of him who occupied the box-seat), and it rejoiced me to let him hoot at a pony-cart, three hundred yards ahead, with a hand on his falsetto scream if his ordinary tones of conversation were unheard or disregarded. Then came a road crossing ours at right angles, and the dear monster seemed to say, 'Yes, yes, — see how obedient and careful I am. I stroll with my hands in my pockets.' Then again a puppy from a farmhouse staggered warlike into the road, and the monster said, 'Poor little chap! get home to your mother, or I'll talk to you in earnest.' The poor little chap did not take the hint, so the monster slackened speed and just said 'Whoof!' Then it chuckled to itself as the puppy scuttled into the hedge, seriously alarmed; and next moment our self-made wind screeched and whistled round us again.

Napoleon, I believe, said that the power of an army lay in its feet: that is true also of the monster. There was a loud bang, and in thirty seconds we were at a standstill. The monster's off fore-foot troubled it, and the chauffeur said, 'Yes, sir — burst.'

So the burst boot was taken off and a new one put on, a boot that had never been on foot before. The foot in question was held up on a jack during this operation, and the new boot laced up with a pump. This took exactly twenty-five minutes. Then the monster got his spoon going again, and said, 'Let me run: oh, let me run!'

And for fifteen miles on a straight and empty road it ran. I timed the miles, but shall not produce their chronology for the benefit of a forsworn constabulary.

But there were no more dithyrambics that morning. We should have reached Hunstanton in time for lunch. Instead, we waited to repair our fourth puncture at 1.45 p.m., twenty-five miles short of our destination. This fourth puncture was caused by a spicule of flint three-quarters of an inch long — sharp, it is true, but weighing perhaps two pennyweights, while we weighed two tons. It seemed an impertinence. So we lunched at a wayside inn, and during lunch the pundits held a consultation, of which the upshot was this:

We had no more boots for our monster, for his off fore-foot had burst once, and punctured once (thus necessitating two socks and one boot). Similarly, but more so, his off hind-foot had burst twice (thus necessitating two boots and two socks). Now, there was no certain shoemaker's shop at Hunstanton, as far as we knew, but there was a regular universal store at King's Lynn, which was about equidistant.

And, so said the chauffeur, there was something wrong with the monster's spoon (ignition), and he didn't rightly know what, and therefore it seemed the prudent part not to go to Hunstanton (lunch, a thing of the preterite, having been the object), but to the well-supplied King's Lynn.

And we all breathed a pious hope that we might get there.

Whizz: hoot: purr! The last boot held, the spoon went busily to the monster's mouth, and we just flowed into King's Lynn. The return journey, so I vaguely gathered, would be made by other roads; but personally, intoxicated with air and movement, I neither asked nor desired to know what those roads would be. This one small but rather salient fact is necessary to record here, that as we waited at King's Lynn, and as we buzzed homewards afterwards, no thought of Bircham entered my head at all. The subsequent hallucination, if hallucination it was, was not, as far as I know, self-suggested. That we had gone out of our way for the sake of the garage, I knew, and that was all. Harry also told me that he did not know where our road would take us.

The rest that follows is the baldest possible narrative of what actually occurred. But it seems to me, a humble student of the occult, to be curious.

While we waited we had tea in an hotel

looking on to a big empty square of houses, and after tea we waited a very long time for our monster to pick us up. Then the telephone from the garage inquired for 'the gentleman on the motor,' and since Harry had strolled out to get a local evening paper with news of the last Test Match, I applied ear and mouth to that elusive instrument. What I heard was not encouraging: the ignition had gone very wrong indeed, and 'perhaps' in an hour we should be able to start. It was then about half-past six, and we were just seventy-eight miles from Dunwich.

Harry came back soon after this, and I told him what the message from the garage had been.

What he said was this: 'Then we shan't get back till long after dinner. We might just as well have camped out to see your ghost.'

As I have already said, no notion of Bircham was in my mind, and I mention this as evidence that, even if it had been, Harry's remark would have implied that we were not going through Bircham.

The hour lengthened itself into an hour and a half. Then the monster, quite well again, came hooting round the corner, and we got in.

'Whack her up, Jack,' said Harry to the chauffeur. 'The roads will be empty. You had better light up at once.'

The monster, with its eyes agleam, was whacked up, and never in my life have I been carried so cautiously and yet so swiftly. Jack never took a risk or the possibility of a risk, but when the road was clear and open he let the monster run just as fast as it was able. Its eyes made day of the road fifty yards ahead, and the romance of night was fairyland round us. Hares started from the roadside, and raced in front of us for a hundred yards, then just wheeled in time to avoid the ear-flaps of the great triumphant brute that carried us. Moths flitted across, struck sometimes by the lenses of its eyes, and the miles peeled over our shoulders. When it occurred we were going top-speed.

And this was It — quite unsensational, but to us quite inexplicable unless my midnight imaginings happened to be true.

As I have said, I was in command of the hooter and of the syren. We were flying along on a straight down-grade, as fast as ever we could go, for the engines were working, though the decline was considerable. Then quite suddenly I saw in front of us a thick cloud of dust, and knew instinctively and on the instant, without thought or reasoning, what that must mean.

Evidently something going very fast (or else

so large a cloud could not have been raised) was in front of us, and going in the same direction as ourselves. Had it been something on the road coming to meet us, we should of course have seen the vehicle first and run into the dust-cloud afterwards. Had it, again, been something of low speed — a horse and dog-cart, for instance — no such dust could have been raised. But, as it was, I knew at once that there was a motor travelling swiftly just ahead of us, also that it was not going as fast as we were, or we should have run into its dust much more gradually. But we went into it as into a suddenly lowered curtain.

Then I shouted to Jack. 'Slow down, and put on the brake,' I shrieked. 'There's something just ahead of us.' As I spoke I wrought a wild concerto on the hooter, and with my right hand groped for the syren, but did not find it. Simultaneously I heard a wild, frightened shriek, just as if I had sounded the syren myself. Jack had felt for it too, and our hands fingered each other. Then we entered the dust-cloud.

We slowed down with extraordinary rapidity, and still peering ahead we went dead-slow through it. I had not put on my goggles after leaving King's Lynn, and the dust stung and smarted in my eyes. It was not, therefore, a belt of fog, but real road-dust. And at the moment we crept through it I felt Harry's hands on my shoulder.

'There's something just ahead,' he said. 'Look! don't you see the tail light?'

As a matter of fact, I did not; and, still going very slow, we came out of that dust-cloud. The broad empty road stretched in front of us; a hedge was on each side, and there was no turning either to right or left. Only, on the right, was a lodge, and gates which were closed. The lodge had no lights in any window.

Then we came to a standstill; the air was dead-calm, not a leaf in the hedgerow trees was moving, not a grain of dust was lifted from the road. But behind, the dust-cloud still hung in the air, and stopped dead-short at the closed lodge-gates. We had moved very slowly for the last hundred yards: it was difficult to suppose that it was of our making. Then Jack spoke, with a curious crack in his voice.

'It must have been a motor, sir,' he said. 'But where is it?'

I had no reply to this, and from behind another voice, Harry's voice, spoke. For the moment I did not recognise it, for it was strained and faltering.

'Did you open the syren?' he asked. 'It didn't sound like our syren. It sounded like, like — '

'I didn't open the syren,' said I.

Then we went on again. Soon we came to scattered lights in houses by the wayside.

'What's this place?' I asked Jack.

'Bircham, sir,' said he.

The Confession of
Charles Linkworth

Dr. Teesdale had occasion to attend the condemned man once or twice during the week before his execution, and found him, as is often the case, when his last hope of life has vanished, quiet and perfectly resigned to his fate, and not seeming to look forward with any dread to the morning that each hour that passed brought nearer and nearer. The bitterness of death appeared to be over for him: it was done with when he was told that his appeal was refused. But for those days while hope was not yet quite abandoned, the wretched man had drunk of death daily. In all his experience the doctor had never seen a man so wildly and passionately tenacious of life, nor one so strongly knit to this material world by the sheer animal lust of living. Then the news that hope could no longer be entertained was told him, and his spirit passed out of the grip of that agony of torture and suspense, and accepted the inevitable with indifference. Yet the change was so extraordinary that it seemed to the doctor rather that the news had completely stunned his powers of feeling, and he was below the numbed surface, still knit into material things as strongly as ever. He had fainted when the result was told him, and Dr. Teesdale had been called in to attend him. But the fit was but transient, and he came out of it into full consciousness of what had happened.

The murder had been a deed of peculiar horror, and there was nothing of sympathy in the mind of the public towards the perpetrator. Charles Linkworth, who now lay under capital sentence, was the keeper of a small stationery store in Sheffield, and there lived with him his wife and mother. The latter was the victim of his atrocious crime; the motive of it being to get possession of the sum of five hundred pounds, which was this woman's property. Linkworth, as came out at the trial, was in debt to the extent of a hundred pounds at the time, and during his wife's absence from home on a visit to relations, he strangled his mother, and during the night buried the body in the small back-garden of his house. On his wife's return, he had a sufficiently plausible tale to account for the elder Mrs. Linkworth's disappearance, for there had been constant jarrings and bickerings between him and his mother for the last year or two, and she had more than once threatened to withdraw herself and the eight shillings a week which she contributed to household expenses, and purchase an annuity with her money. It was true, also, that during the younger Mrs. Linkworth's absence from home, mother and son had had a violent quarrel arising originally from some trivial point in household management, and that in consequence of this, she had actually drawn her money out of the bank, intending to leave Sheffield next day and settle in London, where she had friends. That evening she told him this, and during the night he killed her.

His next step, before his wife's return, was logical and sound. He packed up all his mother's possessions and took them to the station, from which he saw them despatched to town by passenger train, and in the evening he asked several friends in to supper, and told them of his mother's departure. He did not (logically also, and in accordance with what they probably already knew) feign regret, but said that he and she had never got on well together, and that the cause of peace and quietness was furthered by her going. He told that same story to his wife on her return, identical in every detail, adding, however, that the quarrel had been a violent one, and that his mother had not even left him her address. This again was wisely thought of: it would prevent his wife from writing to her. She appeared to accept his story completely: indeed there was nothing strange or suspicious about it.

For a while he behaved with the composure and astuteness which most criminals possess up to a certain point, the lack of which, after that, is generally the cause of their detection. He did not, for instance, immediately pay off his debts, but took into his house a young man as lodger, who occupied his mother's room, and he dismissed the assistant in his shop, and did the entire serving himself. This gave the impression of economy, and at the same time he openly spoke of the great improvement in his trade, and not till a month had passed did he cash any of the bank-notes which he had found in a locked drawer in his mother's room. Then he changed two notes of fifty pounds and paid off his creditors.

At that point his astuteness and composure failed him. He opened a deposit account at a local bank with four more fifty-pound notes, instead of being patient, and increasing his balance at the savings bank pound by pound, and he got uneasy about that which he had buried deep enough for security in the back-garden. Thinking to render himself safer in this regard, he ordered a cartload of slag and stone fragments, and with the help of his lodger employed the summer evenings when work was over in building a sort of rockery over the spot. Then came the chance circumstance which really set match to this dangerous train. There was a fire in the lost luggage office at King's Cross Station (from which he ought to have claimed his mother's property) and one of the two boxes was partially burned. The company was liable for compensation, and his mother's name on her linen, and a letter with the Sheffield address on it, led to the arrival of a purely official and formal notice, stating that the company were prepared to consider claims. It was directed to Mrs. Linkworth's and Charles Linkworth's wife received and read it.

It seemed a sufficiently harmless document, but it was endorsed with his death-warrant. For he could give no explanation at all of the fact of the boxes still lying at King's Cross Station, beyond suggesting that some accident had happened to his mother. Clearly he had to put the matter in the hands of the police, with a view to tracing her movements, and if it proved that she was dead, claiming her property, which she had already drawn out of the bank. Such at least was the course urged on him by his wife and lodger, in whose presence the communication from the railway officials was read out, and it was impossible to refuse to take it. Then the silent, uncreaking machinery of justice, characteristic of England, began to move forward. Quiet men lounged about Smith Street, visited banks, observed the supposed increase in trade, and from a house near by looked into the garden where ferns were already flourishing on the rockery. Then came the arrest and the trial, which did not last very long, and on a certain Saturday night the verdict. Smart women in large hats had made the court bright with colour, and in all the crowd there was not one who felt any sympathy with the young athletic-looking man who was condemned. Many of the audience were elderly and respectable mothers, and the crime had been an outrage on motherhood, and they listened to the unfolding of the flawless evidence with strong approval. They thrilled a little when the judge put on the awful and ludicrous little black cap, and spoke the sentence appointed by God.

Linkworth went to pay the penalty for the atrocious deed, which no one who had heard the evidence could possibly doubt that he had done with the same indifference as had marked his entire demeanour since he knew his appeal had failed. The prison chaplain who had attended him had done his utmost to get him to confess, but his efforts had been quite ineffectual, and to the last he asserted, though without protestation, his innocence. On a bright September morning, when the sun shone warm on the terrible little procession that crossed the prison yard to the shed where was erected the apparatus of death, justice was done, and Dr. Teesdale was satisfied that life was immediately extinct. He had been present on the scaffold, had watched the bolt drawn, and the hooded and pinioned figure drop into the pit. He had heard the chunk and creak of the rope as the sudden weight came on to it, and looking down he had seen the queer twitchings of the hanged body. They had lasted but a second for the execution had been perfectly satisfactory.

An hour later he made the post-mortem examination and found that his view had been correct: the vertebrae of the spine had been broken at the neck, and death must have been absolutely instantaneous. It was hardly necessary even to make that little piece of dissection that proved this, but for the sake of form he did so. And at that moment he had a very curious and vivid mental impression that the spirit of the dead man was close beside him, as if it still dwelt in the broken habitation of its body. But there was no question at all that the body was dead: it had been dead an hour. Then followed another little circumstance that at the first seemed insignificant though curious also. One of the warders entered, and asked if the rope which had been used an hour ago, and was the hangman's perquisite, had by mistake been brought into the mortuary with the body. But there was no trace of it, and it seemed to have vanished altogether, though it was a singular thing to be lost: it was not here; it was not on the scaffold. And though the disappearance was of no particular moment it was quite inexplicable.

Dr. Teesdale was a bachelor and a man of independent means, and lived in a tall-windowed and commodious house in Bedford Square, where a plain cook of surpassing excellence looked after his food, and her husband his person. There was no need for him to practise a profession at all, and he performed his work at the prison for the sake of the study of the minds of criminals.

Most crime — the transgression, that is, of the rule of conduct which the human race has framed for the sake of its own preservation — he held to be either the result of some abnormality, of the brain or of starvation. Crimes of theft, for instance, he would by no means refer to one head; often it is true they were the result of actual want, but more often dictated by some obscure disease of the brain. In marked cases it was labelled as kleptomania, but he was convinced there were many others which did not fall directly under the dictation of physical need. More especially was this the case where the crime in question involved also some deed of violence, and he mentally placed underneath this heading, as he went home that evening, the criminal at whose last moments he had been present that morning. The crime had been abominable, the need of money not so very pressing, and the very abomination and unnaturalness of the murder inclined him to consider the murderer as lunatic rather than criminal. He had been, as far as was known, a man of quiet and kindly disposition, a good husband, a sociable neighbour. And then he had committed a crime, just one, which put him outside all pales. So monstrous a deed, whether perpetrated by a sane man or a mad one, was intolerable; there was no use for the doer of it on this planet at all. But somehow the doctor felt that he would have been more at one with the execution of justice, if the dead man had confessed. It was morally certain that he was guilty, but he wished that when there was no longer any hope for him he had endorsed the verdict himself.

He dined alone that evening, and after

dinner sat in his study which adjoined the dining-room, and feeling disinclined to read, sat in his great red chair opposite the fireplace, and let his mind graze where it would. At once almost, it went back to the curious sensation he had experienced that morning, of feeling that the spirit of Linkworth was present in the mortuary, though life had been extinct for an hour. It was not the first time, especially in cases of sudden death, that he had felt a similar conviction, though perhaps it had never been quite so unmistakable as it had been to-day. Yet the feeling, to his mind, was quite probably formed on a natural and psychical truth.

The spirit — it may be remarked that he was a believer in the doctrine of future life, and the non-extinction of the soul with the death of the body — was very likely unable or unwilling to quit at once and altogether the earthly habitation, very likely it lingered there, earth-bound, for a while.

In his leisure hours Dr. Teesdale was a considerable student of the occult, for like most advanced and proficient physicians, he clearly recognised how narrow was the boundary of separation between soul and body, how tremendous the influence of the intangible was over material things, and it presented no difficulty to his mind that a disembodied spirit should be able to communicate directly with those who still were bounded by the finite and material.

His meditations, which were beginning to group themselves into definite sequence, were interrupted at this moment. On his desk near at hand stood his telephone, and the bell rang, not with its usual metallic insistence, but very faintly, as if the current was weak, or the mechanism impaired. However, it certainly was ringing, and he got up and took the combined ear and mouth-piece off its hook.

'Yes, yes,' he said, 'who is it?'

There was a whisper in reply almost inaudible, and quite unintelligible.

'I can't hear you,' he said.

Again the whisper sounded, but with no greater distinctness. Then it ceased altogether.

He stood there, for some half minute or so, waiting for it to be renewed, but beyond the usual chuckling and croaking, which showed, however, that he was in communication with some other instrument, there was silence. Then he replaced the receiver, rang up the Exchange, and gave his number.

'Can you tell me what number rang me up just now?' he asked.

There was a short pause, then it was given him. It was the number of the prison, where he was doctor.

'Put me on to it, please,' he said.

This was done.

'You rang me up just now,' he said down the tube. 'Yes; I am Doctor Teesdale. What is it? I could not hear what you said.'

The voice came back quite clear and intelligible.

'Some mistake, sir,' it said. 'We haven't rung you up.'

'But the Exchange tells me you did, three minutes ago.'

'Mistake at the Exchange, sir,' said the voice.

'Very odd. Well, good-night. Warder Draycott, isn't it?'

'Yes, sir; good-night, sir.'

Dr. Teesdale went back to his big arm-chair, still less inclined to read. He let his thoughts wander on for a while, without giving them definite direction, but ever and again his mind kept coming back to that strange little incident of the telephone. Often and often he had been rung up by some mistake, often and often he had been put on to the wrong number by the Exchange, but there was something in this very subdued ringing of the telephone bell, and the unintelligible whisperings at the other end that suggested a very curious train of reflection to his mind, and soon he found himself pacing up and down his room, with his thoughts eagerly feeding on a most unusual pasture.

'But it's impossible,' he said, aloud.

He went down as usual to the prison next morning, and once again he was strangely beset with the feeling that there was some unseen presence there. He had before now had some odd psychical experiences, and knew that he was a 'sensitive' — one, that is, who is capable, under certain circumstances, of receiving supernormal impressions, and of having glimpses of the unseen world that lies about us. And this morning the presence of which he was conscious was that of the man who had been executed yesterday morning. It was local, and he felt it most strongly in the little prison yard, and as he passed the door of the condemned cell. So strong was it there that he would not have been surprised if the figure of the man had been visible to him, and as he passed through the door at the end of the passage, he turned round, actually expecting to see it. All the time, too, he was aware of a profound horror at his heart; this unseen presence strangely disturbed him. And the poor soul, he felt, wanted something done for it. Not for a moment did he doubt that this impression of his was objective, it was no imaginative phantom of his own invention that made itself so real. The spirit of Linkworth was there.

He passed into the infirmary, and for a couple of hours busied himself with his work. But all the time he was aware that the same invisible presence was near him, though its force was manifestly less here than in those places which had been more intimately associated with the man. Finally, before he left, in order to test his theory he looked into the execution shed. But next moment with a face suddenly stricken pale, he came out again, closing the door hastily. At the top of the steps stood a figure hooded and pinioned, but hazy of outline and only faintly visible.

But it was visible, there was no mistake about it.

Dr. Teesdale was a man of good nerve, and he recovered himself almost immediately, ashamed of his temporary panic. The terror that had blanched his face was chiefly the effect of startled nerves, not of terrified heart, and yet deeply interested as he was in psychical phenomena, he could not command himself sufficiently to go back there. Or rather he commanded himself, but his muscles refused to act on the message. If this poor earthbound spirit had any communication to make to him, he certainly much preferred that it should be made at a distance. As far as he could understand, its range was circumscribed. It haunted the prison yard, the condemned cell, the execution shed, it was more faintly felt in the infirmary. Then a further point suggested itself to his mind, and he went back to his room and sent for Warder Draycott, who had answered him on the telephone last night.

'You are quite sure,' he asked, 'that nobody rang me up last night, just before I rang you up?'

There was a certain hesitation in the man's manner which the doctor noticed.

'I don't see how it could be possible, sir,' he said. 'I had been sitting close by the telephone for half an hour before, and again before that. I must have seen him, if anyone had been to the instrument.'

'And you saw no one?' said the doctor with a slight emphasis.

The man became more markedly ill at ease.

'No, sir, I saw no one,' he said, with the same emphasis.

Dr. Teesdale looked away from him.

'But you had perhaps the impression that there was some one there?' he asked, carelessly, as if it was a point of no interest.

Clearly Warder Draycott had something on

his mind, which he found it hard to speak of.

'Well, sir, if you put it like that,' he began. 'But you would tell me I was half asleep, or had eaten something that disagreed with me at my supper.'

The doctor dropped his careless manner.

'I should do nothing of the kind,' he said, 'any more than you would tell me that I had dropped asleep last night, when I heard my telephone bell ring. Mind you, Draycott, it did not ring as usual, I could only just hear it ringing, though it was close to me. And I could only hear a whisper when I put my ear to it. But when you spoke I heard you quite distinctly. Now I believe there was something — somebody — at this end of the telephone. You were here, and though you saw no one, you, too, felt there was someone there.'

The man nodded.

'I'm not a nervous man, sir,' he said, 'and I don't deal in fancies. But there was something there. It was hovering about the instrument, and it wasn't the wind, because there wasn't a breath of wind stirring, and the night was warm. And I shut the window to make certain. But it went about the room, sir, for an hour or more. It rustled the leaves of the telephone book, and it ruffled my hair when it came close to me. And it was bitter cold, sir.'

The doctor looked him straight in the face.

'Did it remind you of what had been done yesterday morning?' he asked suddenly.

Again the man hesitated.

'Yes, sir,' he said at length. 'Convict Charles Linkworth.'

Dr. Teesdale nodded reassuringly.

'That's it,' he said. 'Now, are you on duty to-night?'

'Yes, sir, I wish I wasn't.'

'I know how you feel, I have felt exactly the same myself. Now whatever this is, it seems to want to communicate with me. By the way, did you have any disturbance in the prison last night?'

'Yes, sir, there was half a dozen men who had the nightmare. Yelling and screaming they were, and quiet men too, usually. It happens sometimes the night after an execution. I've known it before, though nothing like what it was last night.'

'I see. Now, if this — this thing you can't see wants to get at the telephone again to-night, give it every chance. It will probably come about the same time. I can't tell you why, but that usually happens. So unless you must, don't be in this room where the telephone is, just for an hour to give it plenty of time between half-past nine and half-past ten. I will be ready for it at the other end.

Supposing I am rung up, I will, when it has finished, ring you up to make sure that I was not being called in — in the usual way.'

'And there is nothing to be afraid of, sir?' asked the man.

Dr. Teesdale remembered his own moment of terror this morning, but he spoke quite sincerely.

'I am sure there is nothing to be afraid of,' he said, reassuringly.

Dr. Teesdale had a dinner engagement that night, which he broke, and was sitting alone in his study by half past-nine. In the present state of human ignorance as to the law which governs the movements of spirits severed from the body, he could not tell the warder why it was that their visits are so often periodic, timed to punctuality according to our scheme of hours, but in scenes of tabulated instances of the appearance of revenants, especially if the soul was in sore need of help, as might be the case here, he found that they came at the same hour of day or night. As a rule, too, their power of making themselves seen or heard or felt grew greater for some little while after death, subsequently growing weaker as they became less earthbound, or often after that ceasing altogether, and he was prepared to-night for a less indistinct impression. The spirit apparently for the early hours of its disembodiment is weak, like a moth newly broken out from its chrysalis — and then suddenly the telephone bell rang, not so faintly as the night before, but still not with its ordinary imperative tone.

Dr. Teesdale instantly got up, put the receiver to his ear. And what he heard was heartbroken sobbing, strong spasms that seemed to tear the weeper.

He waited for a little before speaking, himself cold with some nameless fear, and yet profoundly moved to help, if he was able.

'Yes, yes,' he said at length, hearing his own voice tremble. 'I am Dr. Teesdale. What can I do for you? And who are you?' he added, though he felt that it was a needless question.

Slowly the sobbing died down, and the whispers took its place, still broken by crying.

'I want to tell, sir — I want to tell — I must tell.'

'Yes, tell me, what is it?' said the doctor.

'No, not you — another gentleman, who used to come to see me. Will you speak to him what I say to you? — I can't make him hear me or see me.'

'Who are you?' asked Dr. Teesdale suddenly.

'Charles Linkworth. I thought you knew. I am very miserable. I can't leave the prison — and it is cold. Will you send for the other gentleman?'

'Do you mean the chaplain?' asked Dr. Teesdale.

'Yes, the chaplain. He read the service when I went across the yard yesterday. I shan't be so miserable when I have told.'

The doctor hesitated a moment. This was a strange story that he would have to tell Mr. Dawkins, the prison chaplain, that at the other end of the telephone was the spirit of the man executed yesterday. And yet he soberly believed that it was so, that this unhappy spirit was in misery and wanted to 'tell.' There was no need to ask what he wanted to tell.

'Yes, I will ask him to come here,' he said at length.

'Thank you, sir, a thousand times. You will make him come, won't you?'

The voice was growing fainter.

'It must be to-morrow night,' it said. 'I can't speak longer now. I have to go to see — oh, my God, my God.'

The sobs broke out afresh, sounding fainter and fainter. But it was in a frenzy of terrified interest that Dr. Teesdale spoke.

'To see what?' he cried. 'Tell me what you are doing, what is happening to you?'

'I can't tell you; I mayn't tell you,' said the voice very faint. 'That is part — ' and it died away altogether.

Dr. Teesdale waited a little, but there was

96

no further sound of any kind, except the chuckling and croaking of the instrument. He put the receiver on to its hook again, and then became aware for the first time that his forehead was streaming with some cold dew of horror. His ears sang; his heart beat very quick and faint, and he sat down to recover himself. Once or twice he asked himself if it was possible that some terrible joke was being played on him, but he knew that could not be so; he felt perfectly sure that he had been speaking with a soul in torment of contrition for the terrible and irremediable act it had committed. It was no delusion of his senses, either; here in this comfortable room of his in Bedford Square, with London cheerfully roaring round him, he had spoken with the spirit of Charles Linkworth.

But he had no time (nor indeed inclination, for somehow his soul sat shuddering within him) to indulge in meditation. First of all he rang up the prison.

'Warder Draycott?' he asked.

There was a perceptible tremor in the man's voice as he answered.

'Yes, sir. Is it Dr. Teesdale?'

'Yes. Has anything happened here with you?'

Twice it seemed that the man tried to speak and could not. At the third attempt the words came 'Yes, sir. He has been here. I saw him go into the room where the telephone is.'

'Ah! Did you speak to him?'

'No, sir: I sweated and prayed. And there's half a dozen men as have been screaming in their sleep to-night. But it's quiet again now. I think he has gone into the execution shed.'

'Yes. Well, I think there will be no more disturbance now. By the way, please give me Mr. Dawkins's home address.'

This was given him, and Dr. Teesdale proceeded to write to the chaplain, asking him to dine with him on the following night. But suddenly he found that he could not write at his accustomed desk, with the telephone standing close to him, and he went upstairs to the drawing-room which he seldom used, except when he entertained his friends. There he recaptured the serenity of his nerves, and could control his hand. The note simply asked Mr. Dawkins to dine with him next night, when he wished to tell him a very strange history and ask his help. 'Even if you have any other engagement,' he concluded, 'I seriously request you to give it up. To-night, I did the same. 'I should bitterly have regretted it if I had not.'

Next night accordingly, the two sat at their dinner in the doctor's dining-room, and when they were left to their cigarettes and coffee the doctor spoke.

'You must not think me mad, my dear Dawkins,' he said, 'when you hear what I have got to tell you.'

Mr. Dawkins laughed.

'I will certainly promise not to do that,' he said.

'Good. Last night and the night before, a little later in the evening than this, I spoke through the telephone with the spirit of the man we saw executed two days ago. Charles Linkworth.'

The chaplain did not laugh. He pushed back his chair, looking annoyed.

'Teesdale,' he said, 'is it to tell me this — I don't want to be rude — but this bogey-tale that you have brought me here this evening?'

'Yes. You have not heard half of it. He asked me last night to get hold of you. He wants to tell you something. We can guess, I think, what it is.'

Dawkins got up.

'Please let me hear no more of it,' he said. 'The dead do not return. In what state or under what condition they exist has not been revealed to us. But they have done with all material things.'

'But I must tell you more,' said the doctor. 'Two nights ago I was rung up, but very faintly, and could only hear whispers. I instantly inquired where the call came from and was told it came from the prison. I rang up the prison, and Warder Draycott told me that nobody had rung me up. He, too, was conscious of a presence.'

'I think that man drinks,' said Dawkins, sharply.

The doctor paused a moment.

'My dear fellow, you should not say that sort of thing,' he said. 'He is one of the steadiest men we have got. And if he drinks, why not I also?'

The chaplain sat down again.

'You must forgive me,' he said, 'but I can't go into this. These are dangerous matters to meddle with. Besides, how do you know it is not a hoax?'

'Played by whom?' asked the doctor. 'Hark!'

The telephone bell suddenly rang. It was clearly audible to the doctor.

'Don't you hear it?' he said.

'Hear what?'

'The telephone bell ringing.'

'I hear no bell,' said the chaplain, rather angrily. 'There is no bell ringing.'

The doctor did not answer, but went through into his study, and turned on the lights. Then he took the receiver and mouthpiece off its hook.

'Yes?' he said, in a voice that trembled. 'Who is it? Yes: Mr. Dawkins is here. I will try and get him to speak to you.' He went back into the other room.

'Dawkins,' he said, 'there is a soul in agony. I pray you to listen. For God's sake come and listen.'

The chaplain hesitated a moment.

'As you will,' he said.

He took up the receiver and put it to his ear.

'I am Mr. Dawkins,' he said.

He waited.

'I can hear nothing whatever,' he said at length. 'Ah, there was something there. The faintest whisper.'

'Ah, try to hear, try to hear!' said the doctor.

Again the chaplain listened. Suddenly he laid the instrument down, frowning.

'Something — somebody said, 'I killed her, I confess it. I want to be forgiven.' It's a hoax, my dear Teesdale. Somebody knowing your spiritualistic leanings is playing a very grim joke on you. I can't believe it.'

Dr. Teesdale took up the receiver.

'I am Dr. Teesdale,' he said. 'Can you give Mr. Dawkins some sign that it is you?'

Then he laid it down again.

'He says he thinks he can,' he said. 'We must wait.'

The evening was again very warm, and the window into the paved yard at the back of the house was open. For five minutes or so the two men stood in silence, waiting, and nothing happened. Then the chaplain spoke.

'I think that is sufficiently conclusive,' he said.

Even as he spoke a very cold draught of air suddenly blew into the room, making the papers on the desk rustle. Dr. Teesdale went to the window and closed it.

'Did you feel that?' he asked.

'Yes, a breath of air. Chilly.'

Once again in the closed room it stirred again.

'And did you feel that?' asked the doctor.

The chaplain nodded. He felt his heart hammering in his throat suddenly.

'Defend us from all peril and danger of this coming night,' he exclaimed.

'Something is coming!' said the doctor.

As he spoke it came. In the centre of the room not three yards away from them stood the figure of a man with his head bent over on to his shoulder, so that the face was not visible. Then he took his head in both his hands and raised it like a weight, and looked them in the face. The eyes and tongue protruded, a livid mark was round the neck. Then there came a sharp rattle on the boards of the floor, and the figure was no longer there. But on the floor there lay a new rope.

For a long while neither spoke. The sweat poured off the doctor's face, and the chaplain's white lips whispered prayers. Then by a huge effort the doctor pulled himself together. He pointed at the rope.

'It has been missing since the execution,' he said.

Then again the telephone bell rang. This time the chaplain needed no prompting. He went to it at once and the ringing ceased. For a while he listened in silence.

'Charles Linkworth,' he said at length, 'in the sight of God, in whose presence you stand, are you truly sorry for your sin?'

Some answer inaudible to the doctor came, and the chaplain closed his eyes. And Dr. Teesdale knelt as he heard the words of the Absolution.

At the close there was silence again.

'I can hear nothing more,' said the chaplain, replacing the receiver.

Presently the doctor's man-servant came in with the tray of spirits and syphon. Dr. Teesdale pointed without looking to where the apparition had been.

'Take the rope that is there and burn it, Parker,' he said.

There was a moment's silence.

'There is no rope, sir,' said Parker.

At Abdul Ali's Grave

Luxor, as most of those who have been there will allow, is a place of notable charm, and boasts many attractions for the traveller, chief among which he will reckon an excellent hotel containing a billiard-room, a garden fit for the gods to sit in, any quantity of visitors, at least a weekly dance on board a tourist steamer, quail shooting, a climate as of Avilion, and a number of stupendously ancient monuments for those archeologically inclined. But to certain others, few indeed in number, but almost fanatically convinced of their own orthodoxy, the charm of Luxor, like some sleeping beauty, only wakes when these things cease, when the hotel has grown empty and the billiard-marker 'has gone for a long rest' to Cairo, when the decimated quail and the decimating tourist have fled northwards, and the Theban plain, Dana to a tropical sun, is a gridiron across which no man would willingly make a journey by day, not even if Queen Hatasoo herself should signify that she would give him audience on the terraces of Deir-el-Bahari.

A suspicion however that the fanatic few

were right, for in other respects they were men of estimable opinions, induced me to examine their convictions for myself, and thus it came about that two years ago, certain days toward the beginning of June saw me still there, a confirmed convert.

Much tobacco and the length of summer days had assisted us to the analysis of the charm of which summer in the south is possessed, and Weston — one of the earliest of the elect — and myself had discussed it at some length, and though we reserved as the principal ingredient a nameless something which baffled the chemist, and must be felt to be understood, we were easily able to detect certain other drugs of sight and sound, which we were agreed contributed to the whole. A few of them are here sub joined.

The waking in the warm darkness just before dawn to find that the desire for stopping in bed fails with the awakening.

The silent start across the Nile in the still air with our horses, who, like us, stand and sniff at the incredible sweetness of the coming morning without apparently finding it less wonderful in repetition.

The moment infinitesimal in duration but infinite in sensation, just before the sun rises, when the grey shrouded river is struck suddenly out of darkness, and becomes a sheet of green bronze.

The rose flush, rapid as a change of colour in some chemical combination, which shoots across the sky from east to west, followed immediately by the sunlight which catches the peaks of the western hills, and flows down like some luminous liquid.

The stir and whisper which goes through the world: a breeze springs up; a lark soars, and sings; the boatman shouts 'Yallah, Yallah'; the horses toss their heads.

The subsequent ride.

The subsequent breakfast on our return.

The subsequent absence of anything to do.

At sunset the ride into the desert thick with the scent of warm barren sand, which smells like nothing else in the world, for it smells of nothing at all.

The blaze of the tropical night.

Camel's milk.

Converse with the fellahin, who are the most charming and least accountable people on the face of the earth except when tourists are about, and when in consequence there is no thought but backsheesh.

Lastly, and with this we are concerned, the possibility of odd experiences.

The beginning of the things which make this tale occurred four days ago, when Abdul Mi, the oldest man in the village, died suddenly, full of days and riches. Both, some thought, had probably been somewhat exaggerated, but his relations affirmed without variation that he had as many years as he had English pounds, and that each was a hundred. The apt roundness of these numbers was incontestable, the thing was too neat not to be true, and before he had been dead for twenty-four hours it was a matter of orthodoxy. But with regard to his relations, that which turned their bereavement, which must soon have occurred, into a source of blank dismay instead of pious resignation, was that not one of these English pounds, not even their less satisfactory equivalent in notes, which, out of the tourist season, are looked upon at Luxor as a not very dependable variety of Philosopher's stone, though certainly capable of producing gold under favourable circumstances, could be found. Abdul Au with his hundred years was dead, his century of sovereigns — they might as well have been an annuity — were dead with him, and his son Mohamed, who had previously enjoyed a sort of brevet rank in anticipation of the event, was considered to be throwing far more dust in the air than the genuine affection even of a chief mourner wholly justified.

Abdul, it is to be feared, was not a man of stereotyped respectability; though full of years and riches, he enjoyed no great reputation for honour. He drank wine whenever he could get it, he ate food during the days of Ramadan, scornful of the fact, when his appetite desired it, he was supposed to have the evil eye, and in his last moments he was attended by the notorious Achmet, who is well known here to be practised in Black Magic, and has been suspected of the much meaner crime of robbing the bodies of those lately dead. For in Egypt, while to despoil the bodies of ancient kings and priests is a privilege for which advanced and learned societies vie with each other, to rob the corpses of your contemporaries is considered the deed of a dog.

Mohamed, who soon exchanged the throwing of dust in the air for the more natural mode of expressing chagrin, which is to gnaw the nails, told us in confidence that he suspected Achmet of having ascertained the secret of where his father's money was, but it appeared that Achmet had as blank a face as anybody when his patient, who was striving to make some communication to him, went out into the great silence, and the suspicion that he knew where the money was gave way, in the minds, of those who were competent to form an estimate of his character, to a but dubious regret that he had just failed to learn that very important fact.

So Abdul died and was buried, and we all went to the funeral feast, at which we ate more roast meat than one naturally cares about at five in the afternoon on a June day, in consequence of which Weston and I, not requiring dinner, stopped at home after our return from the ride into the desert, and talked to Mohamed, Abdul's son, and Hussein, Abdul's youngest grandson, a boy of about twenty, who is also our valet, cook and housemaid, and they together woefully narrated of the money that had been and was not, and told us scandalous tales about Achmet concerning his weakness for cemeteries. They drank coffee and smoked, for though Hussein was our servant, we had been that day the guests of his father, and shortly after they had gone, up came Machmout.

Machmout, who says he thinks he is twelve, but does not know for certain, is kitchen-maid, groom and gardener, and has to an extraordinary degree some occult power resembling clairvoyance. Weston, who is a member of the Society for Psychical Research, and the tragedy of whose life has been the detection of the fraudulent medium Mrs. Blunt, says that it is all thought-reading, and has made notes of many of Machmout's performances, which may subsequently turn out to be of interest.

112

Thought-reading, however, does not seem to me to fully explain the experience which followed Abdul's funeral, and with Machmout I have to put it down to White Magic, which should be a very inclusive term, or to Pure Coincidence, which is even more inclusive, and will cover all the inexplicable phenomena of the world, taken singly. Machmout's method of unloosing the forces of White Magic is simple, being the ink-mirror known by name to many, and it is as follows.

A little black ink is poured into the palm of Machmout's hand, or, as ink has been at a premium lately owing to the last post-boat from Cairo which contained stationery for us having stuck on a sand-bank, a small piece of black American cloth about an inch in diameter is found to be a perfect substitute. Upon this he gazes. After five or ten minutes his shrewd monkey-like expression is struck from his face, his eyes, wide open, remain fixed on the cloth, a complete rigidity sets in over his muscles, and he tells us of the curious things he sees. In whatever position he is, in that position he remains without the deflection of a hair's breadth until the ink is washed off or the cloth removed. Then he looks up and says 'Khahás,' which means, 'It is finished.'

We only engaged Machmout's services as

second general domestic a fortnight ago, but the first evening he was with us he came upstairs when he had finished his work, and said, 'I will show you White Magic; give me ink,' and proceeded to describe the front hall of our house in London, saying that there were two horses at the door, and that a man and woman soon came out, gave the horses each a piece of bread and mounted. The thing was so probable that by the next mail I wrote asking my mother to write down exactly what she was doing and where at half-past five (English time) on the evening of June 12. At the corresponding time in Egypt Machmout was describing speaking to us of a 'sitt' (lady) having tea in a room which he described with some minuteness, and I am waiting anxiously for her letter. The explanation which Weston gives us of all these phenomena is that a certain picture of people I know is present in my mind, though I may not be aware of it, — present to my subliminal self, I think, he says, — and that I give an unspoken suggestion to the hypnotised Machmout. My explanation is that there isn't any explanation, for no suggestion on my part would make my brother go out and ride at the moment when Machmout says he is so doing (if indeed we find that Machmout's visions are chronologically correct). Consequently I prefer the open mind and am prepared to believe anything. Weston, however, does not speak quite so calmly or scientifically about Machmout's last performance, and since it took place he has almost entirely ceased to urge me to become a member of the Society for Psychical Research, in order that I may no longer be hidebound by vain superstitions.

Machmout will not exercise these powers if his own folk are present, for he says that when he is in this state, if a man who knew Black Magic was in the room, or knew that he was practising White Magic, he could get the spirit who presides over the Black Magic to kill the spirit of White Magic, for the Black Magic is the more potent, and the two are foes. And as the spirit of White Magic is on occasions a powerful friend — he had before now befriended Machmout in a manner which I consider incredible — Machmout is very desirous that he should abide long with him. But Englishmen it appears do not know the Black Magic, so with us he is safe. The spirit of Black Magic, to speak to whom it is death, Machmout saw once 'between heaven and earth, and night and day,' so he phrases it, on the Karnak road. He may be known, he told us, by the fact that he is of paler skin than his people, that he has two long teeth, one in each corner of his mouth, and that his eyes, which are white all over, are as big as the eyes of a horse.

Machmout squatted himself comfortably in the corner, and I gave him the piece of black American cloth. As some minutes must elapse before he gets into the hypnotic state in which the visions begin, I strolled out on to the balcony for coolness. It was the hottest night we had yet had, and though the sun had set three hours, the thermometer still registered close on 100°.

Above, the sky seemed veiled with grey, where it should have been dark velvety blue, and a fitful puffing wind from the south threatened three days of the sandy intolerable khamseen. A little way up the street to the left was a small café in front of which were glowing and waning little glowworm specks of light from the water pipes of Arabs sitting out there in the dark. From inside came the click of brass castanets in the hands of some dancing-girl, sounding sharp and precise against the wailing bagpipe music of the strings and pipes which accompany these movements which Arabs love and Europeans think so unpleasing. Eastwards the sky was paler and luminous, for the moon was imminently rising, and even as I looked the red rim of the enormous disc cut the line of the desert, and on the instant, with a curious aptness, one of the Arabs outside the café broke out into that wonderful chant — 'I cannot sleep for longing for thee, O full moon. Far is thy throne over Mecca, slip down, O beloved, to me.'

Immediately afterwards I heard the piping monotone of Machmout's voice begin, and in a moment or two I went inside.

We have found that the experiments gave the quickest result by contact, a fact which confirmed Weston in his explanation of them by thought transference of some elaborate kind, which I confess I cannot understand. He was writing at a table in the window when I came in, but looked up.

'Take his hand,' he said; 'at present he is quite incoherent.'

'Do you explain that?' I asked.

'It is closely analogous, so Myers thinks, to talking in sleep. He has been saying something about a tomb. Do make a suggestion, and see if he gives it right. He is remarkably sensitive, and he responds quicker to you than to me. Probably Abdul's funeral suggested the tomb!'

A sudden thought struck me.

'Hush!' I said, 'I want to listen.'

Machmout's head was thrown a little back, and he held the hand in which was the piece of cloth rather above his face. As usual he was talking very slowly, and in a high staccato voice, absolutely unlike his usual tones.

'On one side of the grave,' he pipes, 'is a tamarisk tree, and the green beetles make fantasia about it. On the other side is a mud wall. There are many other graves about, but they are all asleep. This is the grave, because it is awake, and it moist and not sandy.'

'I thought so,' said Weston. 'It is Abdul's grave he is talking about.'

'There is a red moon sitting on the desert,' continued Machmout, 'and it is now. There is the puffing of khamseen, and much dust coming. The moon is red with dust, and because it is low.'

'Still sensitive to external conditions,' said Weston. 'That is rather curious. Pinch him, will you?'

I pinched Machmout; he did not pay the slightest attention.

'In the last house of the street, and in the doorway stands a man. Ah! ah!' cried the boy, suddenly, 'it is the Black Magic he knows. Don't let him come. He is going out of the house,' he shrieked, 'he is coming — no, he is going the other way towards the moon and the grave. He has the Black Magic with him, which can raise the dead, and he has a murdering knife, and a spade. I cannot see his face, for the Black Magic is between it and my eyes.'

Weston had got up, and, like me, was hanging on Machmout's words.

'We will go there,' he said. 'Here is an opportunity of testing it. Listen a moment.'

'He is walking, walking, walking,' piped Machmout, 'still walking to the moon and the grave. The moon sits no longer on the desert, but has sprung up a little way.'

I pointed out of the window.

'That at any rate is true,' I said.

Weston took the cloth out of Machmout's hand, and the piping ceased. In a moment he stretched himself, and rubbed his eyes.

'Khalás,' he said.

'Yes, it is Khalás.'

'Did I tell you of the sitt in England?' he asked.

'Yes, oh, yes,' I answered; 'thank you, little Machmout. The White Magic was very good to-night. Get you to bed.'

Machmout trotted obediently out of the room, and Weston closed the door after him.

'We must be quick,' he said. 'It is worth while going and giving the thing a chance, though I wish he had seen something less gruesome. The odd thing is that he was not at the funeral, and yet he describes the grave accurately. What do you make of it?'

'I make that the White Magic has shown Machmout that somebody with Black Magic is going to Abdul's grave, perhaps to rob it,' I answered resolutely.

'What are we to do when we get there?' asked Weston.

'See the Black Magic at work. Personally I am in a blue funk. So are you.'

'There is no such thing as Black Magic,' said Weston. 'Ah, I have it. Give me that orange.'

Weston rapidly skinned it, and cut from the rind two circles as big as a five shilling piece, and two long, white fangs of skin. The first he fixed in his eyes, the two latter in the corners of his mouth.

'The Spirit of Black Magic?' I asked.

'The same.'

He took up a long black burnous and wrapped it round him. Even in the bright lamp light, the spirit of Black Magic was a sufficiently terrific personage.

'I don't believe in Black Magic,' he said, 'but others do. If it is necessary to put a stop to — to anything that is going on, we will hoist the man on his own petard. Come along. Whom do you suspect it is — I mean, of course, who was the person you were thinking of when your thoughts were transferred to Machmout.'

'What Machmout said,' I answered, 'suggested Achmet to me.'

Weston indulged in a laugh of scientific incredulity, and we set off.

The moon, as the boy had told us, was just clear of the horizon, and as it rose higher, its colour at first red and sombre, like the blaze of some distant conflagration, paled to a tawny yellow. The hot wind from the south, blowing no longer fitfully but with a steadily increasing violence, was thick with sand, and of an incredibly scorching heat, and the tops of the palm trees in the garden of the deserted hotel on the right were lashing themselves to and fro with a harsh rattle of dry leaves. The cemetery lay on the outskirts of the village, and, as long as our way lay between the mud walls of the huddling street, the wind came to us only as the heat from behind closed furnace doors. Every now and then with a whisper and whistle rising into a great buffeting flap, a sudden whirlwind of dust would scour some twenty yards along the road, and then break like a shore-quenched wave against one or other of the mud walls or throw itself heavily against a house and fall in a shower of sand. But once free of obstructions we were opposed to the full heat and blast of the wind which blew full in our teeth. It was the first summer khamseen of the year, and for the moment I wished I had gone north with the tourist and the quail and the billiard marker, for khamseen fetches the marrow out of the bones, and turns the body to blotting paper.

We passed no one in the street, and the only sound we heard, except the wind, was the howling of moonstruck dogs.

The cemetery is surrounded by a tall mud-built wall, and sheltering for a few moments under this we discussed our movements. The row of tamarisks close to which the tomb lay went down the centre of the graveyard, and by skirting the wall outside and climbing softly over where they approached it, the fury of the wind might help us to get near the grave without being seen, if anyone happened to be there. We had just decided on this, and were moving on to put the scheme into execution, when the wind dropped for a moment, and in the silence we could hear the chump of the spade being driven into the earth, and what gave me a sudden thrill of intimate horror, the cry of the carrion-feeding hawk from the dusky sky just overhead.

Two minutes later we were creeping up in the shade of the tamarisks, to where Abdul had been buried. The great green beetles which live on the trees were flying about blindly, and once or twice one dashed into my face with a whirr of mail-clad wings. When we were within some twenty yards of the grave we stopped for a moment, and, looking cautiously out from our shelter of tamarisks, saw the figure of a man already waist deep in the earth, digging out the newly turned grave. Weston, who was standing behind me, had adjusted the characteristics of the spirit of Black Magic so as to be ready for emergencies, and turning round suddenly, and finding myself unawares face to face with that realistic impersonation, though my nerves are not precariously strong, I could have found it within me to shriek aloud. But that unsympathetic man of iron only shook with suppressed laughter, and, holding the eyes in his hand, motioned me forward again without speaking to where the trees grew thicker. There we stood not a dozen yards away from the grave.

We waited, I suppose, for some ten minutes, while the man, whom we saw to be Achmet, toiled on at his impious task. He was entirely naked, and his brown skin glistened with the dews of exertion in the moonlight. At times he chattered in a cold uncanny manner to himself, and once or twice he stopped for breath. Then he began scraping the earth away with his hands, and soon afterwards searched in his clothes, which were lying near, for a piece of rope, with which he stepped into the grave, and in a moment reappeared again with both ends in his hands. Then, standing astride the grave, he pulled strongly, and one end of the coffin appeared above the ground. He chipped a piece of the lid away to make sure that he had the right end, and then, setting it upright, wrenched off the top with his knife, and there faced us, leaning against the coffin lid, the small shrivelled figure of the dead Abdul, swathed like a baby in white.

I was just about to motion the spirit of Black Magic to make his appearance, when Machmout's words came into my head: 'He had with him the Black Magic which can raise the dead,' and sudden overwhelming curiosity, which froze disgust and horror into chill unfeeling things, came over me.

'Wait,' I whispered to Weston, 'he will use the Black Magic.'

Again the wind dropped for a moment, and again, in the silence that came with it, I heard the chiding of the hawk overhead, this time nearer, and thought I heard more birds than one.

Achmet meantime had taken the covering from off the face, and had undone the swathing band, which at the moment after death is bound round the chin to close the jaw, and in Arab burial is always left there, and from where we stood I could see that the jaw dropped when the bandage was untied, as if, though the wind blew towards us with a ghastly scent of mortality on it, the muscles were not even now set, though the man had been dead sixty hours. But still a rank and burning curiosity to see what this unclean ghoul would do next stifled all other feelings in my mind. He seemed not to notice, or, at any rate, to disregard that mouth gaping awry, and moved about nimbly in the moonlight.

He took from a pocket of his clothes, which were lying near, two small black objects, which now are safely embedded in the mud at the bottom of the Nile, and rubbed them briskly together.

By degrees they grew luminous with a sickly yellow pallor of light, and from his hands went up a wavy, phosphorescent flame. One of these cubes he placed in the open mouth of the corpse, the other in his own, and, taking the dead man closely in his arms as though he would indeed dance with death, he breathed long breaths from his mouth into that dead cavern which was pressed to his. Suddenly he started back with a quick-drawn breath of wonder and perhaps of horror, and stood for a space as if irresolute, for the cube which the dead man held instead of lying loosely in the jaw was pressed tight between clenched teeth. After a moment of irresolution he stepped back quickly to his clothes again, and took up from near them the knife with which he had stripped off the coffin lid, and holding this in one hand behind his back, with the other he took out the cube from the dead man's mouth, though with a visible exhibition of force, and spoke.

'Abdul,' he said, 'I am your friend, and I swear I will give your money to Mohamed, if you will tell me where it is.'

Certain I am that the lips of the dead moved, and the eyelids fluttered for a moment like the wings of a wounded bird, but at that sight the horror so grew on me that I was physically incapable of stifling the cry that rose to my lips, and Achmet turned round. Next moment the complete Spirit of Black Magic glided out of the shade of the trees, and stood before him. The wretched man stood for a moment without stirring, then, turning with shaking knees to flee, he stepped back and fell into the grave he had just opened.

Weston turned on me angrily, dropping the eyes and the teeth of the Afrit.

'You spoiled it all,' he cried. 'It would perhaps have been the most interesting . . . ' and his eye lighted on the dead Abdul, who peered open-eyed from the coffin, then swayed, tottered, and fell forward, face downwards on the ground close to him. For one moment he lay there, and then the body rolled slowly on to its back without visible cause of movement, and lay staring into the sky. The face was covered with dust, but with the dust was mingled fresh blood. A nail had caught the cloth that wound him, underneath which, as usual, were the clothes in which he had died, for the Arabs do not wash their dead, and it had torn a great rent through them all, leaving the right shoulder bare.

Weston strove to speak once, but failed. Then:

'I will go and inform the police,' he said, 'if you will stop here, and see that Achmet does not get out.'

But this I altogether refused to do, and, after covering the body with the coffin to protect it from the hawks, we secured Achmet's arms with the rope he had already used that night, and took him off to Luxor.

Next morning Mohamed came to see us.

'I thought Achmet knew where the money was,' he said exultantly.

'Where was it?'

'In a little purse tied round the shoulder. The dog had already begun stripping it. See' — and he brought it out of his pocket — 'it is all there in those English notes, five pounds

127

each, and there are twenty of them.'

Our conclusion was slightly different, for even Weston will allow that Achmet hoped to learn from dead lips the secret of the treasure, and then to kill the man anew and bury him. But that is pure conjecture.

The only other point of interest lies in the two black cubes which we picked up, and found to be graven with curious characters. These I put one evening into Machmout's hand, when he was exhibiting to us his curious powers of 'thought transference.' The effect was that he screamed aloud, crying out that the Black Magic had come, and though I did not feel certain about that, I thought they would be safer in mid-Nile. Weston grumbled a little, and said that he had wanted to take them to the British Museum, but that I feel sure was an afterthought.

The Shootings of Achnaleish

The dining-room windows, both front and back, the one looking into Oakley Street, the other into a small back-yard with three sooty shrubs in it (known as the garden), were all open, so that the table stood in mid-stream of such air as there was. But in spite of this the heat was stifling, since, for once in a way, July had remembered that it was the duty of good little summers to be hot. Hot in consequence it had been: heat reverberated from the house-walls, it rose through the boot from the paving-stones, it poured down from a large superheated sun that walked the sky all day long in a benignant and golden manner. Dinner was over, but the small party of four who had eaten it still lingered.

Mabel Armytage — it was she who had laid down the duty of good little summers — spoke first.

'Oh, Jim, it sounds too heavenly,' she said. 'It makes me feel cool to think of it. Just fancy, in a fortnight's time we shall all four of us be there, in our own shooting-lodge — '

'Farm-house,' said Jim.

'Well, I didn't suppose it was Balmoral,

with our own coffee-coloured salmon river roaring down to join the waters of our own loch.'

Jim lit a cigarette.

'Mabel, you mustn't think of shooting-lodges and salmon rivers and lochs,' he said. 'It's a farm-house, rather a big one, though I'm sure we shall find it hard enough to fit in. The salmon river you speak of is a big burn, no more, though it appears that salmon have been caught there.'

'But when I saw it, it would have required as much cleverness on the part of a salmon to fit into it as it will require on our parts to fit into our farm-house. And the loch is a tarn.'

Mabel snatched the 'Guide to Highland Shootings' out of my hand with a rudeness that even a sister should not show her elder brother, and pointed a withering finger at her husband.

''Achnaleish,'' she declaimed, ''is situated in one of the grandest and most remote parts of Sutherlandshire. To be let from August 12 till the end of October, the lodge with shooting and fishing belonging. Proprietor supplies two keepers, fishing-gillie, boat on loch, and dogs. Tenant should secure about 500 head of grouse, and 500 head of mixed game, including partridge, black-game, wood-cock, snipe, roe deer; also rabbits in very large

132

number, especially by ferreting. Large baskets of brown trout can be taken from the loch, and whenever the water is high sea-trout and occasional salmon. Lodge contains' — I can't go on; it's too hot, and you know the rest. Rent only £350!'

Jim listened patiently.

'Well?' he said. 'What then?'

Mabel rose with dignity.

'It is a shooting-lodge with a salmon river and a loch, just as I have said. Come, Madge, let's go out. It is too hot to sit in the house.'

'You'll be calling Buxton 'the major-domo' next,' remarked Jim, as his wife passed him.

I had picked up the 'Guide to Highland Shootings' again which my sister had so unceremoniously plucked from me, and idly compared the rent and attractions of Achnaleish with other places that were to let.

'Seems cheap, too,' I said. 'Why, here's another place, just the same sort of size and bag, for which they ask £500; here's another at £550.'

Jim helped himself to coffee.

'Yes, it does seem cheap,' he said. 'But, of course, it's very remote; it took me a good three hours from Lairg, and I don't suppose I was driving very noticeably below the legal limit. But it's cheap, as you say.'

Now, Madge (who is my wife) has her

prejudices. One of them — an extremely expensive one — is that anything cheap has always some hidden and subtle drawback, which you discover when it is too late. And the drawback to cheap houses is drains or offices — the presence, so to speak, of the former, and the absence of the latter. So I hazarded these.

'No, the drains are all right,' said Jim, 'because I got the certificate of the inspector, and as for offices, really I think the servants' parts are better than ours. No — why it's so cheap, I can't imagine.'

'Perhaps the bag is overstated,' I suggested.

Jim again shook his head.

'No, that's the funny thing about it,' he said. 'The bag, I am sure, is understated. At least, I walked over the moor for a couple of hours, and the whole place is simply crawling with hares. Why, you could shoot five hundred hares alone on it.'

'Hares?' I asked. 'That's rather queer, so far up, isn't it?'

Jim laughed.

'So I thought. And the hares are queer, too; big beasts, very dark in colour. Let's join the others outside. Jove! what a hot night!'

Even as Mabel had said, that day fortnight found us all four, the four who had stifled and sweltered in Chelsea, flying through the cool and invigorating winds of the North. The road was in admirable condition, and I should not wonder if for the second time Jim's big Napier went not noticeably below the legal limit. The servants had gone straight up, starting the same day as we, while we had got out at Perth, motored to Inverness, and were now, on the second day, nearing our goal. Never have I seen so depopulated a road. I do not suppose there was a man to a mile of it.

We had left Lairg about five that afternoon expecting to arrive at Achnaleish by eight, but one disaster after another overtook us. Now it was the engine, and now a tyre that delayed us, till finally we stopped some eight miles short of our destination, to light up, for with evening had come a huge wrack of cloud out of the West, so that we were cheated of the clear post-sunset twilight of the North. Then on again, till, with a little dancing of the car over a bridge, Jim said:

'That's the bridge of our salmon river; so look out for the turning up to the lodge. It is to the right, and only a narrow track. You can send her along, Sefton,' he called to the chauffeur; 'we shan't meet a soul.'

I was sitting in front, finding the speed and the darkness extraordinarily exhilarating. A bright circle of light was cast by our lamps, fading into darkness in front, while at the sides, cut off by the casing of the lamps, the transition into blackness was sharp and sudden. Every now and then, across this circle of illumination some wild thing would pass: now a bird, with hurried flutter of wings when it saw the speed of the luminous monster, would just save itself from being knocked over; now a rabbit feeding by the side of the road would dash on to it and then bounce back again; but more frequently it would be a hare that sprang up from its feeding and raced in front of us. They seemed dazed and scared by the light, unable to wheel into the darkness again, until time and again I thought we must run over one, so narrowly, in giving a sort of desperate sideways leap, did it miss our wheels. Then it seemed that one started up almost from under us, and I saw, to my surprise, it was enormous in size, and in colour apparently quite black. For some hundred yards it raced in front of us, fascinated by the bright light pursuing it, then, like the rest, it dashed for the darkness. But it was too late, and with a horrid jolt we ran over it. At once Sefton slowed down and stopped, for Jim's rule is to go back always and make sure that any poor run-over is dead. So, when we stopped, the chauffeur jumped down and ran back.

'What was it?' Jim asked me, as we waited.
'A hare.'

Sefton came running back.

'Yes, sir, quite dead,' he said. 'I picked it up, sir.'

'What for!'

'Thought you might like to see it, sir. It's the biggest hare I ever see, and it's quite black.'

It was immediately after this that we came to the track up to the house, and in a few minutes we were within doors. There we found that if 'shooting-lodge' was a term unsuitable, so also was 'farm-house,' so roomy, excellently proportioned, and well furnished was our dwelling, while the contentment that beamed from Buxton's face was sufficient testimonial for the offices.

In the hall, too, with its big open fireplace, were a couple of big solemn bookcases, full of serious works, such as some educated minister might have left, and, coming down dressed for dinner before the others, I dipped into the shelves. Then — something must long have been vaguely simmering in my brain, for I pounced on the book as soon as I saw it — I came upon Elwes's 'Folklore of the North-West Highlands,' and looked out 'Hare' in the index. Then I read:

'Nor is it only witches that are believed to

have the power of changing themselves into animals ... Men and women on whom no suspicion of the sort lies are thought to be able to do this, and to don the bodies of certain animals, notably hares ... Such, according to local superstition, are easily distinguishable by their size and colour, which approaches jet black.'

I was up and out early next morning, prey to the vivid desire that attacks many folk in new places — namely, to look on the fresh country and the new horizons — and, on going out, certainly the surprise was great. For I had imagined an utterly lonely and solitary habitation; instead, scarce half a mile away, down the steep brae-side at the top of which stood our commodious farm-house, ran a typically Scotch village street, the hamlet no doubt of Achnaleish.

So steep was this hill-side that the village was really remote; if it was half a mile a way in crow-flying measurement, it must have been a couple of hundred yards below us. But its existence was the odd thing to me: there were some four dozen houses, at the least, while we had not seen half that number since leaving Lairg. A mile away, perhaps, lay the shining shield of the western sea; to the other side, away from the village, I had no difficulty in recognising the river and the loch.

The house, in fact, was set on a hog's back; from all sides it must needs be climbed to. But, as is the custom of the Scots, no house, however small, should be without its due brightness of flowers, and the walls of this were purple with clematis and orange with tropæolum. It all looked very placid and serene and home-like.

I continued my tour of exploration, and came back rather late for breakfast. A slight check in the day's arrangements had occurred, for the head keeper, Maclaren, had not come up, and the second, Sandie Ross, reported that the reason for this had been the sudden death of his mother the evening before. She was not known to be ill, but just as she was going to bed she had thrown up her arms, screamed suddenly as if with fright, and was found to be dead. Sandie, who repeated this news to me after breakfast, was just a slow, polite Scotchman, rather shy, rather awkward. Just as he finished — we were standing about outside the back-door — there came up from the stables the smart, very English-looking Sefton. In one hand he carried the black hare.

He touched his hat to me as he went in.

'Just to show it to Mr. Armytage, sir,' he said. 'She's as black as a boot.'

He turned into the door, but not before

Sandie Ross had seen what he carried, and the slow, polite Scotchman was instantly turned into some furtive, frightened-looking man.

'And where might it be that you found that, sir?' he asked.

Now, the black-hare superstition had already begun to intrigue me.

'Why does that interest you?' I asked.

The slow Scotch look was resumed with an effort.

'It'll no interest me,' he said. 'I just asked. There are unco many black hares in Achnaleish.'

Then his curiosity got the better of him.

'She'd have been nigh to where the road passes by and on to Achnaleish?' he asked.

'The hare? Yes, we found her on the road there.'

Sandie turned away.

'She aye sat there,' he said.

There were a number of little plantations climbing up the steep hill-side from Achnaleish to the moor above, and we had a pleasant slack sort of morning shooting there, walking through and round them with a nondescript tribe of beaters, among whom the serious Buxton figured. We had fair enough sport, but of the hares which Jim had seen in such profusion none that morning came to the gun, till at last, just before lunch, there came out of the apex of one of these plantations, some thirty yards from where Jim was standing, a very large, dark-coloured hare. For one moment I saw him hesitate — for he holds the correct view about long or doubtful shots at hares — then he put up his gun to fire. Sandie, who had walked round outside, after giving the beaters their instructions, was at this moment close to him, and with incredible quickness rushed upon him and with his stick struck up the barrels of the gun before he could fire.

'Black hare!' he cried. 'Ye'd shoot a black hare? There's no shooting of hares at all in Achnaleish, and mark that.'

Never have I seen so sudden and extraordinary a change in a man's face: it was as if he had just prevented some blackguard of the street from murdering his wife.

'An' the sickness about an' all,' he added indignantly. 'When the puir folk escape from their peching fevered bodies an hour or two, to the caller muirs.'

Then he seemed to recover himself.

'I ask your pardon, sir,' he said to Jim. 'I was upset with ane thing an' anither, an' the black hare ye found deid last night — eh, I'm blatherin' again. But there's no a hare shot on Achnaleish, that's sure.'

Jim was still looking in mere speechless astonishment at Sandie when I came up. And, though shooting is dear to me, so too is folk-lore.

'But we've taken the shooting of Achnaleish, Sandie,' I said. 'There was nothing there about not shooting hares.'

Sandie suddenly boiled up again for a minute.

'An' mebbe there was nothing there about shooting the bairns and the weemen!' he cried.

I looked round, and saw that by now the beaters had all come through the wood: of them Buxton and Jim's valet, who was also among them, stood apart: all the rest were standing round us two with gleaming eyes and open mouths, hanging on the debate, and forced, so I imagined, from their imperfect knowledge of English to attend closely in order to catch the drift of what went on. Every now and then a murmur of Gaelic passed between them, and this somehow I found peculiarly disconcerting.

'But what have the hares to do with the children or women of Achnaleish?' I asked.

There was no reply to this beyond the reiterated sentence: 'There's na shooting of hares in Achnaleish whatever,' and then Sandie turned to Jim.

'That's the end of the bit wood, sir,' he said. 'We've been a'roound.'

Certainly the beat had been very satisfactory. A roe had fallen to Jim (one ought also to have fallen to me, but remained, if not standing, at any rate running away). We had a dozen of black-game, four pigeons, six brace of grouse (these were, of course, but outliers, as we had not gone on to the moor proper at all), some thirty rabbits, and four couple of woodcock. This, it must be understood, was just from the fringe of plantations about the house, but this was all we meant to do to-day, making only a morning of it, since our ladies had expressly desired first lessons in the art of angling in the afternoon, so that they too could be busy. Excellently too had Sandie worked the beat, leaving us now, after going, as he said, all round, a couple of hundred yards only from the house, at a few minutes to two.

So, after a little private signalling from Jim to me, he spoke to Sandie, dropping the hare-question altogether.

'Well, the beat has gone excellently,' he said, 'and this afternoon we'll be fishing. Please settle with the beaters every evening, and tell me what you have paid out. Good morning to you all.'

We walked back to the house, but the

moment we had turned a hum of confabulation began behind us, and, looking back, I saw Sandie and all the beaters in close whispering conclave. Then Jim spoke.

'More in your line than mine,' he said; 'I prefer shooting a hare to routing out some cock-and-bull story as to why I shouldn't. What does it all mean?'

I mentioned what I had found in Elwes last night.

'Then do they think it was we who killed the old lady on the road, and that I was going to kill somebody else this morning?' he asked. 'How does one know that they won't say that rabbits are their aunts, and woodcock their uncles, and grouse their children? I never heard such rot, and to-morrow we'll have a hare drive. Blow the grouse! We'll settle this hare-question first.'

Jim by this time was in the frame of mind typical of the English when their rights are threatened. He had the shooting of Achna-leish, on which were hares, sir, hares. And if he chose to shoot hares, neither papal bull nor royal charter could stop him.

'Then there'll be a row,' said I, and Jim sniffed scornfully.

At lunch Sandie's remark about the 'sickness,' which I had forgotten till that moment, was explained.

'Fancy that horrible influenza getting here,' said Madge. 'Mabel and I went down to the village this morning, and, oh, Ted, you can get all sorts of things, from mackintoshes to peppermints, at the most heavenly shop, and there was a child there looking awfully ill and feverish. So we inquired: it was the 'sickness' — that was all they knew. But, from what the woman said, it's clearly influenza. Sudden fever, and all the rest of it.'

'Bad type?' I asked.

'Yes; there have been several deaths already among the old people from pneumonia following it.'

Now, I hope that as an Englishman I too have a notion of my rights, and attempt anyhow to enforce them, as a general rule, if they are wantonly threatened. But if a mad bull wishes to prevent my going across a certain field, I do not insist on my rights, but go round instead, since I see no reasonable hope of convincing the bull that according to the constitution of my country I may walk in this field unmolested. And that afternoon, as Madge and I drifted about the loch, while I was not employed in disentangling her flies from each other or her hair or my coat, I pondered over our position with regard to the hares and men of Achnaleish, and thought that the question of the bull and the field represented our standpoint pretty accurately. Jim had the shooting of Achnaleish, and that undoubtedly included the right to shoot hares: so too he might have the right to walk over a field in which was a mad bull. But it seemed to me not more futile to argue with the bull than to hope to convince these folk of Achnaleish that the hares were — as was assuredly the case — only hares, and not the embodiments of their friends and relations. For that, beyond all doubt, was their belief, and it would take, not half an hour's talk, but perhaps a couple of generations of education to kill that belief, or even to reduce it to the level of a superstition. At present it was no superstition — the terror and incredulous horror on Sandie's face when Jim raised his gun to fire at the hare told me that — it was a belief as sober and commonplace as our own belief that the hares were not incarnations of living folk in Achnaleish.

Also, virulent influenza was raging in the place, and Jim proposed to have a hare-drive to-morrow! What would happen?

That evening Jim raved about it in the smoking-room.

'But, good gracious, man, what can they do?' he cried. 'What's the use of an old gaffer from Achnaleish saying I've shot his grand-daughter and, when he is asked to produce the corpse, telling the jury that we've eaten it, but that he has got the skin as evidence? What skin? A hare-skin! Oh, folklore is all very well in its way, a nice subject for discussion when topics are scarce, but don't tell me it can enter into practical life. What can they do?'

'They can shoot us,' I remarked.

'The canny, God-fearing Scotchmen shoot us for shooting hares?' he asked.

'Well, it's a possibility. However, I don't think you'll have much of a hare-drive in any case.'

'Why not?'

'Because you won't get a single native beater, and you won't get a keeper to come either.'

'You'll have to go with Buxton and your man.'

'Then I'll discharge Sandie,' snapped Jim.

'That would be a pity: he knows his work.'

Jim got up.

'Well, his work to-morrow will be to drive hares for you and me,' said Jim. 'Or do you funk?'

'I funk,' I replied.

The scene next morning was extremely short. Jim and I went out before breakfast, and found Sandie at the back door, silent and respectful. In the yard were a dozen young Highlanders, who had beaten for us the day before.

'Morning, Sandie,' said Jim shortly. 'We'll drive hares to-day. We ought to get a lot in those narrow gorges up above. Get a dozen beaters more, can you?'

'There will be na hare-drive here,' said Sandie quietly.

'I have given you your orders,' said Jim.

Sandie turned to the group of beaters outside and spoke half a dozen words in Gaelic. Next moment the yard was empty, and they were all running down the hillside towards Achnaleish.

One stood on the skyline a moment, waving his arms, making some signal, as I supposed, to the village below. Then Sandie turned again.

'An' whaur are your beaters, sir?' he asked.

For the moment I was afraid Jim was going to strike him. But he controlled himself.

'You are discharged,' he said.

The hare-drive, therefore, since there were neither beaters nor keeper — Maclaren, the head-keeper, having been given this 'dayoff' to bury his mother — was clearly out of the question, and Jim, still blustering rather, but a good bit taken aback at the sudden disciplined defection of the beaters, was in betting humour that they would all return by to-morrow morning. Meanwhile the post which should have arrived before now had not come, though Mabel from her bedroom window had seen the post-cart on its way up the drive a quarter of an hour ago. At that a sudden idea struck me, and I ran to the edge of the hog's back on which the house was set. It was even as I thought: the post-cart was just striking the high-road below, going away from the house and back to the village, without having left our letters.

I went back to the dining-room. Everything apparently was going wrong this morning: the bread was stale, the milk was not fresh, and the bell was rung for Buxton. Quite so: neither milkman nor baker had called.

From the point of view of folk-lore this was admirable.

'There's another cock-and-bull story called 'taboo,'' I said. 'It means that nobody will supply you with anything.'

'My dear fellow, a little knowledge is a dangerous thing,' said Jim, helping himself to marmalade.

I laughed.

'You are irritated,' I said, 'because you are beginning to be afraid that there is something in it.'

'Yes, that's quite true,' he said. 'But who could have supposed there was anything in it? Ah, dash it! there can't be. A hare is a hare.'

'Except when it is your first cousin,' said I.

'Then I shall go out and shoot first cousins by myself,' he said. That, I am glad to say, in the light of what followed, we dissuaded him from doing, and instead he went off with Madge down the burn. And I, I may confess, occupied myself the whole morning, ensconced in a thick piece of scrub on the edge of the steep brae above Achnaleish, in watching through a field-glass what went on there. One could see as from a balloon almost: the street with its houses was spread like a map below.

First, then, there was a funeral — the funeral, I suppose, of the mother of Maclaren, attended, I should say, by the whole village. But after that there was no dispersal of the folk to their work: it was as if it was the Sabbath; they hung about the street talking. Now one group would break up, but it would only go to swell another, and no one went either to his house or to the fields.

Then, shortly before lunch, another idea occurred to me, and I ran down the hill-side, appearing suddenly in the street, to put it to the test. Sandie was there, but he turned his back square on me, as did everybody else, and as I approached any group talk fell dead. But a certain movement seemed to be going on; where they stood and talked before, they now moved and were silent.

Soon I saw what that meant. None would

remain in the street with me: every man was going to his house.

The end house of the street was clearly the 'heavenly shop' we had been told of yesterday.

The door was open and a small child was looking round it as I approached, for my plan was to go in, order something, and try to get into conversation. But, while I was still a yard or two off, I saw through the glass of the door a man inside come quickly up and pull the child roughly away, banging the door and locking it. I knocked and rang, but there was no response: only from inside came the crying of the child.

The street which had been so busy and populous was now completely empty; it might have been the street of some long-deserted place, but that thin smoke curled here and there above the houses. It was as silent, too, as the grave, but, for all that, I knew it was watching. From every house, I felt sure, I was being watched by eyes of mistrust and hate, yet no sign of living being could I see. There was to me something rather eerie about this: to know one is watched by invisible eyes is never, I suppose, quite a comfortable sensation; to know that those eyes are all hostile does not increase the sense of security. So I just climbed back up the hillside again, and from my thicket above the brae again I peered down. Once more the street was full.

Now, all this made me uneasy: the taboo had been started, and — since not a soul had been near us since Sandie gave the word, whatever it was, that morning — was in excellent working order. Then what was the purport of these meetings and colloquies? What else threatened? The afternoon told me.

It was about two o'clock when these meetings finally broke up, and at once the whole village left the street for the hill-sides, much as if they were all returning to work. The only odd thing indeed was that no one remained behind: women and children alike went out, all in little parties of two and three. Some of these I watched rather idly, for I had formed the hasty conclusion that they were all going back to their usual employments, and saw that here a woman and girl were cutting dead bracken and heather. That was reasonable enough, and I turned my glass on others.

Group after group I examined; all were doing the same thing, cutting fuel . . . fuel.

Then vaguely, with a sense of impossibility, a thought flashed across me; again it flashed, more vividly. This time I left my hiding-place with considerable alacrity and went to find Jim down by the burn. I told him exactly what I had seen and what I believed it meant, and I fancy that his belief in the possibility of folk-lore entering the domain of practical life was very considerably quickened. In any case, it was not a quarter of an hour afterwards that the chauffeur and I were going, precisely as fast as the Napier was able, along the road to Lairg. We had not told the women what my conjecture was, because we believed that, making the dispositions we were making, there was no cause for alarm-sounding. One private signal only existed between Jim within the house that night and me outside. If my conjecture proved to be correct, he was to place a light in the window of my room, which I should see returning after dark from Lairg. My ostensible reason for going was to get some local fishing-flies.

As we flowed — there is no other word for the movement of these big cars but that — over the road to Lairg, I ran over everything in my mind. I felt no doubt whatever that all the brushwood and kindling I had seen being gathered in was to be piled after nightfall round our walls and set on fire. This certainly would not be done till after dark; indeed, we both felt sure that it would not be done till it was supposed that we were all abed. It remained to see whether the police at Lairg agreed with my conjecture, and it was to ascertain this that I was now flowing there.

I told my story to the chief constable as soon as I got there, omitting nothing and, I think, exaggerating nothing. His face got graver and graver as I proceeded.

'Yes, sir, you did right to come,' he said. 'The folk at Achnaleish are the dourest and the most savage in all Scotland. You'll have to give up this hare-hunting, though, whatever,' he added.

He rang up his telephone.

'I'll get five men,' he said, 'and I'll be with you in ten minutes.'

Our plan of campaign was simple. We were to leave the car well out of sight of Achnaleish, and — supposing the signal was in my window — steal up from all sides to command the house from every direction. It would not be difficult to make our way unseen through the plantations that ran up close to the house, and hidden at their margins we could see whether the brushwood and heather were piled up round the lodge. There we should wait to see if anybody attempted to fire it. That somebody, whenever he showed his light, would be instantly covered by a rifle and challenged.

It was about ten when we dismounted and stalked our way up to the house. The light burned in my window; all else was quiet. Personally, I was unarmed, and so, when I had planted the men in places of advantageous concealment round the house, my work was over. Then I returned to Sergeant Duncan, the chief constable, at the corner of the hedge by the garden, and waited.

How long we waited I do not know, but it seemed as if æons slipped by over us. Now and then an owl would hoot, now and then a rabbit ran out from cover and nibbled the short sweet grass of the lawn. The night was thickly overcast with clouds, and the house seemed no more than a black dot, with slits of light where windows were lit within. By and by even these slits of illumination were extinguished, and other lights appeared in the top story. After a while they, too, vanished; no sign of life appeared on the quiet house. Then suddenly the end came: I heard a foot grate on the gravel; I saw the gleam of a lantern, and heard Duncan's voice.

'Man,' he shouted, 'if you move hand or foot I fire. My rifle-bead is dead on you.'

Then I blew the whistle; the others ran up, and in less than a minute it was all over. The man we closed in on was Maclaren.

'They killed my mither with that hell-carriage,' he said, 'as she juist sat on the road, puir body, who had niver hurt them.'

And that seemed to him an excellent reason for attempting to burn us all to death.

But it took time to get into the house: their preparations had been singularly workman-like, for every window and door on the ground floor was wired up.

Now, we had Achnaleish for two months, but we had no wish to be burned or otherwise murdered. What we wanted was not a prosecution of our head-keeper, but peace, the necessaries of life, and beaters. For that we were willing to shoot no hares, and release Maclaren. An hour's conclave next morning settled these things; the ensuing two months were most enjoyable, and relations were the friendliest.

But if anybody wants to test how far what Jim still calls cock-and-bull stories can enter into practical life, I should suggest to him to go a-shooting hares at Achnaleish.

How Fear Departed from the Long Gallery

Church-Peveril is a house so beset and frequented by spectres, both visible and audible, that none of the family which it shelters under its acre and a half of green copper roofs takes psychical phenomena with any seriousness. For to the Peverils the appearance of a ghost is a matter of hardly greater significance than is the appearance of the post to those who live in more ordinary houses. It arrives, that is to say, practically every day, it knocks (or makes other noises), it is observed coming up the drive (or in other places). I myself, when staying there, have seen the present Mrs. Peveril, who is rather short-sighted, peer into the dusk, while we were taking our coffee on the terrace after dinner, and say to her daughter:

'My dear, was not that the Blue Lady who has just gone into the shrubbery. I hope she won't frighten Flo. Whistle for Flo, dear.'

(Flo, it may be remarked, is the youngest and most precious of many dachshunds.)

Blanche Peveril gave a cursory whistle, and crunched the sugar left unmelted at the bottom of her coffee-cup between her very white teeth.

'Oh, darling, Flo isn't so silly as to mind,'

she said. 'Poor blue Aunt Barbara is such a bore!'

'Whenever I meet her she always looks as if she wanted to speak to me, but when I say, 'What is it, Aunt Barbara?' she never utters, but only points somewhere towards the house, which is so vague. I believe there was something she wanted to confess about two hundred years ago, but she has forgotten what it is.'

Here Flo gave two or three short pleased barks, and came out of the shrubbery wagging her tail, and capering round what appeared to me to be a perfectly empty space on the lawn.

'There! Flo has made friends with her,' said Mrs. Peveril. 'I wonder why she — in that very stupid shade of blue.'

From this it may be gathered that even with regard to psychical phenomena there is some truth in the proverb that speaks of familiarity. But the Peverils do not exactly treat their ghosts with contempt, since most of that delightful family never despised anybody except such people as avowedly did not care for hunting or shooting, or golf or skating. And as all of their ghosts are of their family, it seems reasonable to suppose that they all, even the poor Blue Lady, excelled at one time in field-sports. So far, then, they harbour no such unkindness or contempt, but only pity. Of one Peveril, indeed, who broke his neck in vainly attempting to ride up the main staircase on a thoroughbred mare after some monstrous and violent deed in the back-garden, they are very fond, and Blanche comes downstairs in the morning with an eye unusually bright when she can announce that Master Anthony was 'very loud' last night. He (apart from the fact of his having been so foul a ruffian) was a tremendous fellow across country, and they like these indications of the continuance of his superb vitality. In fact, it is supposed to be a compliment, when you go to stay at Church-Peveril, to be assigned a bedroom which is frequented by defunct members of the family. It means that you are worthy to look on the august and villainous dead, and you will find yourself shown into some vaulted or tapestried chamber, without benefit of electric light, and are told that great-great-grandmamma Bridget occasion- ally has vague business by the fireplace, but it is better not to talk to her, and that you will hear Master Anthony 'awfully well' if he attempts the front staircase any time before morning. There you are left for your night's repose, and, having quakingly undressed, begin reluctantly to put out your candles. It is draughty in these great chambers, and the solemn tapestry swings and bellows and subsides, and the firelight dances on the forms of huntsmen and warriors and stern pursuits. Then you climb into your bed, a bed so huge that you feel as if the desert of Sahara was spread for you, and pray, like the mariners who sailed with St. Paul, for day. And, all the time, you are aware that Freddy and Harry and Blanche and possibly even Mrs. Peveril are quite capable of dressing up and making disquieting tappings outside your door, so that when you open it some inconjecturable horror fronts you. For myself, I stick steadily to the assertion that I have an obscure valvular disease of the heart, and so sleep undisturbed in the new wing of the house where Aunt Barbara, and great-great-grandmamma Bridget and Master Anthony never penetrate. I forget the details of great-great-grandmamma Bridget, but she certainly cut the throat of some distant relation before she disembowelled herself with the axe that had been used at Agincourt. Before that she had led a very sultry life, crammed with amazing incident.

But there is one ghost at Church-Peveril at which the family never laugh, in which they feel no friendly and amused interest, and of which they only speak just as much as is necessary for the safety of their guests. More properly it should be described as two ghosts, for the 'haunt' in question is that of two very young children, who were twins. These, not without reason, the family take very seriously indeed. The story of them, as told me by Mrs. Peveril, is as follows:

In the year 1602, the same being the last of Queen Elizabeth's reign, a certain Dick Peveril was greatly in favour at Court. He was brother to Master Joseph Peveril, then owner of the family house and lands, who two years previously, at the respectable age of seventy-four, became father of twin boys, first-born of his progeny. It is known that the royal and ancient virgin had said to handsome Dick, who was nearly forty years his brother's junior, "'Tis pity that you are not master of Church-Peveril,' and these words probably suggested to him a sinister design. Be that as it may, handsome Dick, who very adequately sustained the family reputation for wicked-ness, set off to ride down to Yorkshire, and found that, very conveniently, his brother Joseph had just been seized with an apoplexy, which appeared to be the result of a continued spell of hot weather combined with the necessity of quenching his thirst with an augmented amount of sack, and had actually died while handsome Dick, with God knows what thoughts in his mind, was journeying

163

northwards. Thus it came about that he arrived at Church-Peveril just in time for his brother's funeral. It was with great propriety that he attended the obsequies, and returned to spend a sympathetic day or two of mourning with his widowed sister-in-law, who was but a faint-hearted dame, little fit to be mated with such hawks as these. On the second night of his stay, he did that which the Peverils regret to this day. He entered the room where the twins slept with their nurse, and quietly strangled the latter as she slept. Then he took the twins and put them into the fire which warms the long gallery. The weather, which up to the day of Joseph's death had been so hot, had changed suddenly to bitter cold, and the fire was heaped high with burning logs and was exultant with flame. In the core of this conflagration he struck out a cremation-chamber, and into that he threw the two children, stamping them down with his riding-boots. They could just walk, but they could not walk out of that ardent place. It is said that he laughed as he added more logs. Thus he became master of Church-Peveril.

The crime was never brought home to him, but he lived no longer than a year in the enjoyment of his blood-stained inheritance. When he lay a-dying he made his confession to the priest who attended him, but his spirit struggled forth from its fleshly coil before Absolution could be given him. On that very night there began in Church-Peveril the haunting which to this day is but seldom spoken of by the family, and then only in low tones and with serious mien. For only an hour or two after handsome Dick's death, one of the servants passing the door of the long gallery heard from within peals of the loud laughter so jovial and yet so sinister which he had thought would never be heard in the house again. In a moment of that cold courage which is so nearly akin to mortal terror he opened the door and entered, expecting to see he knew not what manifestation of him who lay dead in the room below. Instead he saw two little white-robed figures toddling towards him hand in hand across the moon-lit floor.

The watchers in the room below ran upstairs startled by the crash of his fallen body, and found him lying in the grip of some dread convulsion. Just before morning he regained consciousness and told his tale. Then pointing with trembling and ash-grey finger towards the door, he screamed aloud, and so fell back dead.

During the next fifty years this strange and terrible legend of the twin-babies became fixed and consolidated. Their appearance, luckily for those who inhabit the house, was exceedingly rare, and during these years they seem to have been seen four or five times only. On each occasion they appeared at night, between sunset and sunrise, always in the same long gallery, and always as two toddling children scarcely able to walk. And on each occasion the luckless individual who saw them died either speedily or terribly, or with both speed and terror, after the accursed vision had appeared to him. Sometimes he might live for a few months: he was lucky if he died, as did the servant who first saw them, in a few hours. Vastly more awful was the fate of a certain Mrs. Canning, who had the ill-luck to see them in the middle of the next century, or to be quite accurate, in the year 1760. By this time the hours and the place of their appearance were well known, and, as up till a year ago, visitors were warned not to go between sunset and sunrise into the long gallery.

But Mrs. Canning, a brilliantly clever and beautiful woman, admirer also and friend of the notorious sceptic M. Voltaire, wilfully went and sat night after night, in spite of all protestations, in the haunted place. For four evenings she saw nothing, but on the fifth she had her will, for the door in the middle of the gallery opened, and there came toddling towards her the ill-omened innocent little pair. It seemed that even then she was not frightened, but she thought it good, poor wretch, to mock at them, telling them it was time for them to get back into the fire. They gave no word in answer, but turned away from her crying and sobbing. Immediately after they disappeared from her vision and she rustled downstairs to where the family and guests in the house were waiting for her, with the triumphant announcement that she has seen them both, and must needs write to M. Voltaire, saying that she had spoken to spirits made manifest. It would make him laugh. But when some months later the whole news reached him he did not laugh at all.

Mrs. Canning was one of the great beauties of her day, and in the year 1760 she was at the height and zenith of her blossoming. The chief beauty, if it is possible to single out one point where all was so exquisite, lay in the dazzling colour and incomparable brilliance of her complexion. She was now just thirty years of age, but, in spite of the excesses of her life, retained the snow and roses of girlhood, and she courted the bright light of day which other women shunned, for it but showed to great advantage the splendour of her skin. In consequence she was very considerably dismayed one morning, about a fortnight after her strange experience in the long gallery, to observe on her left cheek, an inch or two below her turquoise-coloured eyes, a little greyish patch of skin, about as big as a threepenny piece. It was in vain that she applied her accustomed washes and unguents: vain, too, were the arts of her fardeuse and of her medical adviser. For a week she kept herself secluded, martyring herself with solitude and unaccustomed physics, and for result at the end of the week she had no amelioration to comfort herself with: instead this woeful grey patch had doubled itself in size. Thereafter the nameless disease, whatever it was, developed in new and terrible ways. From the centre of the discoloured place there sprouted forth little lichen-like tendrils of greenish-grey, and another patch appeared on her lower lip. This, too, soon vegetated, and one morning, on opening her eyes to the horror of a new day, she found that her vision was strangely blurred. She sprang to her looking-glass, and what she saw caused her to shriek aloud with horror. From under her upper eye-lid a fresh growth had sprung up, mushroom-like, in the night, and its filaments extended downwards, screening the pupil of her eye. Soon after, her tongue and throat were attacked: the air passages became obstructed, and death by suffocation was merciful after such suffering.

More terrible yet was the case of a certain Colonel Blantyre who fired at the children with his revolver. What he went through is not to be recorded here.

It is this haunting, then, that the Peverils take quite seriously, and every guest on his arrival in the house is told that the long gallery must not be entered after nightfall on any pretext whatever. By day, however, it is a delightful room and intrinsically merits description, apart from the fact that the due understanding of its geography is necessary for the account that here follows. It is full eighty feet in length, and is lit by a row of six tall windows looking over the gardens at the back of the house. A door communicates with the landing at the top of the main staircase, and about half-way down the gallery in the wall facing the windows is another door communicating with the back staircase and servants' quarters, and thus the gallery forms a constant place of passage for them in going to the rooms on the first landing. It was through this door that the baby-figures came when they appeared to Mrs. Canning, and on several other occasions they have been known to make their entry here, for the room out of which handsome Dick took them lies just beyond at the top of the back stairs. Further on again in the gallery is the fireplace into which he thrust them, and at the far end a large bow-window looks straight down the avenue. Above this fireplace there hangs with grim significance a portrait of handsome Dick, in the insolent beauty of early manhood, attributed to Holbein, and a dozen other portraits of great merit face the windows. During the day this is the most frequented sitting-room in the house, for its other visitors never appear there then, nor does it then ever resound with the harsh jovial laugh of handsome Dick, which sometimes, after dark has fallen, is heard by passers-by on the landing outside. But Blanche does not grow bright-eyed when she hears it: she shuts her ears and hastens to put a greater distance between her and the sound of that atrocious mirth.

But during the day the long gallery is frequented by many occupants, and much laughter in no wise sinister or saturnine resounds there. When summer lies hot over the land, those occupants lounge in the deep window seats, and when winter spreads his icy fingers and blows shrilly between his frozen palms, congregate round the fireplace at the far end, and perch, in companies of cheerful chatterers, upon sofa and chair, and chair-back and floor. Often have I sat there on long August evenings up till dressing-time, but never have I been there when anyone has seemed disposed to linger over-late without hearing the warning: 'It is close on sunset: shall we go?' Later on in the shorter autumn days they often have tea laid there, and sometimes it has happened that, even while merriment was most uproarious, Mrs. Peveril has suddenly looked out of the window and said, 'My dears, it is getting so late: let us finish our nonsense downstairs in the hall.' And then for a moment a curious hush always falls on loquacious family and guests alike, and as if some bad news had just been known, we all make our silent way out of the place.

But the spirits of the Peverils (of the living ones, that is to say) are the most mercurial imaginable, and the blight which the thought of handsome Dick and his doings casts over them passes away again with amazing rapidity.

A typical party, large, young, and peculiarly cheerful, was staying at Church-Peveril shortly after Christmas last year, and as usual on December 31, Mrs. Peveril was giving her annual New Year's Eve ball. The house was quite full, and she had commandeered as well the greater part of the Peveril Arms to provide sleeping-quarters for the overflow from the house. For some days past a black and windless frost had stopped all hunting, but it is an ill windlessness that blows no good (if so mixed a metaphor may be forgiven), and the lake below the house had for the last day or two been covered with an adequate and admirable sheet of ice. Everyone in the house had been occupied all the morning of that day in performing swift and violent manoeuvres on the elusive surface, and as soon as lunch was over we all, with one exception, hurried out again. This one exception was Madge Dalrymple, who had had the misfortune to fall rather badly earlier in the day, but hoped, by resting her injured knee, instead of joining the skaters again, to be able to dance that evening. The hope, it is true, was the most sanguine sort, for she could but hobble ignobly back to the house, but with the breezy optimism which characterises the Peverils (she is Blanche's first cousin), she remarked that it would be but tepid enjoyment that she could, in her present state, derive from further skating, and thus she sacrificed little, but might gain much.

Accordingly, after a rapid cup of coffee which was served in the long gallery, we left Madge comfortably reclined on the big sofa at right-angles to the fireplace, with an attractive book to beguile the tedium till tea. Being of the family, she knew all about handsome Dick and the babies, and the fate of Mrs. Canning and Colonel Blantyre, but as we went out I heard Blanche say to her, 'Don't run it too fine, dear,' and Madge had replied, 'No; I'll go away well before sunset.' And so we left her alone in the long gallery.

Madge read her attractive book for some minutes, but failing to get absorbed in it, put it down and limped across to the window. Though it was still but little after two, it was but a dim and uncertain light that entered, for the crystalline brightness of the morning had given place to a veiled obscurity produced by flocks of thick clouds which were coming sluggishly up from the north-east. Already the whole sky was overcast with them, and occasionally a few snow-flakes fluttered waveringly down past the long windows. From the darkness and bitter cold of the afternoon, it seemed to her that there was like to be a heavy snowfall before long, and these outward signs were echoed inwardly in her by that muffled drowsiness of the brain, which to those who are sensitive to the pressures and lightness of weather portends storm. Madge was peculiarly the prey of such external influences: to her a brisk morning gave an ineffable brightness and briskness of spirit, and correspondingly the approach of heavy weather produced a somnolence in sensation that both drowsed and depressed her.

It was in such mood as this that she limped back again to the sofa beside the log-fire. The whole house was comfortably heated by water-pipes, and though the fire of logs and peat, an adorable mixture, had been allowed to burn low, the room was very warm. Idly she watched the dwindling flames, not opening her book again, but lying on the sofa with face towards the fireplace, intending drowsily and not immediately to go to her own room and spend the hours, until the return of the skaters made gaiety in the house again, in writing one or two neglected letters. Still drowsily she began thinking over what she had to communicate: one letter several days overdue should go to her mother, who was immensely interested in the psychical affairs of the family. She would tell her how Master Anthony had been prodigiously active on the staircase a night or two ago, and how the Blue Lady, regardless of the severity of the weather, had been seen by Mrs. Peveril that morning, strolling about. It was rather interesting: the Blue Lady had gone down the laurel walk and had been seen by her to enter the stables, where, at the moment, Freddy Peveril was inspecting the frost-bound hunters. Identically then, a sudden panic had spread through the stables, and the horses had whinnied and kicked, and shied, and sweated. Of the fatal twins nothing had been seen for many years past, but, as her mother knew, the Peverils never used the long gallery after dark.

Then for a moment she sat up, remembering that she was in the long gallery now. But it was still but a little after half-past two, and if she went to her room in half an hour, she would have ample time to write this and another letter before tea. Till then she would read her book. But she found she had left it on the window-sill, and it seemed scarcely worth while to get it. She felt exceedingly drowsy.

The sofa where she lay had been lately recovered, in a greyish green shade of velvet, somewhat the colour of lichen. It was of very thick soft texture, and she luxuriously stretched her arms out, one on each side of her body, and pressed her fingers into the nap. How horrible that story of Mrs. Canning was: the growth on her face was of the colour of lichen. And then without further transition or blurring of thought Madge fell asleep.

She dreamed. She dreamed that she awoke

and found herself exactly where she had gone to sleep, and in exactly the same attitude. The flames from the logs had burned up again, and leaped on the walls, fitfully illuminating the picture of handsome Dick above the fireplace. In her dream she knew exactly what she had done to-day, and for what reason she was lying here now instead of being out with the rest of the skaters. She remembered also (still dreaming), that she was going to write a letter or two before tea, and prepared to get up in order to go to her room. As she half-rose she caught sight of her own arms lying out on each side of her on the grey velvet sofa.

But she could not see where her hands ended, and where the grey velvet began: her fingers seemed to have melted into the stuff. She could see her wrists quite clearly, and a blue vein on the backs of her hands, and here and there a knuckle. Then, in her dream, she remembered the last thought which had been in her mind before she fell asleep, namely the growth of the lichen-coloured vegetation on the face and the eyes and the throat of Mrs. Canning. At that thought the strangling terror of real nightmare began: she knew that she was being transformed into this grey stuff, and she was absolutely unable to move. Soon the grey would spread up her arms, and over her feet; when they came in from skating they would find here nothing but a huge misshapen cushion of lichen-coloured velvet, and that would be she. The horror grew more acute, and then by a violent effort she shook herself free of the clutches of this very evil dream, and she awoke.

For a minute or two she lay there, conscious only of the tremendous relief at finding herself awake. She felt again with her fingers the pleasant touch of the velvet, and drew them backwards and forwards, assuring herself that she was not, as her dream had suggested, melting into greyness and softness. But she was still, in spite of the violence of her awakening, very sleepy, and lay there till, looking down, she was aware that she could not see her hands at all. It was very nearly dark.

At that moment a sudden flicker of flame came from the dying fire, and a flare of burning gas from the peat flooded the room. The portrait of handsome Dick looked evilly down on her, and her hands were visible again. And then a panic worse than the panic of her dreams seized her.

Daylight had altogether faded, and she knew that she was alone in the dark in the terrible gallery.

This panic was of the nature of nightmare,

for she felt unable to move for terror. But it was worse than nightmare because she knew she was awake. And then the full cause of this frozen fear dawned on her; she knew with the certainty of absolute conviction that she was about to see the twin-babies.

She felt a sudden moisture break out on her face, and within her mouth her tongue and throat went suddenly dry, and she felt her tongue grate along the inner surface of her teeth. All power of movement had slipped from her limbs, leaving them dead and inert, and she stared with wide eyes into the blackness. The spurt of flame from the peat had burned itself out again, and darkness encompassed her.

Then on the wall opposite her, facing the windows, there grew a faint light of dusky crimson.

For a moment she thought it but heralded the approach of the awful vision, then hope revived in her heart, and she remembered that thick clouds had overcast the sky before she went to sleep, and guessed that this light came from the sun not yet quite sunk and set. This sudden revival of hope gave her the necessary stimulus, and she sprang off the sofa where she lay. She looked out of the window and saw the dull glow on the horizon. But before she could take a step forward it was

178

obscured again. A tiny sparkle of light came from the hearth which did no more than illuminate the tiles of the fireplace, and snow falling heavily tapped at the window panes. There was neither light nor sound except these.

But the courage that had come to her, giving her the power of movement, had not quite deserted her, and she began feeling her way down the gallery. And then she found that she was lost. She stumbled against a chair, and, recovering herself, stumbled against another. Then a table barred her way, and, turning swiftly aside, she found herself up against the back of a sofa.

Once more she turned and saw the dim gleam of the firelight on the side opposite to that on which she expected it. In her blind gropings she must have reversed her direction. But which way was she to go now. She seemed blocked in by furniture. And all the time insistent and imminent was the fact that the two innocent terrible ghosts were about to appear to her.

Then she began to pray. 'Lighten our darkness, O Lord,' she said to herself. But she could not remember how the prayer continued, and she had sore need of it. There was something about the perils of the night. All this time she felt about her with groping, fluttering hands. The fire-glimmer which should have been on her left was on her right again; therefore she must turn herself round again. 'Lighten our darkness,' she whispered, and then aloud she repeated, 'Lighten our darkness.'

She stumbled up against a screen, and could not remember the existence of any such screen.

Hastily she felt beside it with blind hands, and touched something soft and velvety. Was it the sofa on which she had lain? If so, where was the head of it. It had a head and a back and feet — it was like a person, all covered with grey lichen. Then she lost her head completely. All that remained to her was to pray; she was lost, lost in this awful place, where no one came in the dark except the babies that cried. And she heard her voice rising from whisper to speech, and speech to scream. She shrieked out the holy words, she yelled them as if blaspheming as she groped among tables and chairs and the pleasant things of ordinary life which had become so terrible.

Then came a sudden and an awful answer to her screamed prayer. Once more a pocket of inflammable gas in the peat on the hearth was reached by the smouldering embers, and the room started into light. She saw the evil eyes of handsome Dick, she saw the little ghostly snow-flakes falling thickly outside. And she saw where she was, just opposite the door through which the terrible twins made their entrance. Then the flame went out again, and left her in blackness once more. But she had gained something, for she had her geography now. The centre of the room was bare of furniture, and one swift dart would take her to the door of the landing above the main staircase and into safety. In that gleam she had been able to see the handle of the door, bright-brassed, luminous like a star. She would go straight for it; it was but a matter of a few seconds now.

She took a long breath, partly of relief, partly to satisfy the demands of her galloping heart.

But the breath was only half-taken when she was stricken once more into the immobility of nightmare.

There came a little whisper, it was no more than that, from the door opposite which she stood, and through which the twin-babies entered. It was not quite dark outside it, for she could see that the door was opening. And there stood in the opening two little white figures, side by side. They came towards her slowly, shufflingly. She could not see face or form at all distinctly, but the two little white figures were advancing. She knew them to be the ghosts of terror, innocent of the awful doom they were bound to bring, even as she was innocent. With the inconceivable rapidity of thought, she made up her mind what to do. She had not hurt them or laughed at them, and they, they were but babies when the wicked and bloody deed had sent them to their burning death. Surely the spirits of these children would not be inaccessible to the cry of one who was of the same blood as they, who had committed no fault that merited the doom they brought. If she entreated them they might have mercy, they might forebear to bring the curse on her, they might allow her to pass out of the place without blight, without the sentence of death, or the shadow of things worse than death upon her.

It was but for the space of a moment that she hesitated, then she sank down on to her knees, and stretched out her hands towards them.

'Oh, my dears,' she said, 'I only fell asleep. I have done no more wrong than that — '

She paused a moment, and her tender girl's heart thought no more of herself, but only of them, those little innocent spirits on whom so awful a doom was laid, that they should bring death where other children bring laughter, and doom for delight. But all those who had seen them before had dreaded and feared them, or had mocked at them.

Then, as the enlightenment of pity dawned on her, her fear fell from her like the wrinkled sheath that holds the sweet folded buds of Spring.

'Dears, I am so sorry for you,' she said. 'It is not your fault that you must bring me what you must bring, but I am not afraid any longer. I am only sorry for you. God bless you, you poor darlings.'

She raised her head and looked at them. Though it was so dark, she could now see their faces, though all was dim and wavering, like the light of pale flames shaken by a draught. But the faces were not miserable or fierce — they smiled at her with shy little baby smiles. And as she looked they grew faint, fading slowly away like wreaths of vapour in frosty air.

Madge did not at once move when they had vanished, for instead of fear there was wrapped round her a wonderful sense of peace, so happy and serene that she would not willingly stir, and so perhaps disturb it. But before long she got up, and feeling her way, but without any sense of nightmare pressing her on, or frenzy of fear to spur her, she went out of the long gallery, to find Blanche just coming upstairs whistling and swinging her skates.

'How's the leg, dear,' she asked. 'You're not limping any more.'

Till that moment Madge had not thought of it.

'I think it must be all right,' she said; 'I had forgotten it, anyhow. Blanche, dear, you won't be frightened for me, will you, but — but I have seen the twins.'

For a moment Blanche's face whitened with terror.

'What?' she said in a whisper.

'Yes, I saw them just now. But they were kind, they smiled at me, and I was so sorry for them. And somehow I am sure I have nothing to fear.'

It seems that Madge was right, for nothing has come to touch her. Something, her attitude to them, we must suppose, her pity, her sympathy, touched and dissolved and annihilated the curse.

Indeed, I was at Church-Peveril only last week, arriving there after dark. Just as I passed the gallery door, Blanche came out.

'Ah, there you are,' she said: 'I've just been seeing the twins. They looked too sweet and stopped nearly ten minutes. Let us have tea at once.'

184

Caterpillars

I saw a month or two ago in an Italian paper that the Villa Cascana, in which I once stayed, had been pulled down, and that a manufactory of some sort was in process of erection on its site.

There is therefore no longer any reason for refraining from writing of those things which I myself saw (or imagined I saw) in a certain room and on a certain landing of the villa in question, nor from mentioning the circumstances which followed, which may or may not (according to the opinion of the reader) throw some light on or be somehow connected with this experience.

The Villa Cascana was in all ways but one a perfectly delightful house, yet, if it were standing now, nothing in the world — I use the phrase in its literal sense — would induce me to set foot in it again, for I believe it to have been haunted in a very terrible and practical manner.

Most ghosts, when all is said and done, do not do much harm; they may perhaps terrify, but the person whom they visit usually gets over their visitation. They may on the other hand be entirely friendly and beneficent. But the appearances in the Villa Cascana were not beneficent, and had they made their 'visit' in a very slightly different manner, I do not suppose I should have got over it any more than Arthur Inglis did.

The house stood on an ilex-clad hill not far from Sestri di Levante on the Italian Riviera, looking out over the iridescent blues of that enchanted sea, while behind it rose the pale green chestnut woods that climb up the hillsides till they give place to the pines that, black in contrast with them, crown the slopes. All round it the garden in the luxuriance of mid-spring bloomed and was fragrant, and the scent of magnolia and rose, borne on the salt freshness of the winds from the sea, flowed like a stream through the cool vaulted rooms.

On the ground floor a broad pillared loggia ran round three sides of the house, the top of which formed a balcony for certain rooms of the first floor. The main staircase, broad and of grey marble steps, led up from the hall to the landing outside these rooms, which were three in number, namely, two big sitting-rooms and a bedroom arranged en suite. The latter was unoccupied, the sitting-rooms were in use. From these the main staircase was continued to the second floor, where were situated certain bedrooms, one of which I occupied, while from the other side of the first-floor landing some half-dozen steps led to another suite of rooms, where, at the time I am speaking of, Arthur Inglis, the artist, had his bedroom and studio. Thus the landing outside my bedroom at the top of the house commanded both the landing of the first floor and also the steps that led to Inglis' rooms. Jim Stanley and his wife, finally (whose guest I was), occupied rooms in another wing of the house, where also were the servants' quarters.

I arrived just in time for lunch on a brilliant noon of mid-May. The garden was shouting with colour and fragrance, and not less delightful after my broiling walk up from the marina, should have been the coming from the reverberating heat and blaze of the day into the marble coolness of the villa. Only (the reader has my bare word for this, and nothing more), the moment I set foot in the house I felt that something was wrong. This feeling, I may say, was quite vague, though very strong, and I remember that when I saw letters waiting for me on the table in the hall I felt certain that the explanation was here: I was convinced that there was bad news of some sort for me. Yet when I opened them I found no such explanation of my premonition: my correspondents all reeked of prosperity. Yet this clear miscarriage of a presentiment did not dissipate my uneasiness. In that cool fragrant house there was something wrong.

I am at pains to mention this because to the general view it may explain that though I am as a rule so excellent a sleeper that the extinction of my light on getting into bed is apparently contemporaneous with being called on the following morning, I slept very badly on my first night in the Villa Cascana. It may also explain the fact that when I did sleep (if it was indeed in sleep that I saw what I thought I saw) I dreamed in a very vivid and original manner, original, that is to say, in the sense that something that, as far as I knew, had never previously entered into my consciousness, usurped it then. But since, in addition to this evil premonition, certain words and events occurring during the rest of the day might have suggested something of what I thought happened that night, it will be well to relate them.

After lunch, then, I went round the house with Mrs. Stanley, and during our tour she referred, it is true, to the unoccupied bedroom on the first floor, which opened out of the room where we had lunched.

'We left that unoccupied,' she said, 'because Jim and I have a charming bedroom

190

and dressing-room, as you saw, in the wing, and if we used it ourselves we should have to turn the dining-room into a dressing-room and have our meals downstairs. As it is, however, we have our little flat there, Arthur Inglis has his little flat in the other passage; and I remembered (aren't I extraordinary?) that you once said that the higher up you were in a house the better you were pleased. So I put you at the top of the house, instead of giving you that room.'

It is true, that a doubt, vague as my uneasy premonition, crossed my mind at this. I did not see why Mrs. Stanley should have explained all this, if there had not been more to explain. I allow, therefore, that the thought that there was something to explain about the unoccupied bedroom was momentarily present to my mind.

The second thing that may have borne on my dream was this.

At dinner the conversation turned for a moment on ghosts. Inglis, with the certainty of conviction, expressed his belief that anybody who could possibly believe in the existence of supernatural phenomena was unworthy of the name of an ass. The subject instantly dropped. As far as I can recollect, nothing else occurred or was said that could bear on what follows.

We all went to bed rather early, and personally I yawned my way upstairs, feeling hideously sleepy. My room was rather hot, and I threw all the windows wide, and from without poured in the white light of the moon, and the love-song of many nightingales. I undressed quickly, and got into bed, but though I had felt so sleepy before, I now felt extremely wide-awake. But I was quite content to be awake: I did not toss or turn, I felt perfectly happy listening to the song and seeing the light. Then, it is possible, I may have gone to sleep, and what follows may have been a dream. I thought, anyhow, that after a time the nightingales ceased singing and the moon sank. I thought also that if, for some unexplained reason, I was going to lie awake all night, I might as well read, and I remembered that I had left a book in which I was interested in the dining-room on the first floor. So I got out of bed, lit a candle, and went downstairs. I went into the room, saw on a side-table the book I had come to look for, and then, simultaneously, saw that the door into the unoccupied bedroom was open. A curious grey light, not of dawn nor of moonshine, came out of it, and I looked in. The bed stood just opposite the door, a big four-poster, hung with tapestry at the head. Then I saw that the greyish light of the bedroom came from the bed, or rather from what was on the bed. For it was covered with great caterpillars, a foot or more in length, which crawled over it. They were faintly luminous, and it was the light from them that showed me the room. Instead of the sucker-feet of ordinary caterpillars they had rows of pincers like crabs, and they moved by grasping what they lay on with their pincers, and then sliding their bodies forward. In colour these dreadful insects were yellowish-grey, and they were covered with irregular lumps and swellings. There must have been hundreds of them, for they formed a sort of writhing, crawling pyramid on the bed. Occasionally one fell off on to the floor, with a soft fleshy thud, and though the floor was of hard concrete, it yielded to the pincerfeet as if it had been putty, and, crawling back, the caterpillar would mount on to the bed again, to rejoin its fearful companions. They appeared to have no faces, so to speak, but at one end of them there was a mouth that opened sideways in respiration.

Then, as I looked, it seemed to me as if they all suddenly became conscious of my presence.

All the mouths, at any rate, were turned in my direction, and next moment they began dropping off the bed with those soft fleshy thuds on to the floor, and wriggling towards me. For one second a paralysis as of a dream was on me, but the next I was running upstairs again to my room, and I remember feeling the cold of the marble steps on my bare feet. I rushed into my bedroom, and slammed the door behind me, and then — I was certainly wide-awake now — I found myself standing by my bed with the sweat of terror pouring from me. The noise of the banged door still rang in my ears. But, as would have been more usual, if this had been mere nightmare, the terror that had been mine when I saw those foul beasts crawling about the bed or dropping softly on to the floor did not cease then. Awake, now, if dreaming before, I did not at all recover from the horror of dream: it did not seem to me that I had dreamed. And until dawn, I sat or stood, not daring to lie down, thinking that every rustle or movement that I heard was the approach of the caterpillars. To them and the claws that bit into the cement the wood of the door was child's play: steel would not keep them out.

But with the sweet and noble return of day the horror vanished: the whisper of wind became benignant again: the nameless fear, whatever it was, was smoothed out and terrified me no longer. Dawn broke, hueless at first; then it grew dove-coloured, then the flaming pageant of light spread over the sky.

The admirable rule of the house was that everybody had breakfast where and when he pleased, and in consequence it was not till lunch-time that I met any of the other members of our party, since I had breakfast on my balcony, and wrote letters and other things till lunch. In fact, I got down to that meal rather late, after the other three had begun. Between my knife and fork there was a small pill-box of cardboard, and as I sat down Inglis spoke.

'Do look at that,' he said, 'since you are interested in natural history. I found it crawling on my counterpane last night, and I don't know what it is.'

I think that before I opened the pill-box I expected something of the sort which I found in it.

Inside it, anyhow, was a small caterpillar, greyish-yellow in colour, with curious bumps and excrescences on its rings. It was extremely active, and hurried round the box, this way and that.

Its feet were unlike the feet of any caterpillar I ever saw: they were like the pincers of a crab. I looked, and shut the lid down again.

'No, I don't know it,' I said, 'but it looks

rather unwholesome. What are you going to do with it?'

'Oh, I shall keep it,' said Inglis. 'It has begun to spin: I want to see what sort of a moth it turns into.'

I opened the box again, and saw that these hurrying movements were indeed the beginning of the spinning of the web of its cocoon. Then Inglis spoke again.

'It has got funny feet, too,' he said. 'They are like crabs' pincers. What's the Latin for crab?'

'Oh, yes, Cancer. So in case it is unique, let's christen it: 'Cancer Inglisensis.'' Then something happened in my brain, some momentary piecing together of all that I had seen or dreamed. Something in his words seemed to me to throw light on it all, and my own intense horror at the experience of the night before linked itself on to what he had just said. In effect, I took the box and threw it, caterpillar and all, out of the window. There was a gravel path just outside, and beyond it, a fountain playing into a basin. The box fell on to the middle of this.

Inglis laughed.

'So the students of the occult don't like solid facts,' he said. 'My poor caterpillar!'

The talk went off again at once on to other subjects, and I have only given in detail, as they happened, these trivialities in order to be sure myself that I have recorded everything that could have borne on occult subjects or on the subject of caterpillars. But at the moment when I threw the pill-box into the fountain, I lost my head: my only excuse is that, as is probably plain, the tenant of it was, in miniature, exactly what I had seen crowded on to the bed in the unoccupied room. And though this translation of those phantoms into flesh and blood — or whatever it is that caterpillars are made of — ought perhaps to have relieved the horror of the night, as a matter of fact it did nothing of the kind. It only made the crawling pyramid that covered the bed in the unoccupied room more hideously real.

After lunch we spent a lazy hour or two strolling about the garden or sitting in the loggia, and it must have been about four o'clock when Stanley and I started off to bathe, down the path that led by the fountain into which I had thrown the pill-box. The water was shallow and clear, and at the bottom of it I saw its white remains. The water had disintegrated the cardboard, and it had become no more than a few strips and shreds of sodden paper. The centre of the fountain was a marble Italian Cupid which squirted the water out of a wine-skin held under its arm. And crawling up its leg was the caterpillar. Strange and scarcely credible as it seemed, it must have survived the falling-to-bits of its prison, and made its way to shore, and there it was, out of arm's reach, weaving and waving this way and that as it evolved its cocoon.

Then, as I looked at it, it seemed to me again that, like the caterpillar I had seen last night, it saw me, and breaking out of the threads that surrounded it, it crawled down the marble leg of the Cupid and began swimming like a snake across the water of the fountain towards me. It came with extraordinary speed (the fact of a caterpillar being able to swim was new to me), and in another moment was crawling up the marble lip of the basin. Just then Inglis joined us.

'Why, if it isn't old 'Cancer Inglisensis' again,' he said, catching sight of the beast. 'What a tearing hurry it is in!'

We were standing side by side on the path, and when the caterpillar had advanced to within about a yard of us, it stopped, and began waving again as if in doubt as to the direction in which it should go. Then it appeared to make up its mind, and crawled on to Inglis' shoe.

'It likes me best,' he said, 'but I don't really know that I like it. And as it won't drown I think perhaps — '

He shook it off his shoe on to the gravel path and trod on it.

All afternoon the air got heavier and heavier with the Sirocco that was without doubt coming up from the south, and that night again I went up to bed feeling very sleepy; but below my drowsiness, so to speak, there was the consciousness, stronger than before, that there was something wrong in the house, that something dangerous was close at hand. But I fell asleep at once, and — how long after I do not know — either woke or dreamed I awoke, feeling that I must get up at once, or I should be too late. Then (dreaming or awake) I lay and fought this fear, telling myself that I was but the prey of my own nerves disordered by Sirocco or what not, and at the same time quite clearly knowing in another part of my mind, so to speak, that every moment's delay added to the danger. At last this second feeling became irresistible, and I put on coat and trousers and went out of my room on to the landing. And then I saw that I had already delayed too long, and that I was now too late.

The whole of the landing of the first floor below was invisible under the swarm of caterpillars that crawled there. The folding doors into the sitting-room from which opened the bedroom where I had seen them last night were shut, but they were squeezing through the cracks of it and dropping one by one through the keyhole, elongating themselves into mere string as they passed, and growing fat and lumpy again on emerging. Some, as if exploring, were nosing about the steps into the passage at the end of which were Inglis' rooms, others were crawling on the lowest steps of the staircase that led up to where I stood. The landing, however, was completely covered with them: I was cut off. And of the frozen horror that seized me when I saw that I can give no idea in words.

Then at last a general movement began to take place, and they grew thicker on the steps that led to Inglis' room. Gradually, like some hideous tide of flesh, they advanced along the passage, and I saw the foremost, visible by the pale grey luminousness that came from them, reach his door. Again and again I tried to shout and warn him, in terror all the time that they would turn at the sound of my voice and mount my stair instead, but for all my efforts I felt that no sound came from my throat. They crawled along the hinge-crack of his door, passing through as they had done before, and still I stood there, making impotent efforts to shout to him, to bid him escape while there was time.

At last the passage was completely empty: they had all gone, and at that moment I was conscious for the first time of the cold of the marble landing on which I stood barefooted. The dawn was just beginning to break in the Eastern sky.

Six months after I met Mrs. Stanley in a country house in England. We talked on many subjects and at last she said:

'I don't think I have seen you since I got that dreadful news about Arthur Inglis a month ago.'

'I haven't heard,' said I.

'No? He has got cancer. They don't even advise an operation, for there is no hope of a cure: he is riddled with it, the doctors say.'

Now during all these six months I do not think a day had passed on which I had not had in my mind the dreams (or whatever you like to call them) which I had seen in the Villa Cascana.

'It is awful, is it not?' she continued, 'and I feel I can't help feeling, that he may have — '

'Caught it at the villa?' I asked.

She looked at me in blank surprise.

'Why did you say that?' she asked. 'How did you know?'

Then she told me. In the unoccupied bedroom a year before there had been a fatal case of cancer. She had, of course, taken the best advice and had been told that the utmost dictates of prudence would be obeyed so long as she did not put anybody to sleep in the room, which had also been thoroughly disinfected and newly white-washed and painted. But —

The Cat

Many people will doubtless remember that exhibition at the Royal Academy, not so many seasons ago which came to be known as Alingham's year, when Dick Alingham vaulted, with one bound, as it were, out of the crowd of strugglers and seated himself with admirably certain poise on the very topmost pinnacle of contemporary fame. He exhibited three portraits, each a masterpiece, which killed every picture within range. But since that year nobody cared anything for pictures whether in or out of range except those three, it did not signify so greatly. The phenomenon of his appearance was as sudden as that of the meteor, coming from nowhere and sliding large and luminous across the remote and star-sown sky, as inexplicable as the bursting of a spring on some dust-ridden rocky hillside. Some fairy godmother, one might conjecture, had bethought herself of her forgotten godson, and with a wave of her hand bestowed on him this transcendent gift. But, as the Irish say, she held her wand in her left hand, for her gift had another side to it. Or perhaps, again, Jim Merwick is right, and the theory he propounds in his monograph, 'On certain obscure lesions of the nerve centres,' says the final word on the subject.

Dick Alingham himself, as was indeed natural, was delighted with his fairy godmother or his obscure lesion (whichever was responsible), and (the monograph spoken of above was written after Dick's death) confessed frankly to his friend Merwick, who was still struggling through the crowd of rising young medical practitioners, that it was all quite as inexplicable to himself as it was to anyone else.

'All I know about it,' he said, 'is that last autumn I went through two months of mental depression so hideous that I thought again and again that I must go off my head. For hours daily, I sat here, waiting for something to crack, which as far as I am concerned would end everything.

'Yes, there was a cause; you know it.'

He paused a moment and poured into his glass a fairly liberal allowance of whisky, filled it half up from a syphon, and lit a cigarette. The cause, indeed, had no need to be enlarged on, for Merwick quite well remembered how the girl Dick had been engaged to threw him over with an abruptness that was almost superb, when a more eligible suitor made his appearance. The latter was certainly very eligible indeed with his good looks, his title, and his million of money, and Lady Madingley — ex-future Mrs. Alingham — was perfectly content with what she had done.

She was one of those blonde, lithe, silken girls, who, happily for the peace of men's minds, are rather rare, and who remind one of some humanised yet celestial and bestial cat.

'I needn't speak of the cause,' Dick continued, 'but, as I say, for those two months I soberly thought that the only end to it would be madness. Then one evening when I was sitting here alone — I was always sitting alone — something did snap in my head. I know I wondered, without caring at all, whether this was the madness which I had been expecting, or whether (which would be preferable) some more fatal breakage had happened. And even while I wondered, I was aware that I was not depressed or unhappy any longer.'

He paused for so long in a smiling retrospect that Merwick indicated to him that he had a listener.

'Well?' he said.

'It was well indeed. I haven't been unhappy since. I have been riotously happy instead. Some divine doctor, I suppose, just wiped off that stain on my brain that hurt so. Heavens, how it hurt! Have a drink, by the way?'

'No, thanks,' said Merwick. 'But what has all this got to do with your painting?'

'Why, everything. For I had hardly realised the fact that I was happy again, when I was aware that everything looked different. The colours of all I saw were twice as vivid as they had been, shape and outline were intensified too. The whole visible world had been dusty and blurred before, and seen in a half-light. But now the lights were turned up, and there was a new heaven and a new earth. And in the same flash, I knew that I could paint things as I saw them. Which,' he concluded, 'I have done.'

There was something rather sublime about this, and Merwick laughed.

'I wish something would snap in my brain, if it kindles the perceptions in that way,' said he, 'but it is just possible that the snapping of things in one's brain does not always produce just that effect.'

'That is possible. Also, as I gather, things don't snap unless you have gone through some such hideous period as I have been through. And I tell you frankly that I wouldn't go through that again even to ensure a snap that would make me see things like Titian.'

'What did the snapping feel like?' asked Merwick.

Dick considered a moment.

'Do you know when a parcel comes, tied up with string, and you can't find a knife,' he said, 'and therefore you burn the string through, holding it taut? Well, it was like that: quite painless, only something got weaker and weaker, and then parted, softly without effort. Not very lucid, I'm afraid, but it was just like that. It had been burning a couple of months, you see.'

He turned away and hunted among the letters and papers which littered his writing-table till he found an envelope with a coronet on it. He chuckled to himself as he took it up.

'Commend me to Lady Madingley,' he said, 'for a brazen impudence in comparison with which brass is softer than putty. She wrote to me yesterday, asking me if I would finish the portrait I had begun of her last year, and let her have it at my own price.

'Then I think you have had a lucky escape,' remarked Merwick. 'I suppose you didn't even answer her.'

'Oh, yes, I did: why not? I said the price would be two thousand pounds, and I was ready to go on at once. She has agreed, and sent me a cheque for a thousand this evening.'

Merwick stared at him in blank astonishment. 'Are you mad?' he asked.

'I hope not, though one can never be sure about little points like that. Even doctors like you don't know exactly what constitutes madness.'

Merwick got up.

'But is it possible that you don't see what a terrible risk you run?' he asked. 'To see her again, to be with her like that, having to look at her — I saw her this afternoon, by the way, hardly human — may not that so easily revive again all that you felt before? It is too dangerous: much too dangerous.'

Dick shook his head.

'There is not the slightest risk,' he said; 'everything within me is utterly and absolutely indifferent to her. I don't even hate her: if I hated her there might be a possibility of my again loving her. As it is, the thought of her does not arouse in me any emotion of any kind. And really such stupendous calmness deserves to be rewarded. I respect colossal things like that.'

He finished his whisky as he spoke, and instantly poured himself out another glass.

'That's the fourth,' said his friend.

'Is it? I never count. It shows a sordid attention to uninteresting detail. Funnily enough, too, alcohol does not have the smallest effect on me now.'

'Why drink then?'

'Because if I give it up this entrancing vividness of colour and clarity of outline is a little diminished.

'Can't be good for you,' said the doctor.

Dick laughed.

'My dear fellow, look at me carefully,' he said, 'and then if you can conscientiously declare that I show any signs of indulging in stimulants, I'll give them up altogether.'

Certainly it would have been hard to find a point in which Dick did not present the appearance of perfect health. He had paused, and stood still a moment, his glass in one hand, the whisky-bottle in the other, black against the front of his shirt, and not a tremor of unsteadiness was there. His face of wholesome sun-burnt hue was neither puffy nor emaciated, but firm of flesh and of a wonderful clearness of skin. Clear too was his eye, with eyelids neither baggy nor puckered; he looked indeed a model of condition, hard and fit, as if he was in training for some athletic event. Lithe and active too was his figure, his movements were quick and precise, and even Merwick, with his doctor's eye trained to detect any symptom, however slight, in which the drinker must betray himself, was bound to confess that no such

211

was here present. His appearance contradicted it authoritatively, so also did his manner; he met the eye of the man he was talking to without sideway glances; he showed no signs, however small, of any disorder of the nerves. Yet Dick was altogether an abnormal fellow; the history he had just been recounting was abnormal, those weeks of depression, followed by the sudden snap in his brain which had apparently removed, as a wet cloth removes a stain, all the memory of his love and of the cruel bitterness that resulted from it. Abnormal too was his sudden leap into high artistic achievement from a past of very mediocre performance. Why should there then not be a similar abnormality here?

'Yes, I confess you show no sign of taking excessive stimulant,' said Merwick, 'but if I attended you professionally — ah, I'm not touting — I should make you give up all stimulant, and go to bed for a month.'

'Why in the name of goodness?' asked Dick.

'Because, theoretically, it must be the best thing you could do. You had a shock, how severe, the misery of those weeks of depression tells you. Well, common sense says, 'Go slow after a shock; recoup.' Instead of which you go very fast indeed and produce. I grant it seems to suit you; you also became suddenly capable of feats which — oh, it's sheer nonsense, man.'

'What's sheer nonsense?'

'You are. Professionally, I detest you, because you appear to be an exception to a theory that I am sure must be right. Therefore I have got to explain you away, and at present I can't.'

'What's the theory?' asked Dick.

'Well, the treatment of shock first of all. And secondly, that in order to do good work, one ought to eat and drink very little and sleep a lot. How long do you sleep, by the way?'

Dick considered.

'Oh, I go to bed about three usually,' he said; 'I suppose I sleep for about four hours.'

'And live on whisky, and eat like a Strasburg goose, and are prepared to run a race tomorrow.'

'Go away, or at least I will. Perhaps you'll break down, though. That would satisfy me.

'But even if you don't, it still remains quite interesting.'

Merwick found it more than quite interesting in fact, and when he got home that night he searched in his shelves for a certain dusky volume in which he turned up a chapter called 'Shock.' The book was a treatise on obscure diseases and abnormal conditions of the nervous system. He had often read it before, for in his profession he was a special student of the rare and curious. And the following paragraph which had interested him much before, interested him more than ever this evening.

'The nervous system also can act in a way that must always even to the most advanced student be totally unexpected. Cases are known, and well-authenticated ones, when a paralytic person has jumped out of bed on the cry of 'Fire.' Cases too are known when a great shock, which produces depression so profound as to amount to lethargy, is followed by abnormal activity, and the calling into use of powers which were previously unknown to exist, or at any rate existed in a quite ordinary degree. Such a hyper-sensitised state, especially since the desire for sleep or rest is very often much diminished, demands much stimulant in the way of food and alcohol. It would appear also that the patient suffering from this rare form of the after-consequences of shock has sooner or later some sudden and complete break-down. It is impossible, however, to conjecture what form this will take. The digestion, however, may become suddenly atrophied, delirium tremens may, without warning, supervene, or he may go completely off his head . . . '

But the weeks passed on, the July suns made London reel in a haze of heat, and yet Alingham remained busy, brilliant, and altogether exceptional. Merwick, unknown to him, was watching him closely, and at present was completely puzzled. He held Dick to his word that if he could detect the slightest sign of over-indulgence in stimulant, he would cut it off altogether, but he could see absolutely none. Lady Madingley meantime had given him several sittings, and in this connection again Merwick was utterly mistaken in the view he had expressed to Dick as to the risks he ran. For, strangely enough, the two had become great friends. Yet Dick was quite right, all emotion with regard to her on his part was dead, it might have been a piece of still-life that he was painting, instead of a woman he had wildly worshipped.

One morning in mid-July she had been sitting to him in his studio, and contrary to custom he had been rather silent, biting the ends of his brushes, frowning at his canvas, frowning too at her.

Suddenly he gave a little impatient exclamation.

'It's so like you,' he said, 'but it just isn't you. There's a lot of difference! I can't help making you look as if you were listening to a hymn, one of those in four sharps, don't you know, written by an organist, probably after eating muffins. And that's not characteristic of you!'

She laughed.

'You must be rather ingenious to put all that in,' she said.

'I am.'

'Where do I show it all?'

Dick sighed.

'Oh, in your eyes of course,' he said. 'You show everything by your eyes, you know. It is entirely characteristic of you. You are a throw-back; don't you remember we settled that ever so long ago, to the brute creation, who likewise show everything by their eyes.'

'Oh-h. I should have thought that dogs growled at you, and cats scratched.'

'Those are practical measures, but short of that you and animals use their eyes only, whereas people use their mouths and foreheads and other things. A pleased dog, an expectant dog, a hungry dog, a jealous dog, a disappointed dog — one gathers all that from a dog's eyes. Their mouths are comparatively immobile, and a cat's is even more so.

'You have often told me that I belong to the genus cat,' said Lady Madingley, with complete composure.

'By Jove, yes,' said he. 'Perhaps looking at

the eyes of a cat would help me to see what I miss. Many thanks for the hint.'

He put down his palette and went to a side table on which stood bottles and ice and syphons.

'No drink of any kind on this Sahara of a morning?' he asked.

'No, thanks. Now when will you give me the final sitting? You said you only wanted one more.'

Dick helped himself.

'Well, I go down to the country with this,' he said, 'to put in the background I told you of.

'With luck it will take me three days' hard painting, without luck a week or more. Oh, my mouth waters at the thought of the background. So shall we say to-morrow week?'

Lady Madingley made a note of this in a minute gold and jewelled memorandum book.

'And I am to be prepared to see cat's eyes painted there instead of my own when I see it next?' she asked, passing by the canvas.

Dick laughed.

'Oh, you will hardly notice the difference,' he said. 'How odd it is that I always have detested cats so — they make me feel actually faint, although you always reminded me of a cat.'

'You must ask your friend Mr. Merwick

about these metaphysical mysteries,' said she.

The background to the picture was at present only indicated by a few vague splashes close to the side of the head of brilliant purple and brilliant green, and the artist's mouth might well water at the thought of the few days painting that lay before him. For behind the figure in the long panel-shaped canvas was to be painted a green trellis, over which, almost hiding the wood-work, there was to sprawl a great purple clematis in full flaunting glory of varnished leaf and starry flower.

At the top would be just a strip of pale summer sky, at her feet just a strip of grey-green grass, but all the rest of the background, greatly daring, would be this diaper of green and purple. For the purpose of putting this in, he was going down to a small cottage of his near Godalming, where he had built in the garden a sort of outdoor studio, an erection betwixt a room and a mere shelter, with the side to the north entirely open, and flanked by this green trellis which was now one immense constellation of purple stars. Framed in this, he well knew how the strange pale beauty of his sitter would glow on the canvas, how she would start out of the background, she and her huge grey hat, and shining grey dress, and yellow hair and ivory white skin and pale eyes, now blue, now grey, now green. This was indeed a thing to look forward to, for there is probably no such unadulterated rapture known to men as creation, and it was small wonder that Dick's mood, as he travelled down to Godalming, was buoyant and effervescent. For he was going, so to speak, to realise his creation: every purple star of clematis, every green leaf and piece of trellis-work that he put in, would cause what he had painted to live and shine, just as it is the layers of dusk that fall over the sky at evening which make the stars to sparkle there, jewel-like.

His scheme was assured, he had hung his constellation — the figure of Lady Madingley — in the sky: and now he had to surround it with the green and purple night, so that it might shine.

His garden was but a circumscribed plot, but walls of old brick circumscribed it, and he had dealt with the space at his command with a certain originality. At no time had his grass plot (you could scarcely call it 'lawn') been spacious; now the outdoor studio, twenty-five feet by thirty, took up the greater part of it. He had a solid wooden wall on one side and two trellis walls to the south and east, which creepers were beginning to clothe and which were faced internally by hangings of Syrian and Oriental work. Here in the summer he passed the greater part of the day, painting or idling, and living an outdoor existence. The floor, which had once been grass, which had withered completely under the roof, was covered with Persian rugs; a writing-table and a dining-table were there, a bookcase full of familiar friends and a half-dozen of basket chairs. One corner, too, was frankly given up to the affairs of the garden, and a mowing machine, a hose for watering, shears, and spade stood there. For like many excitable persons, Dick found that in gardening, that incessant process of plannings and designings to suit the likings of plants, and make them gorgeous in colour and high of growth, there was a wonderful calm haven of refuge for the brain that had been tossing on emotional seas. Plants, too, were receptive, so responsive to kindness; thought given to them was never thought wasted, and to come back now after a month's absence in London was to be assured of fresh surprise and pleasure in each foot of garden-bed. And here, with how regal a generosity was the purple clematis to repay him for the care lavished on it. Every flower would show its practical gratitude by standing model for the background of his picture.

The evening was very warm, warm not with any sultry premonition of thunder, but with the clear, clean heat of summer, and he dined alone in his shelter, with the after-flames of the sunset for his lamp. These slowly faded into a sky of velvet blue, but he lingered long over his coffee, looking northwards across the garden towards the row of trees that screened him from the house beyond. These were acacias, most graceful and feminine of all green things that grow, summer-plumaged now, yet still fresh of leaf. Below them ran a little raised terrace of turf and nearer the beds of the beloved garden; clumps of sweet-peas made an inimitable fragrance, and the rose-beds were pink with Baroness Rothschild and La France, and copper-coloured with Beauté inconstante, and the Richardson rose. Then, nearer at hand, was the green trellis foaming with purple.

He was sitting there, hardly looking, but unconsciously drinking in this great festival of colour, when his eye was arrested by a dark slinking form that appeared among the roses, and suddenly turned two shining luminous orbs on him. At this he started up, but his movement caused no perturbation in the animal, which continued with back arched for stroking, and poker-like tail, to advance towards him, purring. As it came closer Dick felt that shuddering faintness, which often affected him in the presence of cats, come over him, and he stamped and clapped his hands. At this it turned tail quickly: a sort of dark shadow streaked the garden-wall for a moment, and it vanished. But its appearance had spoiled for him the sweet spell of the evening, and he went indoors.

The next morning was pellucid summer: a faint north wind blew, and a sun worthy to illumine the isles of Greece flooded the sky. Dick's dreamless and (for him) long sleep had banished from his mind that rather disquieting incident of the cat, and he set up his canvas facing the trellis-work and purple clematis with a huge sense of imminent ecstasy. Also the garden, which at present he had only seen in the magic of sunset, was gloriously rewarding, and glowed with colour, and though life — this was present to his mind for the first time for months — in the shape of Lady Madingley had not been very propitious, yet a man, he argued to himself, must be a very poor hand at living if, with a passion for plants and a passion for art, he cannot fashion a life that shall be full of content. So breakfast being finished, and his model ready and glowing with beauty, he quickly sketched in the broad lines of flowers and foliage and began to paint.

Purple and green, green and purple: was

there ever such a feast for the eye? Gourmetlike and greedy as well, he was utterly absorbed in it. He was right too: as soon as he put on the first brush of colour he knew he was right. It was just those divine and violent colours which would cause his figure to step out from the picture, it was just that pale strip of sky above which would focus her again, it was just that strip of grey-green grass below her feet that would prevent her, so it seemed, from actually leaving the canvas. And with swift eager sweeps of the brush which never paused and never hurried, he lost himself in his work.

He stopped at length with a sense of breathlessness, feeling too as if he had been suddenly called back from some immense distance off. He must have been working some three hours, for his man was already laying the table for lunch, yet it seemed to him that the morning had gone by in one flash. The progress he had made was extraordinary, and he looked long at his picture.

Then his eye wandered from the brightness of the canvas to the brightness of the garden-beds.

There, just in front of the bed of sweet-peas, not two yards from him, stood a very large grey cat, watching him.

Now the presence of a cat was a thing that

usually produced in Dick a feeling of deadly faintness, yet, at this moment, as he looked at the cat and the cat at him, he was conscious of no such feeling, and put down the absence of it, in so far as he consciously thought about it, to the fact that he was in the open air, not in the atmosphere of a closed room. Yet, last night out here, the cat had made him feel faint. But he hardly gave a thought to this, for what filled his mind was that he saw in the rather friendly interested look of the beast that expression in the eye which had so baffled him in his portrait of Lady Madingley. So, slowly, and without any sudden movement that might startle the cat, he reached out his hand for the palette he had just put down, and in a corner of the canvas not yet painted over, recorded in half a dozen swift intuitive touches, what he wanted. Even in the broad sunlight where the animal stood, its eyes looked as if they were internally smouldering as well as being lit from without: it was just so that Lady Madingley looked. He would have to lay colour very thinly over white . . .

For five minutes or so he painted them with quiet eager strokes, drawing the colour thinly over the background of white, and then looked long at that sketch of the eye to see if he had got what he wanted. Then he looked back at the cat which had stood so charmingly for him. But there was no cat there. That, however, since he detested them, and this one had served his purpose, was no matter for regret, and he merely wondered a little at the suddenness of its disappearance. But the legacy it had left on the canvas could not vanish thus, it was his own, a possession, an achievement. Truly this was to be a portrait which would altogether out-distance all he had ever done before. A woman, real, alive, wearing her soul in her eyes, should stand there, and summer riot round her.

An extraordinary clearness of vision was his all day, and towards sunset an empty whisky-bottle.

But this evening he was conscious for the first time of two feelings, one physical, one mental, altogether strange to him: the first an impression that he had drunk as much as was good for him, the second a sort of echo in his mind of those tortures he had undergone in the autumn, when he had been tossed aside by the girl, to whom he had given his soul, like a soiled glove.

Neither was at all acutely felt, but both were present to him.

The evening altogether belied the brilliance of the day, and about six o'clock thick clouds had driven up over the sky, and the clear heat of summer had given place to a heat no less intense, but full of the menace of storm. A few big hot drops, too, of rain warned him further, and he pulled his easel into shelter, and gave orders that he would dine indoors. As was usual with him when he was at work, he shunned the distracting influence of any companionship, and he dined alone. Dinner finished, he went into his sitting-room prepared to enjoy his solitary evening. His servant had brought him in the tray, and till he went to bed he would be undisturbed. Outside the storm was moving nearer, the reverberation of the thunder, though not yet close, kept up a continual growl: any moment it might move up and burst above in riot of fire and sound.

Dick read a book for a while, but his thoughts wandered. The poignancy of his trouble last autumn, which he thought had passed away from him for ever, grew suddenly and strangely more acute, also his head was heavy, perhaps with the storm, but possibly with what he had drunk. So, intending to go to bed and sleep off his disquietude, he closed his book, and went across to the window to close that also. But, half-way towards it, he stopped. There on the sofa below it sat a large grey cat with yellow gleaming eyes. In its mouth it held a young thrush, still alive.

Then horror woke in him: his feeling of sick-faintness was there, and he loathed and was terrified at this dreadful feline glee in the torture of its prey, a glee so great that it preferred the postponement of its meal to a shortening of the other. More than all, the resemblance of the eyes of this cat to those of his portrait suddenly struck him as something hellish. For one moment this all held him bound, as if with paralysis, the next his physical shuddering could be withstood no longer, and he threw the glass he carried at the cat, missing it. For one second the animal paused there glaring at him with an intense and dreadful hostility, then it made one spring of it out of the open window. Dick shut it with a bang that startled himself, and then searched on the sofa and the floor for the bird which he thought the cat had dropped. Once or twice he thought he heard it feebly fluttering, but this must have been an illusion, for he could not find it.

All this was rather shaky business, so before going to bed he steadied himself, as his unspoken phrase ran, with a final drink. Outside the thunder had ceased, but the rain beat hissing on to the grass. Then another sound mingled with it the mewing of a cat, not the long-drawn screeches and cries that are usual, but the plaintive calls of the beast that wants to be admitted into its own home. The blind was down, but after a while he could not resist peeping out. There on the window-sill was seated the large grey cat. Though it was raining heavily its fur seemed dry, for it was standing stiffly away from its body. But when it saw him it spat at him, scratching angrily at the glass, and vanished.

Lady Madingley . . . heavens, how he had loved her! And, infernally as she had treated him, how passionately he wanted her now! Was all his trouble, then, to begin over again? Had that nightmare dawned anew on him? It was the cat's fault: the eyes of the cat had done it. Yet just now all his desire was blurred by this dullness of brain that was as unaccountable as the re-awakening of his desire. For months now he had drunk far more than he had drunk to-day, yet evening had seen him clear-headed, acute, master of himself, and revelling in the liberty that had come to him, and in the cool joy of creative vision. But to-night he stumbled and groped across the room.

The neutral-coloured light of dawn awoke him, and he got up at once, feeling still very drowsy, but in answer to some silent imperative call. The storm had altogether passed away, and a jewel of a morning star hung in a pale heaven. His room looked strangely unfamiliar to him, his own sensations were unfamiliar, there was a vagueness about things, a barrier between him and the world. One desire alone possessed him, to finish the portrait. All else, so he felt, he left to chance, or whatever laws regulate the world, those laws which choose that a certain thrush shall be caught by a certain cat, and choose one scapegoat out of a thousand, and let the rest go free.

Two hours later his servant called him, and found him gone from his room. So as the morning was so fair, he went out to lay breakfast in the shelter. The portrait was there, it had been dragged back into position by the clematis, but it was covered with strange scratches, as if the claws of some enraged animal or the nails perhaps of a man had furiously attacked it. Dick Alingham was there, too, lying very still in front of the disfigured canvas. Claws, also, or nails had attacked him, his throat was horribly mangled by them. But his hands were covered with paint, the nails of his fingers too were choked with it.

The Bus-Conductor

My friend, Hugh Grainger, and I had just returned from a two days' visit in the country, where we had been staying in a house of sinister repute which was supposed to be haunted by ghosts of a peculiarly fearsome and truculent sort. The house itself was all that such a house should be, Jacobean and oak-panelled, with long dark passages and high vaulted rooms. It stood, also, very remote, and was encompassed by a wood of sombre pines that muttered and whispered in the dark, and all the time that we were there a southwesterly gale with torrents of scolding rain had prevailed, so that by day and night weird voices moaned and fluted in the chimneys, a company of uneasy spirits held colloquy among the trees, and sudden tattoos and tappings beckoned from the window-panes. But in spite of these surroundings, which were sufficient in themselves, one would almost say, to spontaneously generate occult phenomena, nothing of any description had occurred. I am bound to add, also, that my own state of mind was peculiarly well adapted to receive or even to invent the sights and sounds we had gone to seek, for I was, I confess, during the whole time that we were there, in a state of abject apprehension, and lay awake both nights through hours of terrified unrest, afraid of the dark, yet more afraid of what a lighted candle might show me.

Hugh Grainger, on the evening after our return to town, had dined with me, and after dinner our conversation, as was natural, soon came back to these entrancing topics.

'But why you go ghost-seeking I cannot imagine,' he said, 'because your teeth were chattering and your eyes starting out of your head all the time you were there, from sheer fright.'

'Or do you like being frightened?'

Hugh, though generally intelligent, is dense in certain ways; this is one of them.

'Why, of course, I like being frightened,' I said. 'I want to be made to creep and creep and creep. Fear is the most absorbing and luxurious of emotions. One forgets all else if one is afraid.'

'Well, the fact that neither of us saw anything,' he said, 'confirms what I have always believed.'

'And what have you always believed?'

'That these phenomena are purely objective, not subjective, and that one's state of mind has nothing to do with the perception that perceives them, nor have circumstances or surroundings anything to do with them either. Look at Osburton. It has had the reputation of being a haunted house for years, and it certainly has all the accessories of one. Look at yourself, too, with all your nerves on edge, afraid to look round or light a candle for fear of seeing something! Surely there was the right man in the right place then, if ghosts are subjective.'

He got up and lit a cigarette, and looking at him — Hugh is about six feet high, and as broad as he is long — I felt a retort on my lips, for I could not help my mind going back to a certain period in his life, when, from some cause which, as far as I knew, he had never told anybody, he had become a mere quivering mass of disordered nerves. Oddly enough, at the same moment and for the first time, he began to speak of it himself.

'You may reply that it was not worth my while to go either,' he said, 'because I was so clearly the wrong man in the wrong place. But I wasn't. You for all your apprehensions and expectancy have never seen a ghost. But I have, though I am the last person in the world you would have thought likely to do so, and, though my nerves are steady enough again now, it knocked me all to bits.'

He sat down again in his chair.

'No doubt you remember my going to bits,' he said, 'and since I believe that I am sound again now, I should rather like to tell you about it. But before I couldn't; I couldn't speak of it at all to anybody. Yet there ought to have been nothing frightening about it; what I saw was certainly a most useful and friendly ghost. But it came from the shaded side of things; it looked suddenly out of the night and the mystery with which life is surrounded.

'I want first to tell you quite shortly my theory about ghost-seeing,' he continued, 'and I can explain it best by a simile, an image. Imagine then that you and I and everybody in the world are like people whose eye is directly opposite a little tiny hole in a sheet of cardboard which is continually shifting and revolving and moving about. Back to back with that sheet of cardboard is another, which also, by laws of its own, is in perpetual but independent motion. In it too there is another hole, and when, fortuitously it would seem, these two holes, the one through which we are always looking, and the other in the spiritual plane, come opposite one another, we see through, and then only do the sights and sounds of the spiritual world become visible or audible to us. With most people these holes never come opposite each other during their life. But at the hour of death they do, and then they remain stationary. That, I fancy, is how we 'pass over.'

'Now, in some natures, these holes are comparatively large, and are constantly coming into opposition. Clairvoyants, mediums are like that. But, as far as I knew, I had no clairvoyant or mediumistic powers at all. I therefore am the sort of person who long ago made up his mind that he never would see a ghost. It was, so to speak, an incalculable chance that my minute spy-hole should come into opposition with the other. But it did: and it knocked me out of time.'

I had heard some such theory before, and though Hugh put it rather picturesquely, there was nothing in the least convincing or practical about it. It might be so, or again it might not.

'I hope your ghost was more original than your theory,' said I, in order to bring him to the point.

'Yes, I think it was. You shall judge.'

I put on more coal and poked up the fire. Hugh has got, so I have always considered, a great talent for telling stories, and that sense of drama which is so necessary for the narrator. Indeed, before now, I have suggested to him that he should take this up as a profession, sit by the fountain in Piccadilly Circus, when times are, as usual, bad, and tell stories to the passers-by in the street, Arabian fashion, for reward. The most part of mankind, I am aware, do not like long stories, but to the few, among whom I number myself, who really like to listen to lengthy accounts of experiences, Hugh is an ideal narrator. I do not care for his theories, or for his similes, but when it comes to facts, to things that happened, I like him to be lengthy.

'Go on, please, and slowly,' I said. 'Brevity may be the soul of wit, but it is the ruin of story-telling. I want to hear when and where and how it all was, and what you had for lunch and where you had dined and what — '

Hugh began:

'It was the 24th of June, just eighteen months ago,' he said. 'I had let my flat, you may remember, and came up from the country to stay with you for a week. We had dined alone here — '

I could not help interrupting.

'Did you see the ghost here?' I asked. 'In this square little box of a house in a modern street?'

'I was in the house when I saw it.' I hugged myself in silence.

'We had dined alone here in Graeme Street,' he said, 'and after dinner I went out to some party, and you stopped at home. At dinner your man did not wait, and when I asked where he was, you told me he was ill, and, I thought, changed the subject rather abruptly.

'You gave me your latch-key when I went out, and on coming back, I found you had gone to bed. There were, however, several letters for me, which required answers. I wrote them there and then, and posted them at the pillar-box opposite. So I suppose it was rather late when I went upstairs.

'You had put me in the front room, on the third floor, overlooking the street, a room which I thought you generally occupied yourself. It was a very hot night, and though there had been a moon when I started to my party, on my return the whole sky was cloud-covered, and it both looked and felt as if we might have a thunderstorm before morning. I was feeling very sleepy and heavy, and it was not till after I had got into bed that I noticed by the shadows of the window-frames on the blind that only one of the windows was open. But it did not seem worth while to get out of bed in order to open it, though I felt rather airless and uncomfortable, and I went to sleep.

'What time it was when I awoke I do not know, but it was certainly not yet dawn, and I never remember being conscious of such an extraordinary stillness as prevailed. There was no sound either of foot-passengers or wheeled traffic; the music of life appeared to be absolutely mute. But now, instead of being sleepy and heavy, I felt, though I must have slept an hour or two at most, since it was not yet dawn, perfectly fresh and wide-awake, and the effort which had seemed not worth making before, that of getting out of bed and opening the other window, was quite easy now and I pulled up the blind, threw it wide open, and leaned out, for somehow I parched and pined for air. Even outside the oppression was very noticeable, and though, as you know, I am not easily given to feel the mental effects of climate, I was aware of an awful creepiness coming over me. I tried to analyse it away, but without success; the past day had been pleasant, I looked forward to another pleasant day to-morrow, and yet I was full of some nameless apprehension. I felt, too, dreadfully lonely in this stillness before the dawn.

'Then I heard suddenly and not very far away the sound of some approaching vehicle; I could distinguish the tread of two horses walking at a slow foot's pace. They were, though not yet visible, coming up the street, and yet this indication of life did not abate that dreadful sense of loneliness which I have spoken of. Also in some dim unformulated way that which was coming seemed to me to have something to do with the cause of my oppression.

'Then the vehicle came into sight. At first I could not distinguish what it was. Then I saw that the horses were black and had long tails, and that what they dragged was made of glass, but had a black frame. It was a hearse. Empty.

'It was moving up this side of the street. It stopped at your door.

'Then the obvious solution struck me. You had said at dinner that your man was ill, and you were, I thought, unwilling to speak more about his illness. No doubt, so I imagined now, he was dead, and for some reason, perhaps because you did not want me to know anything about it, you were having the body removed at night. This, I must tell you, passed through my mind quite instantaneously, and it did not occur to me how unlikely it really was, before the next thing happened.

'I was still leaning out of the window, and I remember also wondering, yet only momentarily, how odd it was that I saw things — or rather the one thing I was looking at — so very distinctly. Of course, there was a moon behind the clouds, but it was curious how every detail of the hearse and the horses was visible. There was only one man, the driver, with it, and the street was otherwise absolutely empty. It was at him I was looking now. I could see every detail of his clothes, but from where I was, so high above him, I could not see his face. He had on grey trousers, brown boots, a black coat buttoned all the way up, and a straw hat. Over his shoulder there was a strap, which seemed to support some sort of little bag. He looked exactly like — well, from my description what did he look exactly like?'

'Why — a bus-conductor,' I said instantly.

'So I thought, and even while I was thinking this, he looked up at me. He had a rather long thin face, and on his left cheek there was a mole with a growth of dark hair on it. All this was as distinct as if it had been noonday, and as if I was within a yard of him. But — so instantaneous was all that takes so long in the telling — I had not time to think it strange that the driver of a hearse should be so unfunereally dressed.

'Then he touched his hat to me, and jerked his thumb over his shoulder.

'Just room for one inside, sir,' he said.

'There was something so odious, so coarse, so unfeeling about this that I instantly drew my head in, pulled the blind down again, and then, for what reason I do not know, turned on the electric light in order to see what time it was. The hands of my watch pointed to half-past eleven.

'It was then for the first time, I think, that a doubt crossed my mind as to the nature of what I had just seen. But I put out the light again, got into bed, and began to think. We had dined; I had gone to a party, I had come back and written letters, had gone to bed and had slept. So how could it be half-past eleven? . . . Or — what half-past eleven was it?

'Then another easy solution struck me; my watch must have stopped. But it had not; I could hear it ticking.

'There was stillness and silence again. I expected every moment to hear muffled footsteps on the stairs, footsteps moving slowly and smally under the weight of a heavy burden, but from inside the house there was no sound whatever. Outside, too, there was the same dead silence, while the hearse waited at the door. And the minutes ticked on and ticked on, and at length I began to see a difference in the light in the room, and knew that the dawn was beginning to break outside. But how had it happened, then, that if the corpse was to be removed at night it had not gone, and that the hearse still waited, when morning was already coming?

'Presently I got out of bed again, and with the sense of strong physical shrinking I went to the window and pulled back the blind. The dawn was coming fast; the whole street was lit by that silver hueless light of morning. But there was no hearse there.

'Once again I looked at my watch. It was just a quarter-past four. But I would swear that not half an hour had passed since it had told me that it was half-past eleven.

'Then a curious double sense, as if I was living in the present and at the same moment had been living in some other time, came over me. It was dawn on June 25th, and the street, as natural, was empty. But a little while ago the driver of a hearse had spoken to me, and it was half-past eleven. What was that driver, to what plane did he belong? And again what half-past eleven was it that I had seen recorded on the dial of my watch?

'And then I told myself that the whole thing had been a dream. But if you ask me whether I believed what I told myself, I must confess that I did not.

'Your man did not appear at breakfast next morning, nor did I see him again before I left that afternoon. I think if I had, I should have told you about all this, but it was still possible, you see, that what I had seen was a real hearse, driven by a real driver, for all the ghastly gaiety of the face that had looked up to mine, and the levity of his pointing hand. I might possibly have fallen asleep soon after seeing him, and slumbered through the removal of the body and the departure of the hearse. So I did not speak of it to you.'

There was something wonderfully straightforward and prosaic in all this; here were no Jacobean houses oak-panelled and surrounded by weeping pine-trees, and somehow the very absence of suitable surroundings made the story more impressive. But for a moment a doubt assailed me.

'Don't tell me it was all a dream,' I said.

'I don't know whether it was or not. I can only say that I believe myself to have been wide awake. In any case the rest of the story is — odd.

'I went out of town again that afternoon,' he continued, 'and I may say that I don't think that even for a moment did I get the haunting sense of what I had seen or dreamed that night out of my mind. It was present to me always as some vision unfulfilled. It was as if some clock had struck the four quarters, and I was still waiting to hear what the hour would be.

'Exactly a month afterwards I was in

London again, but only for the day. I arrived at Victoria about eleven, and took the underground to Sloane Square in order to see if you were in town and would give me lunch. It was a baking hot morning, and I intended to take a bus from the King's Road as far as Graeme Street. There was one standing at the corner just as I came out of the station, but I saw that the top was full, and the inside appeared to be full also. Just as I came up to it the conductor, who, I suppose, had been inside, collecting fares or what not, came out on to the step within a few feet of me. He wore grey trousers, brown boots, a black coat buttoned, a straw hat, and over his shoulder was a strap on which hung his little machine for punching tickets. I saw his face, too; it was the face of the driver of the hearse, with a mole on the left cheek. Then he spoke to me, jerking his thumb over his shoulder.

'' Just room for one inside, sir,' he said.

'At that a sort of panic-terror took possession of me, and I knew I gesticulated wildly with my arms, and cried, 'No, no!' But at that moment I was living not in the hour that was then passing, but in that hour which had passed a month ago, when I leaned from the window of your bedroom here just before the dawn broke. At this moment too I knew that my spy-hole had been opposite the spy-hole into the spiritual world. What I had seen there had some significance, now being fulfilled, beyond the significance of the trivial happenings of to-day and to-morrow. The Powers of which we know so little were visibly working before me. And I stood there on the pavement shaking and trembling.

'I was opposite the post-office at the corner, and just as the bus started my eye fell on the clock in the window there. I need not tell you what the time was.

'Perhaps I need not tell you the rest, for you probably conjecture it, since you will not have forgotten what happened at the corner of Sloane Square at the end of July, the summer before last. The bus pulled out from the pavement into the street in order to get round a van that was standing in front of it. At that moment there came down the King's Road a big motor going at a hideously dangerous pace. It crashed full into the bus, burrowing into it as a gimlet burrows into a board.'

He paused.

'And that's my story,' he said.

The Man Who Went Too Far

The little village of St. Faith's nestles in a hollow of wooded till up on the north bank of the river Fawn in the country of Hampshire, huddling close round its grey Norman church as if for spiritual protection against the fays and fairies, the trolls and 'little people,' who might be supposed still to linger in the vast empty spaces of the New Forest, and to come after dusk and do their doubtful businesses. Once outside the hamlet you may walk in any direction (so long as you avoid the high road which leads to Brockenhurst) for the length of a summer afternoon without seeing sign of human habitation, or possibly even catching sight of another human being.

Shaggy wild ponies may stop their feeding for a moment as you pass, the white scuts of rabbits will vanish into their burrows, a brown viper perhaps will glide from your path into a clump of heather, and unseen birds will chuckle in the bushes, but it may easily happen that for a long day you will see nothing human. But you will not feel in the least lonely; in summer, at any rate, the sunlight will be gay with butterflies, and the air thick with all those woodland sounds which like instruments in an orchestra combine to play the great symphony of the yearly festival of June.

Winds whisper in the birches, and sigh among the firs; bees are busy with their redolent labour among the heather, a myriad birds chirp in the green temples of the forest trees, and the voice of the river prattling over stony places, bubbling into pools, chuckling and gulping round corners, gives you the sense that many presences and companions are near at hand.

Yet, oddly enough, though one would have thought that these benign and cheerful influences of wholesome air and spaciousness of forest were very healthful comrades for a man, in so far as Nature can really influence this wonderful human genus which has in these centuries learned to defy her most violent storms in its well-established houses, to bridle her torrents and make them light its streets, to tunnel her mountains and plough her seas, the inhabitants of St. Faith's will not willingly venture into the forest after dark. For in spite of the silence and loneliness of the hooded night it seems that a man is not sure in what company he may suddenly find himself, and though it is difficult to get from these villagers any very clear story of occult appearances, the feeling is widespread. One story indeed I have heard with some definiteness, the tale of a monstrous goat that has been seen to skip with hellish glee about the woods and shady places, and this perhaps is connected with the story which I have here attempted to piece together. It too is well-known to them; for all remember the young artist who died here not long ago, a young man, or so he struck the beholder, of great personal beauty, with something about him that made men's faces to smile and brighten when they looked on him. His ghost they will tell you 'walks' constantly by the stream and through the woods which he loved so, and in especial it haunts a certain house, the last of the village, where he lived, and its garden in which he was done to death. For my part I am inclined to think that the terror of the forest dates chiefly from that day.

So, such as the story is, I have set it forth in connected form. It is based partly on the accounts of the villagers, but mainly on that of Darcy, a friend of mine and a friend of the man with whom these events were chiefly concerned.

The day had been one of untarnished midsummer splendour, and as the sun drew near to its setting, the glory of the evening grew every moment more crystalline, more miraculous.

Westward from St. Faith's the beechwood which stretched for some miles toward the heathery upland beyond already cast its veil of clear shadow over the red roofs of the village, but the spire of the grey church, over-topping all, still pointed a flaming orange finger into the sky. The river Fawn, which runs below, lay in sheets of sky-reflected blue, and wound its dreamy devious course round the edge of this wood, where a rough two-planked bridge crossed from the bottom of the garden of the last house in the village, and communicated by means of a little wicker gate with the wood itself. Then once out of the shadow of the wood the stream lay in flaming pools of the molten crimson of the sunset, and lost itself in the haze of woodland distances.

This house at the end of the village stood outside the shadow, and the lawn which sloped down to the river was still flecked with sunlight. Garden-beds of dazzling colour lined its gravel walks, and down the middle of it ran a brick pergola, half-hidden in clusters of rambler-rose and purple with starry clematis. At the bottom end of it, between two of its pillars, was slung a hammock containing a shirtsleeved figure.

The house itself lay somewhat remote from the rest of the village, and a footpath leading across two fields, now tall and fragrant with hay, was its only communication with the high road.

It was low-built, only two stories in height, and like the garden, its walls were a mass of flowering roses. A narrow stone terrace ran along the garden front, over which was stretched an awning, and on the terrace a young silent-footed man-servant was busied with the laying of the table for dinner. He was neat-handed and quick with his job, and having finished it he went back into the house, and reappeared again with a large rough bath-towel on his arm. With this he went to the hammock in the pergola.

'Nearly eight, sir,' he said.

'Has Mr. Darcy come yet?' asked a voice from the hammock.

'No, sir.'

'If I'm not back when he comes, tell him that I'm just having a bathe before dinner.'

The servant went back to the house, and after a moment or two Frank Halton struggled to a sitting posture, and slipped out on to the grass. He was of medium height and rather slender in build, but the supple ease and grace of his movements gave the impression of great physical strength: even his descent from the hammock was not an awkward performance. His face and hands were of very dark complexion, either from constant exposure to wind and sun, or, as his black hair and dark eyes tended to show, from some strain of southern blood. His head was small, his face of an exquisite beauty of modelling, while the smoothness of its contour would have led you to believe that he was a beardless lad still in his teens. But something, some look which living and experience alone can give, seemed to contradict that, and finding yourself completely puzzled as to his age, you would next moment probably cease to think about that, and only look at this glorious specimen of young manhood with wondering satisfaction.

He was dressed as became the season and the heat, and wore only a shirt open at the neck, and a pair of flannel trousers. His head, covered very thickly with a somewhat rebellious crop of short curly hair, was bare as he strolled across the lawn to the bathing-place that lay below. Then for a moment there was silence, then the sound of splashed and divided waters, and presently after, a great shout of ecstatic joy, as he swam up-stream with the foamed water standing in a frill round his neck. Then after some five minutes of limb-stretching struggle with the flood, he turned over on his back, and with arms thrown wide, floated down-stream, ripple-cradled and inert.

His eyes were shut, and between half-parted lips he talked gently to himself.

'I am one with it,' he said to himself, 'the river and I, I and the river. The coolness and splash of it is I, and the water-herbs that wave in it are I also. And my strength and my limbs are not mine but the river's. It is all one, all one, dear Fawn.' A quarter of an hour later he appeared again at the bottom of the lawn, dressed as before, his wet hair already drying into its crisp short curls again. There he paused a moment, looking back at the stream with the smile with which men look on the face of a friend, then turned towards the house. Simultaneously his servant came to the door leading on to the terrace, followed by a man who appeared to be some half-way through the fourth decade of his years. Frank and he saw each other across the bushes and garden-beds, and each quickening his step, they met suddenly face to face round an angle of the garden walk, in the fragrance of syringa.

'My dear Darcy,' cried Frank, 'I am charmed to see you.' But the other stared at him in amazement.

'Frank!' he exclaimed.

'Yes, that is my name,' he said, laughing; 'what is the matter?' Darcy took his hand.

'What have you done to yourself?' he asked.

'You are a boy again.'

'Ah, I have a lot to tell you,' said Frank.

'Lots that you will hardly believe, but I shall convince you — '

He broke off suddenly, and held up his hand.

'Hush, there is my nightingale,' he said.

The smile of recognition and welcome with which he had greeted his friend faded from his face, and a look of rapt wonder took its place, as of a lover listening to the voice of his beloved.

His mouth parted slightly, showing the white line of teeth, and his eyes looked out and out till they seemed to Darcy to be focussed on things beyond the vision of man. Then something perhaps startled the bird, for the song ceased.

'Yes, lots to tell you,' he said. 'Really I am delighted to see you. But you look rather white and pulled down; no wonder after that fever. And there is to be no nonsense about this visit. It is June now, you stop here till you are fit to begin work again. Two months at least.'

'Ah, I can't trespass quite to that extent.'

Frank took his arm and walked him down the grass.

'Trespass? Who talks of trespass? I shall tell you quite openly when I am tired of you, but you know when we had the studio together, we used not to bore each other. However, it is ill talking of going away on the moment of your arrival. Just a stroll to the river, and then it will be dinner-time.'

Darcy took out his cigarette case, and offered it to the other.

Frank laughed.

'No, not for me. Dear me, I suppose I used to smoke once. How very odd!'

'Given it up?'

'I don't know. I suppose I must have. Anyhow I don't do it now. I would as soon think of eating meat.'

'Another victim on the smoking altar of vegetarianism?'

'Victim?' asked Frank. 'Do I strike you as such?'

He paused on the margin of the stream and whistled softly. Next moment a moor-hen made its splashing flight across the river, and ran up the bank. Frank took it very gently in his hands and stroked its head, as the creature lay against his shirt.

'And is the house among the reeds still secure?' he half-crooned to it. 'And is the missus quite well, and are the neighbours flourishing? There, dear, home with you,' and he flung it into the air.

'That bird's very tame,' said Darcy, slightly bewildered.

'It is rather,' said Frank, following its flight.

During dinner Frank chiefly occupied himself in bringing himself up-to-date in the movements and achievements of this old friend whom he had not seen for six years. Those six years, it now appeared, had been full of incident and success for Darcy; he had made a name for himself as a portrait painter which bade fair to outlast the vogue of a couple of seasons, and his leisure time had been brief. Then some four months previously he had been through a severe attack of typhoid, the result of which as concerns this story was that he had come down to this sequestered place to recruit.

'Yes, you've got on,' said Frank at the end. 'I always knew you would. A.R.A. with more in prospect. Money? You roll in it, I suppose, and, O Darcy, how much happiness have you had all these years? That is the only imperishable possession. And how much have you learned? Oh, I don't mean in Art. Even I could have done well in that.'

Darcy laughed.

'Done well? My dear fellow, all I have learned in these six years you knew, so to speak, in your cradle. Your old pictures fetch huge prices. Do you never paint now?'

Frank shook his head.

'No, I'm too busy,' he said.

'Doing what? Please tell me. That is what everyone is for ever asking me.'

'Doing? I suppose you would say I do nothing.'

Darcy glanced up at the brilliant young face opposite him.

'It seems to suit you, that way of being busy,' he said. 'Now, it's your turn. Do you read? Do you study? I remember you saying that it would do us all — all us artists, I mean — a great deal of good if we would study any one human face carefully for a year, without recording a line.'

'Have you been doing that?'

Frank shook his head again.

'I mean exactly what I say,' he said. 'I have been doing nothing. And I have never been so occupied. Look at me; have I not done something to myself to begin with?'

'You are two years younger than I,' said Darcy, 'at least you used to be. You therefore are thirty-five. But had I never seen you before I should say you were just twenty. But was it worth while to spend six years of greatly-occupied life in order to look twenty? Seems rather like a woman of fashion.'

Frank laughed boisterously.

'First time I've ever been compared to that particular bird of prey,' he said. 'No, that has not been my occupation — in fact I am only very rarely conscious that one effect of my occupation has been that. Of course, it must have been if one comes to think of it. It is not very important.'

'Quite true my body has become young. But that is very little; I have become young.'

Darcy pushed back his chair and sat sideways to the table looking at the other.

'Has that been your occupation then?' he asked.

'Yes, that anyhow is one aspect of it. Think what youth means! It is the capacity for growth, mind, body, spirit, all grow, all get stronger, all have a fuller, firmer life every day. That is something, considering that every day that passes after the ordinary man reaches the full-blown flower of his strength, weakens his hold on life. A man reaches his prime, and remains, we say, in his prime for ten years, or perhaps twenty. But after his primest prime is reached, he slowly, insensibly weakens. These are the signs of age in you, in your body, in your art probably, in your mind. You are less electric than you were. But I, when I reach my prime — I am nearing it — ah, you shall see.' The stars had begun to appear in the blue velvet of the sky, and to the east the horizon seen above the black silhouette of the village was growing dove-coloured with the approach of moon-rise.

White moths hovered dimly over the garden-beds, and the footsteps of night tip-toed through the bushes. Suddenly Frank rose.

'Ah, it is the supreme moment,' he said softly. 'Now more than at any other time the current of life, the eternal imperishable current runs so close to me that I am almost enveloped in it. Be silent a minute.'

He advanced to the edge of the terrace and looked out, standing stretched with arms outspread. Darcy heard him draw a long breath into his lungs, and after many seconds expel it again. Six or eight times he did this, then turned back into the lamplight.

'It will sound to you quite mad, I expect,' he said, 'but if you want to hear the soberest truth I have ever spoken and shall ever speak, I will tell you about myself. But come into the garden if it is not damp for you. I have never told anyone yet, but I shall like to tell you. It is long, in fact, since I have even tried to classify what I have learned.'

They wandered into the fragrant dimness of the pergola, and sat down. Then Frank began:

'Years ago, do you remember,' he said, 'we used often to talk about the decay of joy in the world. Many impulses, we settled, had contributed to this decay, some of which were

263

good in themselves, others that were quite completely bad. Among the good things, I put what we may call certain Christian virtues, renunciation, resignation, sympathy with suffering, and the desire to relieve sufferers, but out of those things spring very bad ones, useless renunciation, asceticism for its own sake, mortification of the flesh with nothing to follow, no corresponding gain that is, and that awful and terrible disease which devastated England some centuries ago, and from which by heredity of spirit we suffer now, Puritanism. That was a dreadful plague, the brutes held and taught that joy and laughter and merriment were evil: it was a doctrine the most profane and wicked. Why, what is the commonest crime one sees? A sullen face. That is the truth of the matter. Now all my life I have believed that we are intended to be happy, that joy is of all gifts the most divine. And when I left London, abandoned my career, such as it was, I did so because I intended to devote my life to the cultivation of joy, and, by continuous and unsparing effort to be happy. Among people, and in constant intercourse with others, I did not find it possible; there were too many distractions in towns and work-rooms, and also too much suffering. So I took one step backwards or forwards, as you may choose to put it, and went straight to Nature, to trees, birds, animals, to all those things which quite clearly pursue one aim only, which blindly follow the great native instinct to be happy without any care at all for morality, or human law or divine law. I wanted, you understand, to get all joy first-hand and unadulterated, and I think it scarcely exists among men; it is obsolete.'

Darcy turned in his chair.

'Ah, but what makes birds and animals happy?' he asked. 'Food, food and mating.'

Frank laughed gently in the stillness.

'Do not think I became a sensualist,' he said. 'I did not make that mistake. For the sensualist carries his miseries pick-a-back, and round his feet is wound the shroud that shall soon enwrap him. I may be mad, it is true, but I am not so stupid anyhow as to have tried that. No, what is it that makes puppies play with their own tails, that sends cats on their prowling ecstatic errands at night?'

He paused a moment.

'So I went to Nature,' he said. 'I sat down here in this New Forest, sat down fair and square, and looked. That was my first difficulty, to sit here quiet without being bored, to wait without being impatient, to be receptive and very alert, though for a long time nothing particular happened. The change in fact was slow in those early stages.'

'Nothing happened?' asked Darcy, rather impatiently, with the sturdy revolt against any new idea which to the English mind is synonymous with nonsense. 'Why, what in the world should happen?'

Now Frank as he had known him was the most generous but most quick-tempered of mortal men; in other words his anger would flare to a prodigious beacon, under almost no provocation, only to be quenched again under a gust of no less impulsive kindliness. Thus the moment Darcy had spoken, an apology for his hasty question was half-way up his tongue. But there was no need for it to have travelled even so far, for Frank laughed again with kindly, genuine mirth.

'Oh, how I should have resented that a few years ago,' he said. 'Thank goodness that resentment is one of the things I have got rid of. I certainly wish that you should believe my story — in fact, you are going to — but that you at this moment should imply that you do not does not concern me.'

'Ah, your solitary sojournings have made you inhuman,' said Darcy, still very English.

'No, human,' said Frank. 'Rather more human, at least rather less of an ape.'

'Well, that was my first quest,' he

continued, after a moment, 'the deliberate and unswerving pursuit of joy, and my method, the eager contemplation of Nature. As far as motive went, I daresay it was purely selfish, but as far as effect goes, it seems to me about the best thing one can do for one's follow-creatures, for happiness is more infectious than smallpox. So, as I said, I sat down and waited; I looked at happy things, zealously avoided the sight of anything unhappy, and by degrees a little trickle of the happiness of this blissful world began to filter into me. The trickle grew more abundant, and now, my dear fellow, if I could for a moment divert from me into you one half of the torrent of joy that pours through me day and night, you would throw the world, art, everything aside, and just live, exist. When a man's body dies, it passes into trees and flowers. Well, that is what I have been trying to do with my soul before death.'

The servant had brought into the pergola a table with syphons and spirits, and had set a lamp upon it. As Frank spoke he leaned forward towards the other, and Darcy for all his matter-of-fact common sense could have sworn that his companion's face shone, was luminous in itself. His dark brown eyes glowed from within, the unconscious smile of a child irradiated and transformed his face.

Darcy felt suddenly excited, exhilarated.

'Go on,' he said. 'Go on. I can feel you are somehow telling me sober truth. I daresay you are mad; but I don't see that matters.'

Frank laughed again.

'Mad?' he said. 'Yes, certainly, if you wish. But I prefer to call it sane. However, nothing matters less than what anybody chooses to call things. God never labels his gifts; He just puts them into our hands; just as he put animals in the garden of Eden, for Adam to name if he felt disposed.

'So by the continual observance and study of things that were happy,' continued he, 'I got happiness, I got joy. But seeking it, as I did, from Nature, I got much more which I did not seek, but stumbled upon originally by accident. It is difficult to explain, but I will try.

'About three years ago I was sitting one morning in a place I will show you to-morrow. It is down by the river brink, very green, dappled with shade and sun, and the river passes there through some little clumps of reeds. Well, as I sat there, doing nothing, but just looking and listening, I heard the sound quite distinctly of some flute-like instrument playing a strange unending melody. I thought at first it was some musical yokel on the highway and did not pay much

268

attention. But before long the strangeness and indescribable beauty of the tune struck me.

'It never repeated itself, but it never came to an end, phrase after phrase ran its sweet course, it worked gradually and inevitably up to a climax, and having attained it, it went on; another climax was reached and another and another. Then with a sudden gasp of wonder I localised where it came from. It came from the reeds and from the sky and from the trees. It was everywhere, it was the sound of life. It was, my dear Darcy, as the Greeks would have said, it was Pan playing on his pipes, the voice of Nature. It was the life-melody, the world-melody.'

Darcy was far too interested to interrupt, though there was a question he would have liked to ask, and Frank went on:

'Well, for the moment I was terrified, terrified with the impotent horror of nightmare, and I stopped my ears and just ran from the place and got back to the house panting, trembling, literally in a panic. Unknowingly, for at that time I only pursued joy, I had begun, since I drew my joy from Nature, to get in touch with Nature. Nature, force, God, call it what you will, had drawn across my face a little gossamer web of essential life. I saw that when I emerged from my terror, and I went very humbly back to where I had heard the Pan-pipes. But it was nearly six months before I heard them again.'

'Why was that?' asked Darcy.

'Surely because I had revolted, rebelled, and worst of all been frightened. For I believe that just as there is nothing in the world which so injures one's body as fear, so there is nothing that so much shuts up the soul. I was afraid, you see, of the one thing in the world which has real existence. No wonder its manifestation was withdrawn.'

'And after six months?'

'After six months one blessed morning I heard the piping again. I wasn't afraid that time.'

'And since then it has grown louder, it has become more constant. I now hear it often, and I can put myself into such an attitude towards Nature that the pipes will almost certainly sound. And never yet have they played the same tune, it is always something new, something fuller, richer, more complete than before.'

'What do you mean by 'such an attitude towards Nature'?' asked Darcy.

'I can't explain that; but by translating it into a bodily attitude it is this.'

Frank sat up for a moment quite straight in his chair, then slowly sunk back with arms outspread and head drooped.

'That;' he said, 'an effortless attitude, but open, resting, receptive. It is just that which you must do with your soul.'

Then he sat up again.

'One word more,' he said, 'and I will bore you no further. Nor unless you ask me questions shall I talk about it again. You will find me, in fact, quite sane in my mode of life. Birds and beasts you will see behaving somewhat intimately to me, like that moorhen, but that is all. I will walk with you, ride with you, play golf with you, and talk with you on any subject you like. But I wanted you on the threshold to know what has happened to me. And one thing more will happen.'

He paused again, and a slight look of fear crossed his eyes.

'There will be a final revelation,' he said, 'a complete and blinding stroke which will throw open to me, once and for all, the full knowledge, the full realisation and comprehension that I am one, just as you are, with life. In reality there is no 'me,' no 'you,' no 'it.' Everything is part of the one and only thing which is life. I know that that is so, but the realisation of it is not yet mine.

'But it will be, and on that day, so I take it, I shall see Pan. It may mean death, the death of my body, that is, but I don't care. It may mean immortal, eternal life lived here and now and for ever.

'Then having gained that, ah, my dear Darcy, I shall preach such a gospel of joy, showing myself as the living proof of the truth, that Puritanism, the dismal religion of sour faces, shall vanish like a breath of smoke, and be dispersed and disappear in the sunlit air. But first the full knowledge must be mine.'

Darcy watched his face narrowly.

'You are afraid of that moment,' he said. Frank smiled at him.

'Quite true; you are quick to have seen that. But when it comes I hope I shall not be afraid.'

For some little time there was silence; then Darcy rose. 'You have bewitched me, you extraordinary boy,' he said. 'You have been telling me a fairy-story, and I find myself saying, 'Promise me it is true.'

'I promise you that,' said the other.

'And I know I shan't sleep,' added Darcy.

Frank looked at him with a sort of mild wonder as if he scarcely understood.

'Well, what does that matter?' he said.

'I assure you it does. I am wretched unless I sleep.'

'Of course I can make you sleep if I want,' said Frank in a rather bored voice.

272

'Well, do.'

'Very good: go to bed. I'll come upstairs in ten minutes.'

Frank busied himself for a little after the other had gone, moving the table back under the awning of the verandah and quenching the lamp. Then he went with his quick silent tread upstairs and into Darcy's room. The latter was already in bed, but very wide-eyed and wakeful, and Frank with an amused smile of indulgence, as for a fretful child, sat down on the edge of the bed.

'Look at me,' he said, and Darcy looked.

'The birds are sleeping in the brake,' said Frank softly, 'and the winds are asleep. The sea sleeps, and the tides are but the heaving of its breast. The stars swing slow, rocked in the great cradle of the Heavens, and — '

He stopped suddenly, gently blew out Darcy's candle, and left him sleeping.

Morning brought to Darcy a flood of hard common sense, as clear and crisp as the sunshine that filled his room. Slowly as he woke he gathered together the broken threads of the memories of the evening which had ended, so he told himself, in a trick of common hypnotism. That accounted for it all; the whole strange talk he had had was under a spell of suggestion from the extraordinary vivid boy who had once been a

273

man; all his own excitement, his acceptance of the incredible had been merely the effect of a stronger, more potent will imposed on his own. How strong that will was, he guessed from his own instantaneous obedience to Frank's suggestion of sleep. And armed with impenetrable common sense he came down to breakfast. Frank had already begun, and was consuming a large plateful of porridge and milk with the most prosaic and healthy appetite.

'Slept well?' he asked.

'Yes, of course. Where did you learn hypnotism?'

'By the side of the river.'

'You talked an amazing quantity of nonsense last night,' remarked Darcy, in a voice prickly with reason.

'Rather. I felt quite giddy. Look, I remembered to order a dreadful daily paper for you. You can read about money markets or politics or cricket matches.' Darcy looked at him closely. In the morning light Frank looked even fresher, younger, more vital than he had done the night before, and the sight of him somehow dinted Darcy's armour of common sense.

'You are the most extraordinary fellow I ever saw,' he said. 'I want to ask you some more questions.'

'Ask away,' said Frank.

For the next day or two Darcy plied his friend with many questions, objections and criticisms on the theory of life, and gradually got out of him a coherent and complete account of his experience. In brief, then, Frank believed that 'by lying naked,' as he put it, to the force which controls the passage of the stars, the breaking of a wave, the budding of a tree, the love of a youth and maiden, he had succeeded in a way hitherto undreamed of in possessing himself of the essential principle of life. Day by day, so he thought, he was getting nearer to, and in closer union with, the great power itself which caused all life to be, the spirit of nature, of force, or the spirit of God. For himself, he confessed to what others would call paganism; it was sufficient for him that there existed a principle of life. He did not worship it, he did not pray to it, he did not praise it. Some of it existed in all human beings, just as it existed in trees and animals; to realise and make living to himself the fact that it was all one, was his sole aim and object.

Here perhaps Darcy would put in a word of warning.

'Take care,' he said. 'To see Pan meant death, did it not.'

Frank's eyebrows would rise at this.

'What does that matter?' he said. 'True, the

Greeks were always right, and they said so, but there is another possibility. For the nearer I get to it, the more living, the more vital and young I become.'

'What then do you expect the final revelation will do for you?'

'I have told you,' said he. 'It will make me immortal.'

But it was not so much from speech and argument that Darcy grew to grasp his friend's conception, as from the ordinary conduct of his life. They were passing, for instance, one morning down the village street, when an old woman, very bent and decrepit, but with an extraordinary cheerfulness of face, hobbled out from her cottage. Frank instantly stopped when he saw her.

'You old darling! How goes it all?' he said.

But she did not answer, her dim old eyes were riveted on his face; she seemed to drink in like a thirsty creature the beautiful radiance which shone there. Suddenly she put her two withered old hands on his shoulders.

'You're just the sunshine itself,' she said, and he kissed her and passed on.

But scarcely a hundred yards further a strange contradiction of such tenderness occurred. A child running along the path towards them fell on its face and set up a dismal cry of fright and pain. A look of horror came into Frank's eyes, and, putting his fingers in his ears, he fled at full speed down the street, and did not pause till he was out of hearing. Darcy, having ascertained that the child was not really hurt, followed him in bewilderment.

'Are you without pity then?' he asked. Frank shook his head impatiently.

'Can't you see?' he asked. 'Can't you understand that that sort of thing, pain, anger, anything unlovely, throws me back, retards the coming of the great hour! Perhaps when it comes I shall be able to piece that side of life on to the other, on to the true religion of joy. At present I can't.'

'But the old woman. Was she not ugly?'

Frank's radiance gradually returned.

'Ah, no. She was like me. She longed for joy, and knew it when she saw it, the old darling.'

Another question suggested itself.

'Then what about Christianity?' asked Darcy.

'I can't accept it. I can't believe in any creed of which the central doctrine is that God who is Joy should have had to suffer. Perhaps it was so; in some inscrutable way I believe it may have been so, but I don't understand how it was possible. So I leave it alone; my affair is joy.'

They had come to the weir above the

village, and the thunder of riotous cool water was heavy in the air. Trees dipped into the translucent stream with slender trailing branches, and the meadow where they stood was starred with midsummer blossomings. Larks shot up carolling into the crystal dome of blue, and a thousand voices of June sang round them. Frank, bare-headed as was his wont, with his coat slung over his arm and his shirt sleeves rolled up above the elbow, stood there like some beautiful wild animal with eyes half-shut and mouth half-open, drinking in the scented warmth of the air. Then suddenly he flung himself face downwards on the grass at the edge of the stream, burying his face in the daisies and cowslips, and lay stretched there in wide-armed ecstasy, with his long fingers pressing and stroking the dewy herbs of the field. Never before had Darcy seen him thus fully possessed by his idea; his caressing fingers, his half-buried face pressed close to the grass, even the clothed lines of his figure were instinct with a vitality that somehow was different from that of other men. And some faint glow from it reached Darcy, some thrill, some vibration from that charged recumbent body passed to him, and for a moment he understood as he had not understood before, despite his persistent questions and the candid answers they received, how real, and how realised by Frank, his idea was.

Then suddenly the muscles in Frank's neck became stiff and alert, and he half-raised his head.

'The Pan-pipes, the Pan-pipes,' he whispered. 'Close, oh, so close.'

Very slowly, as if a sudden movement might interrupt the melody, he raised himself and leaned on the elbow of his bent arm. His eyes opened wider, the lower lids drooped as if he focussed his eyes on something very far away, and the smile on his face broadened and quivered like sunlight on still water, till the exultance of its happiness was scarcely human. So he remained motionless and rapt for some minutes, then the look of listening died from his face, and he bowed his head, satisfied.

'Ah, that was good,' he said. 'How is it possible you did not hear? Oh, you poor fellow! Did you really hear nothing?'

A week of this outdoor and stimulating life did wonders in restoring to Darcy the vigour and health which his weeks of fever had filched from him, and as his normal activity and higher pressure of vitality returned, he seemed to himself to fall even more under the spell which the miracle of Frank's youth cast over him. Twenty times a day he found himself saying to himself suddenly at the end of some ten minutes silent resistance to the absurdity of Frank's idea: 'But it isn't possible; it can't be possible,' and from the fact of his having to assure himself so frequently of this, he knew that he was struggling and arguing with a conclusion which already had taken root in his mind. For in any case a visible living miracle confronted him, since it was equally impossible that this youth, this boy, trembling on the verge of manhood, was thirty-five.

Yet such was the fact.

July was ushered in by a couple of days of blustering and fretful rain, and Darcy, unwilling to risk a chill, kept to the house. But to Frank this weeping change of weather seemed to have no bearing on the behaviour of man, and he spent his days exactly as he did under the suns of June, lying in his hammock, stretched on the dripping grass, or making huge rambling excursions into the forest, the birds hopping from tree to tree after him, to return in the evening, drenched and soaked, but with the same unquenchable flame of joy burning within him.

'Catch cold?' he would ask; 'I've forgotten how to do it, I think I suppose it makes one's body more sensible always to sleep out-of-doors. People who live indoors always remind me of something peeled and skinless.'

'Do you mean to say you slept out-of-doors last night in that deluge?' asked Darcy. 'And where, may I ask?'

Frank thought a moment.

'I slept in the hammock till nearly dawn,' he said. 'For I remember the light blinked in the east when I awoke. Then I went — where did I go — oh, yes, to the meadow where the Pan-pipes sounded so close a week ago. You were with me, do you remember? But I always have a rug if it is wet.'

And he went whistling upstairs.

Somehow that little touch, his obvious effort to recall where he had slept, brought strangely home to Darcy the wonderful romance of which he was the still half-incredulous beholder. Sleep till close on dawn in a hammock, then the tramp — or probably scamper — underneath the windy and weeping heavens to the remote and lonely meadow by the weir! The picture of other such nights rose before him; Frank sleeping perhaps by the bathing-place under the filtered twilight of the stars, or the white blaze of moon-shine, a stir and awakening at some dead hour, perhaps a space of silent wide-eyed thought, and then awandering through the hushed woods to some other dormitory, alone with his happiness, alone

281

with the joy and the life that suffused and enveloped him, without other thought or desire or aim except the hourly and never-ceasing communion with the joy of nature.

They were in the middle of dinner that night, talking on indifferent subjects, when Darcy suddenly broke off in the middle of a sentence.

'I've got it,' he said. 'At last I've got it.'

'Congratulate you,' said Frank. 'But what?'

'The radical unsoundness of your idea. It is this: 'All Nature from highest to lowest is full, crammed full of suffering; every living organism in Nature preys on another, yet in your aim to get close to, to be one with Nature, you leave suffering altogether out; you run away from it, you refuse to recognise it. And you are waiting, you say, for the final revelation.'

Frank's brow clouded slightly.

'Well,' he asked, rather wearily.

'Cannot you guess then when the final revelation will be? In joy you are supreme, I grant you that; I did not know a man could be so master of it. You have learned perhaps practically all that Nature can teach. And if, as you think, the final revelation is coming to you, it will be the revelation of horror, suffering, death, pain in all its hideous forms. Suffering does exist: you hate it and fear it.'

Frank held up his hand.

'Stop; let me think,' he said.

There was silence for a long minute.

'That never struck me,' he said at length. 'It is possible that what you suggest is true. Does the sight of Pan mean that, do you think? Is it that Nature, take it altogether, suffers horribly, suffers to a hideous inconceivable extent? Shall I be shown all the suffering?' He got up and came round to where Darcy sat.

'If it is so, so be it,' he said. 'Because, my dear fellow, I am near, so splendidly near to the final revelation. To-day the pipes have sounded almost without pause. I have even heard the rustle in the bushes, I believe, of Pan's coming. I have seen, yes, I saw to-day, the bushes pushed aside as if by a hand, and piece of a face, not human, peered through. But I was not frightened, at least I did not run away this time.'

He took a turn up to the window and back again.

'Yes, there is suffering all through,' he said, 'and I have left it all out of my search. Perhaps, as you say, the revelation will be that. And in that case, it will be good-bye. I have gone on one line. I shall have gone too far along one road, without having explored the other. But I can't go back now. I wouldn't if I could; not a step would I retrace! In any case, whatever the revelation is, it will be God. I'm sure of that.'

The rainy weather soon passed, and with the return of the sun Darcy again joined Frank in long rambling days. It grew extraordinarily hotter, and with the fresh bursting of life, after the rain, Frank's vitality seemed to blaze higher and higher. Then, as is the habit of the English weather, one evening clouds began to bank themselves up in the west, the sun went down in a glare of coppery thunder-rack, and the whole earth broiling under an unspeakable oppression and sultriness paused and panted for the storm. After sunset the remote fires of lightning began to wink and flicker on the horizon, but when bed-time came the storm seemed to have moved no nearer, though a very low unceasing noise of thunder was audible. Weary and oppressed by the stress of the day, Darcy fell at once into a heavy uncomforting sleep.

He woke suddenly into full consciousness, with the din of some appalling explosion of thunder in his ears, and sat up in bed with racing heart. Then for a moment, as he recovered himself from the panic-land which lies between sleeping and waking, there was silence, except for the steady hissing of rain on the shrubs outside his window. But suddenly that silence was shattered and shredded into fragments by a scream from somewhere close at hand outside in the black garden, a scream of supreme and despairing terror. Again and once again it shrilled up, and then a babble of awful words was interjected. A quivering sobbing voice that he knew said:

'My God, oh, my God; oh, Christ!'

And then followed a little mocking, bleating laugh. Then was silence again; only the rain hissed on the shrubs.

All this was but the affair of a moment, and without pause either to put on clothes or light a candle, Darcy was already fumbling at his door-handle. Even as he opened it he met a terror-stricken face outside, that of the man-servant who carried a light.

'Did you hear?' he asked.

The man's face was bleached to a dull shining whiteness. 'Yes, sir,' he said. 'It was the master's voice.'

Together they hurried down the stairs and through the dining-room where an orderly table for breakfast had already been laid, and out on to the terrace. The rain for the moment had been utterly stayed, as if the tap of the heavens had been turned off, and under the lowering black sky, not quite dark, since the moon rode somewhere serene behind the conglomerated thunder-clouds, Darcy stumbled into the garden, followed by the servant with the candle. The monstrous leaping shadow of himself was cast before him on the lawn; lost and wandering odours of rose and lily and damp earth were thick about him, but more pungent was some sharp and acrid smell that suddenly reminded him of a certain chalet in which he had once taken refuge in the Alps. In the blackness of the hazy light from the sky, and the vague tossing of the candle behind him, he saw that the hammock in which Frank so often lay was tenanted. A gleam of white shirt was there, as if a man were sitting up in it, but across that there was an obscure dark shadow, and as he approached the acrid odour grew more intense.

He was now only some few yards away, when suddenly the black shadow seemed to jump into the air, then came down with tappings of hard hoofs on the brick path that ran down the pergola, and with frolicsome skippings galloped off into the bushes. When that was gone Darcy could see quite clearly that a shirted figure sat up in the hammock. For one moment, from sheer terror of the unseen, he hung on his step, and the servant joining him they walked together to the hammock.

It was Frank. He was in shirt and trousers only, and he sat up with braced arms. For one half-second he stared at them, his face a mask of horrible contorted terror. His upper lip was drawn back so that the gums of the teeth appeared, and his eyes were focussed not on the two who approached him, but on something quite close to him; his nostrils were widely expanded, as if he panted for breath, and terror incarnate and repulsion and deathly anguish ruled dreadful lines on his smooth cheeks and forehead. Then even as they looked the body sank backwards, and the ropes of the hammock wheezed and strained.

Darcy lifted him out and carried him indoors. Once he thought there was a faint convulsive stir of the limbs that lay with so dead a weight in his arms, but when they got inside, there was no trace of life. But the look of supreme terror and agony of fear had gone from his face, a boy tired with play but still smiling in his sleep was the burden he laid on the floor. His eyes had closed, and the beautiful mouth lay in smiling curves, even as when a few mornings ago, in the meadow by the weir, it had quivered to the music of the unheard melody of Pan's pipes. Then they looked further.

Frank had come back from his bathe before

dinner that night in his usual costume of shirt and trousers only. He had not dressed, and during dinner, so Darcy remembered, he had rolled up the sleeves of his shirt to above the elbow. Later, as they sat and talked after dinner on the close sultriness of the evening, he had unbuttoned the front of his shirt to let what little breath of wind there was play on his skin. The sleeves were rolled up now, the front of the shirt was unbuttoned, and on his arms and on the brown skin of his chest were strange discolorations which grew momently more clear and defined, till they saw that the marks were pointed prints, as if caused by the hoofs of some monstrous goat that had leaped and stamped upon him.

Between the Lights

The day had been one unceasing fall of snow from sunrise until the gradual withdrawal of the vague white light outside indicated that the sun had set again. But as usual at this hospitable and delightful house of Everard Chandler where I often spent Christmas, and was spending it now, there had been no lack of entertainment, and the hours had passed with a rapidity that had surprised us. A short billiard tournament had filled up the time between breakfast and lunch, with Badminton and the morning papers for those who were temporarily not engaged, while afterwards, the interval till tea-time had been occupied by the majority of the party in a huge game of hide-and-seek all over the house, barring the billiard-room, which was sanctuary for any who desired peace. But few had done that; the enchantment of Christmas, I must suppose, had, like some spell, made children of us again, and it was with palsied terror and trembling misgivings that we had tip-toed up and down the dim passages, from any corner of which some wild screaming form might dart out on us. Then, wearied with exercise and emotion, we had assembled again for tea in the hall, a room of shadows and panels on which the light from the wide open fireplace, where there burned a divine mixture of peat and logs, flickered and grew bright again on the walls. Then, as was proper, ghost-stories, for the narration of which the electric light was put out, so that the listeners might conjecture anything they pleased to be lurking in the corners, succeeded, and we vied with each other in blood, bones, skeletons, armour and shrieks. I had just given my contribution, and was reflecting with some complacency that probably the worst was now known, when Everard, who had not yet administered to the horror of his guests, spoke. He was sitting opposite me in the full blaze of the fire, looking, after the illness he had gone through during the autumn, still rather pale and delicate. All the same he had been among the boldest and best in the exploration of dark places that afternoon, and the look on his face now rather startled me.

'No, I don't mind that sort of thing,' he said. 'The paraphernalia of ghosts has become somehow rather hackneyed, and when I hear of screams and skeletons I feel I am on familiar ground, and can at least hide my head under the bed-clothes.'

'Ah, but the bed-clothes were twitched away by my skeleton,' said I, in self-defence.

'I know, but I don't even mind that. Why, there are seven, eight skeletons in this room now, covered with blood and skin and other horrors. No, the nightmares of one's child-hood were the really frightening things, because they were vague. There was the true atmosphere of horror about them because one didn't know what one feared. Now if one could recapture that — '

Mrs. Chandler got quickly out of her seat.

'Oh, Everard,' she said, 'surely you don't wish to recapture it again. I should have thought once was enough.'

This was enchanting. A chorus of invitation asked him to proceed: the real true ghost-story first-hand, which was what seemed to be indicated, was too precious a thing to lose.

Everard laughed. 'No, dear, I don't want to recapture it again at all,' he said to his wife.

Then to us: 'But really the — well, the nightmare perhaps, to which I was referring, is of the vaguest and most unsatisfactory kind. It has no apparatus about it at all. You will probably all say that it was nothing, and wonder why I was frightened. But I was; it frightened me out of my wits. And I only just saw something, without being able to swear what it was, and heard something which might have been a falling stone.'

'Anyhow, tell us about the falling stone,' said I.

There was a stir of movement about the circle round the fire, and the movement was not of purely physical order. It was as if — this is only what I personally felt — it was as if the childish gaiety of the hours we had passed that day was suddenly withdrawn; we had jested on certain subjects, we had played hide-and-seek with all the power of earnestness that was in us. But now — so it seemed to me — there was going to be real hide-and-seek, real terrors were going to lurk in dark corners, or if not real terrors, terrors so convincing as to assume the garb of reality, were going to pounce on us. And Mrs. Chandler's exclamation as she sat down again, 'Oh, Everard, won't it excite you?' tended in any case to excite us. The room still remained in dubious darkness except for the sudden lights disclosed on the walls by the leaping flames on the hearth, and there was wide field for conjecture as to what might lurk in the dim corners. Everard, moreover, who had been sitting in bright light before, was banished by the extinction of some flaming log into the shadows. A voice alone spoke to us, as he sat back in his low chair, a voice rather slow but very distinct.

'Last year,' he said, 'on the twenty-fourth of December, we were down here, as usual, Amy and I, for Christmas. Several of you who are here now were here then. Three or four of you at least.'

I was one of these, but like the others kept silence, for the identification, so it seemed to me, was not asked for. And he went on again without a pause.

'Those of you who were here then,' he said, 'and are here now, will remember how very warm it was this day year. You will remember, too, that we played croquet that day on the lawn. It was perhaps a little cold for croquet, and we played it rather in order to be able to say — with sound evidence to back the statement — that we had done so.'

Then he turned and addressed the whole little circle.

'We played ties of half-games,' he said, 'just as we have played billiards to-day, and it was certainly as warm on the lawn then as it was in the billiard-room this morning directly after breakfast, while to-day I should not wonder if there was three feet of snow outside. More, probably; listen.'

A sudden draught fluted in the chimney, and the fire flared up as the current of air caught it.

The wind also drove the snow against the windows, and as he said, 'Listen,' we heard a soft scurry of the falling flakes against the panes, like the soft tread of many little people who stepped lightly, but with the persistence of multitudes who were flocking to some rendezvous. Hundreds of little feet seemed to be gathering outside; only the glass kept them out. And of the eight skeletons present four or five, anyhow, turned and looked at the windows. These were small-paned, with leaden bars. On the leaden bars little heaps of snow had accumulated, but there was nothing else to be seen.

'Yes, last Christmas Eve was very warm and sunny,' went on Everard. 'We had had no frost that autumn, and a temerarious dahlia was still in flower. I have always thought that it must have been mad.'

He paused a moment.

'And I wonder if I were not mad too,' he added.

No one interrupted him; there was something arresting, I must suppose, in what he was saying; it chimed in anyhow with the hide-and-seek, with the suggestions of the lonely snow.

Mrs. Chandler had sat down again, but I heard her stir in her chair. But never was there a gay party so reduced as we had been in the last five minutes. Instead of laughing at ourselves for playing silly games, we were all taking a serious game seriously.

'Anyhow, I was sitting out,' he said to me, 'while you and my wife played your half-game of croquet. Then it struck me that it was not so warm as I had supposed, because quite suddenly I shivered. And shivering I looked up. But I did not see you and her playing croquet at all. I saw something which had no relation to you and her — at least I hope not.'

Now the angler lands his fish, the stalker kills his stag, and the speaker holds his audience.

And as the fish is gaffed, and as the stag is shot, so were we held. There was no getting away till he had finished with us.

'You all know the croquet lawn,' he said, 'and how it is bounded all round by a flower border with a brick wall behind it, through which, you will remember, there is only one gate.

'Well, I looked up and saw that the lawn — I could for one moment see it was still a lawn — was shrinking, and the walls closing in upon it. As they closed in too, they grew higher, and simultaneously the light began to fade and be sucked from the sky, till it grew quite dark overhead and only a glimmer of light came in through the gate.

'There was, as I told you, a dahlia in flower that day, and as this dreadful darkness and bewilderment came over me, I remember that my eyes sought it in a kind of despair, holding on, as it were, to any familiar object. But it was no longer a dahlia, and for the red of its petals I saw only the red of some feeble firelight. And at that moment the hallucination was complete. I was no longer sitting on the lawn watching croquet, but I was in a low-roofed room, something like a cattle-shed, but round. Close above my head, though I was sitting down, ran rafters from wall to wall. It was nearly dark, but a little light came in from the door opposite to me, which seemed to lead into a passage that communicated with the exterior of the place. Little, however, of the wholesome air came into this dreadful den; the atmosphere was oppressive and foul beyond all telling, it was as if for years it had been the place of some human menagerie, and for those years had been uncleaned and unsweetened by the winds of heaven. Yet that oppressiveness was nothing to the awful horror of the place from the view of the spirit. Some dreadful atmosphere of crime and abomination dwelt heavy in it, its denizens, whoever they were, were scarce human, so it seemed to me, and though men and women, were akin more to the beasts of the field. And in addition there was present to me some sense of the weight of years; I had been taken and thrust down into some epoch of dim antiquity.'

He paused a moment, and the fire on the hearth leaped up for a second and then died down again. But in that gleam I saw that all faces were turned to Everard, and that all wore some look of dreadful expectancy. Certainly I felt it myself, and waited in a sort of shrinking horror for what was coming.

'As I told you,' he continued, 'where there had been that unseasonable dahlia, there now burned a dim firelight, and my eyes were drawn there. Shapes were gathered round it; what they were I could not at first see. Then perhaps my eyes got more accustomed to the dusk, or the fire burned better, for I perceived that they were of human form, but very small, for when one rose with a horrible chattering, to his feet, his head was still some inches off the low roof. He was dressed in a sort of shirt that came to his knees, but his arms were bare and covered with hair.

'Then the gesticulation and chattering increased, and I knew that they were talking about me, for they kept pointing in my direction. At that my horror suddenly deepened, for I became aware that I was powerless and could not move hand or foot; a helpless, nightmare impotence had possession of me. I could not lift a finger or turn my head. And in the paralysis of that fear I tried to scream, but not a sound could I utter.

'All this I suppose took place with the instantaneousness of a dream, for at once, and without transition, the whole thing had vanished, and I was back on the lawn again, while the stroke for which my wife was aiming was still unplayed. But my face was dripping with perspiration, and I was trembling all over.

'Now you may all say that I had fallen asleep, and had a sudden nightmare. That may be so; but I was conscious of no sense of sleepiness before, and I was conscious of none afterwards. It was as if someone had held a book before me, whisked the pages open for a second and closed them again.'

Somebody, I don't know who, got up from his chair with a sudden movement that made me start, and turned on the electric light. I do not mind confessing that I was rather glad of this.

Everard laughed.

'Really I feel like Hamlet in the play-scene,' he said, 'and as if there was a guilty uncle present. Shall I go on?'

I don't think anyone replied, and he went on.

'Well, let us say for the moment that it was not a dream exactly, but a hallucination.

'Whichever it was, in any case it haunted me; for months, I think, it was never quite out of my mind, but lingered somewhere in the dusk of consciousness, sometimes sleeping quietly, so to speak, but sometimes stirring in its sleep. It was no good my telling myself that I was disquieting myself in vain, for it was as if something had actually entered into my very soul, as if some seed of horror had been planted there. And as the weeks went on the seed began to sprout, so that I could no longer even tell myself that that vision had been a moment's disorderment only. I can't say that it actually affected my health. I did not, as far as I know, sleep or eat insufficiently, but morning after morning I used to wake, not gradually and through pleasant dozings into full consciousness, but with absolute suddenness, and find myself plunged in an abyss of despair.

'Often too, eating or drinking, I used to pause and wonder if it was worth while.

'Eventually, I told two people about my trouble, hoping that perhaps the mere communication would help matters, hoping also, but very distantly, that though I could not believe at present that digestion or the obscurities of the nervous system were at fault, a doctor by some simple dose might convince me of it. In other words I told my wife, who laughed at me, and my doctor, who laughed also, and assured me that my health was quite unnecessarily robust.

'At the same time he suggested that change of air and scene does wonders for the delusions that exist merely in the imagination. He also told me, in answer to a direct question, that he would stake his reputation on the certainty that I was not going mad.

'Well, we went up to London as usual for the season, and though nothing whatever occurred to remind me in any way of that single moment on Christmas Eve, the reminding was seen to all right, the moment itself took care of that, for instead of fading as is the way of sleeping or waking dreams, it grew every day more vivid, and ate, so to speak, like some corrosive acid into my mind, etching itself there. And to London succeeded Scotland.

'I took last year for the first time a small forest up in Sutherland, called Glen Callan, very remote and wild, but affording excellent stalking. It was not far from the sea, and the gillies used always to warn me to carry a compass on the hill, because sea-mists were liable to come up with frightful rapidity, and there was always a danger of being caught by one, and of having perhaps to wait hours till it cleared again. This at first I always used to do, but, as everyone knows, any precaution that one takes which continues to be unjustified gets gradually relaxed, and at the end of a few weeks, since the weather had been uniformly clear, it was natural that, as often as not, my compass remained at home.

'One day the stalk took me on to a part of my ground that I had seldom been on before, a very high table-land on the limit of my forest, which went down very steeply on one side to a loch that lay below it, and on the other, by gentler gradations, to the river that came from the loch, six miles below which stood the lodge. The wind had necessitated our climbing up — or so my stalker had insisted — not by the easier way, but up the crags from the loch. I had argued the point with him for it seemed to me that it was impossible that the deer could get our scent if we went by the more natural path, but he still held to his opinion; and therefore, since after all this was his part of the job, I yielded. A dreadful climb we had of it, over big boulders with deep holes in between, masked by clumps of heather, so that a wary eye and a prodding stick were necessary for each step if one wished to avoid broken bones. Adders also literally swarmed in the heather; we must have seen a dozen at least on our way up, and adders are a beast for which I have no manner of use. But a couple of hours saw us to the top, only to find that the stalker had been utterly at fault, and that the deer must quite infallibly have got wind of us, if they had remained in the place where we last saw them. That, when we could spy the ground again, we saw had happened; in any case they had gone. The man insisted the wind had changed, a palpably stupid excuse, and I wondered at that moment what other reason he had — for reason I felt sure there must be — for not wishing to take what would clearly now have been a better route. But this piece of bad management did not spoil our luck, for within an hour we had spied more deer, and about two o'clock I got a shot, killing a heavy stag. Then sitting on the heather I ate lunch, and enjoyed a well-earned bask and smoke in the sun. The pony meantime had been saddled with the stag, and was plodding homewards.

'The morning had been extraordinarily warm, with a little wind blowing off the sea, which lay a few miles off sparkling beneath a blue haze, and all morning in spite of our abominable climb I had had an extreme sense of peace, so much so that several times I had probed my mind, so to speak, to find if the horror still lingered there. But I could scarcely get any response from it.

'Never since Christmas had I been so free of fear, and it was with a great sense of repose, both physical and spiritual, that I lay looking up into the blue sky, watching my smoke-whorls curl slowly away into nothingness. But I was not allowed to take my ease long, for Sandy came and begged that I would move. The weather had changed, he said, the wind had shifted again, and he wanted me to be off this high ground and on the path again as soon as possible, because it looked to him as if a sea-mist would presently come up.'

''And yon's a bad place to get down in the mist,' he added, nodding towards the crags we had come up.

'I looked at the man in amazement, for to our right lay a gentle slope down on to the river, and there was now no possible reason for again tackling those hideous rocks up which we had climbed this morning. More than ever I was sure he had some secret reason for not wishing to go the obvious way. But about one thing he was certainly right, the mist was coming up from the sea, and I felt in my pocket for the compass, and found I had forgotten to bring it.

'Then there followed a curious scene which

305

lost us time that we could really ill afford to waste, I insisting on going down by the way that common sense directed, he imploring me to take his word for it that the crags were the better way. Eventually, I marched off to the easier descent, and told him not to argue any more but follow. What annoyed me about him was that he would only give the most senseless reasons for preferring the crags. There were mossy places, he said, on the way I wished to go, a thing patently false, since the summer had been one spell of unbroken weather; or it was longer, also obviously untrue; or there were so many vipers about.

'But seeing that none of these arguments produced any effect, at last he desisted, and came after me in silence.

'We were not yet half down when the mist was upon us, shooting up from the valley like the broken water of a wave, and in three minutes we were enveloped in a cloud of fog so thick that we could barely see a dozen yards in front of us. It was therefore another cause for self-congratulation that we were not now, as we should otherwise have been, precariously clambering on the face of those crags up which we had come with such difficulty in the morning, and as I rather prided myself on my powers of generalship in the matter of direction, I continued leading, feeling sure that before long we should strike the track by the river. More than all, the absolute freedom from fear elated me; since Christmas I had not known the instinctive joy of that; I felt like a schoolboy home for the holidays. But the mist grew thicker and thicker, and whether it was that real rain-clouds had formed above it, or that it was of an extraordinary density itself, I got wetter in the next hour than I have ever been before or since. The wet seemed to penetrate the skin, and chill the very bones. And still there was no sign of the track for which I was making.

'Behind me, muttering to himself, followed the stalker, but his arguments and protestations were dumb, and it seemed as if he kept close to me, as if afraid.

'Now there are many unpleasant companions in this world; I would not, for instance, care to be on the hill with a drunkard or a maniac, but worse than either, I think, is a frightened man, because his trouble is infectious, and, insensibly, I began to be afraid of being frightened too.

'From that it is but a short step to fear. Other perplexities too beset us. At one time we seemed to be walking on flat ground, at another I felt sure we were climbing again, whereas all the time we ought to have been descending, unless we had missed the way very badly indeed. Also, for the month was October, it was beginning to get dark, and it was with a sense of relief that I remembered that the full moon would rise soon after sunset. But it had grown very much colder, and soon, instead of rain, we found we were walking through a steady fall of snow.

'Things were pretty bad, but then for the moment they seemed to mend, for, far away to the left, I suddenly heard the brawling of the river. It should, it is true, have been straight in front of me and we were perhaps a mile out of our way, but this was better than the blind wandering of the last hour, and turning to the left, I walked towards it. But before I had gone a hundred yards, I heard a sudden choked cry behind me, and just saw Sandy's form flying as if in terror of pursuit, into the mists. I called to him, but got no reply, and heard only the spurned stones of his running.

'What had frightened him I had no idea, but certainly with his disappearance, the infection of his fear disappeared also, and I went on, I may almost say, with gaiety. On the moment, however, I saw a sudden well-defined blackness in front of me, and before I knew what I was doing I was half stumbling, half walking up a very steep grass slope.

'During the last few minutes the wind had got up, and the driving snow was peculiarly uncomfortable, but there had been a certain consolation in thinking that the wind would soon disperse these mists, and I had nothing more than a moonlight walk home. But as I paused on this slope, I became aware of two things, one, that the blackness in front of me was very close, the other that, whatever it was, it sheltered me from the snow. So I climbed on a dozen yards into its friendly shelter, for it seemed to me to be friendly.

'A wall some twelve feet high crowned the slope, and exactly where I struck it there was a hole in it, or door rather, through which a little light appeared. Wondering at this I pushed on, bending down, for the passage was very low, and in a dozen yards came out on the other side.

'Just as I did this the sky suddenly grew lighter, the wind, I suppose, having dispersed the mists, and the moon, though not yet visible through the flying skirts of cloud, made sufficient illumination.

'I was in a circular enclosure, and above me there projected from the walls some four feet from the ground, broken stones which must have been intended to support a floor. Then simultaneously two things occurred.

'The whole of my nine months' terror

came back to me, for I saw that the vision in the garden was fulfilled, and at the same moment I saw stealing towards me a little figure as of a man, but only about three foot six in height. That my eyes told me; my ears told me that he stumbled on a stone; my nostrils told me that the air I breathed was of an overpowering foulness, and my soul told me that it was sick unto death. I think I tried to scream, but could not; I know I tried to move and could not. And it crept closer.

'Then I suppose the terror which held me spellbound so spurred me that I must move, for next moment I heard a cry break from my lips, and was stumbling through the passage. I made one leap of it down the grass slope, and ran as I hope never to have to run again. What direction I took I did not pause to consider, so long as I put distance between me and that place. Luck, however, favoured me, and before long I struck the track by the river, and an hour afterwards reached the lodge.

'Next day I developed a chill, and as you know pneumonia laid me on my back for six weeks.

'Well, that is my story, and there are many explanations. You may say that I fell asleep on the lawn, and was reminded of that by finding myself, under discouraging circumstances, in an old Picts' castle, where a sheep or a goat that, like myself, had taken shelter from the storm, was moving about. Yes, there are hundreds of ways in which you may explain it. But the coincidence was an odd one, and those who believe in second sight might find an instance of their hobby in it.'

'And that is all?' I asked.

'Yes, it was nearly too much for me. I think the dressing-bell has sounded.'

Outside the Door

The rest of the small party staying with my friend Geoffrey Aldwych in the charming old house which he had lately bought at a little village north of Sheringham on the Norfolk coast had drifted away soon after dinner to bridge and billiards, and Mrs. Aldwych and myself had for the time been left alone in the drawing-room, seated one on each side of a small round table which we had very patiently and unsuccessfully been trying to turn. But such pressure, psychical or physical, as we had put upon it, though of the friendliest and most encouraging nature, had not overcome in the smallest degree the very slight inertia which so small an object might have been supposed to possess, and it had remained as fixed as the most constant of the stars. No tremor even had passed through its slight and spindle-like legs. In consequence we had, after a really considerable period of patient endeavour, left it to its wooden repose, and proceeded to theorise about psychical matters instead, with no stupid table to contradict in practice all our ideas on the subject.

This I had added with a certain bitterness

born of failure, for if we could not move so insignificant an object, we might as well give up all idea of moving anything. But hardly were the words out of my mouth when there came from the abandoned table a single peremptory rap, loud and rather startling.

'What's that?' I asked.

'Only a rap,' said she. 'I thought something would happen before long.'

'And do you really think that is a spirit rapping?' I asked.

'Oh dear no. I don't think it has anything whatever to do with spirits.'

'More perhaps with the very dry weather we have been having. Furniture often cracks like that in the summer.'

Now this, in point of fact, was not quite the case. Neither in summer nor in winter have I ever heard furniture crack as the table had cracked, for the sound, whatever it was, did not at all resemble the husky creak of contracting wood. It was a loud sharp crack like the smart concussion of one hard object with another.

'No, I don't think it had much to do with dry weather either,' said she, smiling. 'I think, if you wish to know, that it was the direct result of our attempt to turn the table. Does that sound nonsense?'

'At present, yes,' said I, 'though I have no

doubt that if you tried you could make it sound sense. There is, I notice, a certain plausibility about you and your theories — '

'Now you are being merely personal,' she observed.

'For the good motive, to goad you into explanations and enlargements. Please go on.'

'Let us stroll outside, then,' said she, 'and sit in the garden, if you are sure you prefer my plausibilities to bridge. It is deliciously warm, and — '

'And the darkness will be more suitable for the propagation of psychical phenomena. As at séances,' said I.

'Oh, there is nothing psychical about my plausibilities,' said she. 'The phenomena I mean are purely physical, according to my theory.'

So we wandered out into the transparent half light of multitudinous stars. The last crimson feather of sunset, which had hovered long in the West, had been blown away with the breath of the night wind, and the moon, which would presently rise, had not yet cut the dim horizon of the sea, which lay very quiet, breathing gently in its sleep with stir of whispering ripples. Across the dark velvet of the close-cropped lawn, which stretched seawards from the house, blew a little breeze full of the savour of salt and the freshness of night, with, every now and then, a hint so subtly conveyed as to be scarcely perceptible of its travel across the sleeping fragrance of drowsy garden-beds, over which the white moths hovered seeking their night-honey. The house itself, with its two battlemented towers of Elizabethan times, gleamed with many windows, and we passed out of sight of it, and into the shadow of a box-hedge, clipped into shapes and monstrous fantasies, and found chairs by the striped tent at the top of the sheltered bowling-alley.

'And this is all very plausible,' said I. 'Theories, if you please, at length, and, if possible, a full length illustration also.'

'By which you mean a ghost-story, or something to that effect?'

'Precisely: and, without presuming to dictate, if possible, firsthand.'

'Oddly enough, I can supply that also,' said she. 'So first I will tell you my general theory, and follow it by a story that seems to bear it out. It happened to me, and it happened here.'

'I am sure it will fill the bill,' said I.

She paused a moment while I lit a cigarette, and then began in her very clear, pleasant voice.

She has the most lucid voice I know, and to me sitting there in the deep-dyed dusk, the words seemed the very incarnation of clarity, for they dropped into the still quiet of the darkness, undisturbed by impressions conveyed to other senses.

'We are only just beginning to conjecture,' she said, 'how inextricable is the interweaving between mind, soul, life — call it what you will — and the purely material part of the created world. That such interweaving existed has, of course, been known for centuries; doctors, for instance, knew that a cheerful optimistic spirit on the part of their patients conducted towards recovery; that fear, the mere emotion, had a definite effect on the beat of the heart, that anger produced chemical changes in the blood, that anxiety led to indigestion, that under the influence of strong passion a man can do things which in his normal state he is physically incapable of performing. Here we have mind, in a simple and familiar manner, producing changes and effects in tissue, in that which is purely material. By an extension of this — though, indeed, it is scarcely an extension — we may expect to find that mind can have an effect, not only on what we call living tissue, but on dead things, on pieces of wood or stone. At least it is hard to see why that should not be so.'

'Table-turning, for instance?' I asked.

'That is one instance of how some force, out of that innumerable cohort of obscure mysterious forces with which we human beings are garrisoned, can pass, as it is constantly doing, into material things. The laws of its passing we do not know; sometimes we wish it to pass and it does not. Just now, for instance, when you and I tried to turn the table, there was some impediment in the path, though I put down that rap which followed as an effect of our efforts. But nothing seems more natural to my mind than that these forces should be transmissible to inanimate things. Of the manner of its passing we know next to nothing, any more than we know the manner of the actual process by which fear accelerates the beating of the heart, but as surely as a Marconi message leaps along the air by no visible or tangible bridge, so through some subtle gateway of the body these forces can march from the citadel of the spirit into material forms, whether that material is a living part of ourselves or that which we choose to call inanimate nature.' She paused a moment.

'Under certain circumstances,' she went on, 'it seems that the force which has passed from us into inanimate things can manifest its presence there. The force that passes into a table can show itself in movements or in noises coming from the table. The table has been charged with physical energy. Often and often I have seen a table or a chair move apparently of its own accord, but only when some outpouring of force, animal magnetism — call it what you will — has been received by it. A parallel phenomenon to my mind is exhibited in what we know as haunted houses, houses in which, as a rule, some crime or act of extreme emotion or passion has been committed, and in which some echo or re-enactment of the deed is periodically made visible or audible. A murder has been committed, let us say, and the room where it took place is haunted. The figure of the murdered, or less commonly of the murderer, is seen there by sensitives, and cries are heard, or steps run to and fro. The atmosphere has somehow been charged with the scene, and the scene in whole or part repeats itself, though under what laws we do not know, just as a phonograph will repeat, when properly handled, what has been said into it.'

'This is all theory,' I remarked.

'But it appears to me to cover a curious set of facts, which is all we ask of a theory.

'Otherwise, we must frankly state our disbelief in haunted houses altogether, or suppose that the spirit of the murdered, poor wretch, is bound under certain circumstances to re-enact the horror of its body's tragedy. It was not enough that its body was killed there, its soul has to be dragged back and live through it all again with such vividness that its anguish becomes visible or audible to the eyes or ears of the sensitive. That to me is unthinkable, whereas my theory is not. Do I make it at all clear?'

'It is clear enough,' said I, 'but I want support for it, the full-sized illustration.'

'I promised you that, a ghost-story of my own experience.'

Mrs. Aldwych paused again, and then began the story which was to illustrate her theory.

'It is just a year,' she said, 'since Jack bought this house from old Mrs. Denison. We had both heard, both he and I, that it was supposed to be haunted, but neither of us knew any particulars of the haunt whatever. A month ago I heard what I believe to have been the ghost, and, when Mrs. Denison was staying with us last week, I asked her exactly what it was, and found it tallied completely with my experience. I will tell you my experience first, and give her account of the haunt afterwards.

'A month ago Jack was away for a few days and I remained here alone. One Sunday evening I, in my usual health and spirits, as far as I am aware, both of which are serenely excellent, went up to bed about eleven. My room is on the first floor, just at the foot of the staircase that leads to the floor above. There are four more rooms on my passage, all of which that night were empty, and at the far end of it a door leads into the landing at the top of the front staircase. On the other side of that, as you know, are more bedrooms, all of which that night were also unoccupied; I, in fact, was the only sleeper on the first floor.

'The head of my bed is close behind my door, and there is an electric light over it. This is controlled by a switch at the bed-head, and another switch there turns on a light in the passage just outside my room. That was Jack's plan: if by chance you want to leave your room when the house is dark, you can light up the passage before you go out, and not grope blindly for a switch outside.

'Usually I sleep solidly: it is very rarely indeed that I wake, when once I have gone to sleep, before I am called. But that night I woke, which was rare; what was rarer was that I woke in a state of shuddering and unaccountable terror; I tried to localise my panic, to run it to earth and reason it away, but without any success. Terror of something

I could not guess at stared me in the face, white, shaking terror. So, as there was no use in lying quaking in the dark, I lit my lamp, and, with the view of composing this strange disorder of my fear, began to read again in the book I had brought up with me. The volume happened to be 'The Green Carnation,' a work one would have thought to be full of tonic to twittering nerves. But it failed of success, even as my reasoning had done, and after reading a few pages, and finding that the heart-hammer in my throat grew no quieter, and that the grip of terror was in no way relaxed, I put out my light and lay down again. I looked at my watch, however, before doing this, and remember that the time was ten minutes to two.

'Still matters did not mend: terror, that was slowly becoming a little more definite, terror of some dark and violent deed that was momently drawing nearer to me held me in its vice.

'Something was coming, the advent of which was perceived by the sub-conscious sense, and was already conveyed to my conscious mind. And then the clock struck two jingling chimes, and the stable-clock outside clanged the hour more sonorously.

'I still lay there, abject and palpitating. Then I heard a sound just outside my room on the stairs that lead, as I have said, to the second story, a sound which was perfectly commonplace and unmistakable. Feet feeling their way in the dark were coming downstairs to my passage: I could hear also the groping hand slip and slide along the bannisters. The footfalls came along the few yards of passage between the bottom of the stairs and my door, and then against my door itself came the brush of drapery, and on the panels the blind groping of fingers. The handle rattled as they passed over it, and my terror nearly rose to screaming point.

'Then a sensible hope struck me. The midnight wanderer might be one of the servants, ill or in want of something, and yet — why the shuffling feet and the groping hand? But on the instant of the dawning of that hope (for I knew that it was of the step and that which was moving in the dark passage of which I was afraid) I turned on both the light at my bed-head, and the light of the passage outside, and, opening the door, looked out. The passage was quite bright from end to end, but it was perfectly empty. Yet as I looked, seeing nothing of the walker, I still heard. Down the bright boards I heard the shuffle growing fainter as it receded, until, judging by the ear, it turned into the gallery at the end and died away. And with it there died also all my sense of terror. It was It of which I had been afraid: now It and my terror had passed. And I went back to bed and slept till morning.'

Again Mrs. Aldwych paused, and I was silent. Somehow it was in the extreme simplicity of her experience that the horror lay. She went on almost immediately.

'Now for the sequel,' she said, 'of what I choose to call the explanation. Mrs. Denison, as I told you, came down to stay with us not long ago, and I mentioned that we had heard, though only vaguely, that the house was supposed to be haunted, and asked for an account of it. This is what she told me:

'In the year 1610 the heiress to the property was a girl Helen Denison, who was engaged to be married to young Lord Southern. In case therefore of her having children, the property would pass away from Denisons. In case of her death, childless, it would pass to her first cousin. A week before the marriage took place, he and a brother of his entered the house, riding here from thirty miles away, after dark, and made their way to her room on the second story. There they gagged her and attempted to kill her, but she escaped from them, groped her way along this passage, and into the room at the end of the gallery. They followed her there, and killed her. The facts were known by the younger brother turning king's evidence.'

'Now Mrs. Denison told me that the ghost had never been seen, but that it was occasionally heard coming downstairs or going along the passage. She told me that it was never heard except between the hours of two and three in the morning, the hour during which the murder took place.'

'And since then have you heard it again?' I asked.

'Yes, more than once. But it has never frightened me again. I feared, as we all do, what was unknown.'

'I feel that I should fear the known, if I knew it was that,' said I.

'I don't think you would for long. Whatever theory you adopt about it, the sounds of the steps and the groping hand, I cannot see that there is anything to shock or frighten one. My own theory you know — '

'Please apply it to what you heard,' I asked.

'Simply enough. The poor girl felt her way along this passage in the despair of her agonised terror, hearing no doubt the soft footsteps of her murderers gaining on her, as she groped along her lost way. The waves of that terrible brainstorm raging within her, impressed themselves in some subtle yet physical manner on the place. It would only be by those people whom we call sensitives that the wrinkles, so to speak, made by those breaking waves on the sands would be perceived, and by them not always. But they are there, even as when a Marconi apparatus is working the waves are there, though they can only be perceived by a receiver that is in tune. If you believe in brain-waves at all, the explanation is not so difficult.'

'Then the brain-wave is permanent?'

'Every wave of whatever kind leaves its mark, does it not? If you disbelieve the whole thing, shall I give you a room on the route of that poor murdered harmless walker?'

I got up.

'I am very comfortable, thanks, where I am,' I said.

The Other Bed

I had gone out to Switzerland just before Christmas, expecting, from experience, a month of divinely renovating weather, of skating all day in brilliant sun, and basking in the hot frost of that windless atmosphere. Occasionally, as I knew, there might be a snowfall, which would last perhaps for forty-eight hours at the outside, and would be succeeded by another ten days of cloudless perfection, cold even to zero at night, but irradiated all day long by the unflecked splendour of the sun.

Instead the climatic conditions were horrible. Day after day a gale screamed through this upland valley that should have been so windless and serene, bringing with it a tornado of sleet that changed to snow by night. For ten days there was no abatement of it, and evening after evening, as I consulted my barometer, feeling sure that the black finger would show that we were coming to the end of these abominations, I found that it had sunk a little lower yet, till it stayed, like a homing pigeon, on the S of storm. I mention these things in depredation of the story that follows, in order that the intelligent reader may say at once, if he wishes, that all that occurred was merely a result of the malaise of nerves and digestion that perhaps arose from those storm-bound and disturbing conditions. And now to go back to the beginning again.

I had written to engage a room at the Hotel Beau Site, and had been agreeably surprised on arrival to find that for the modest sum of twelve francs a day I was allotted a room on the first floor with two beds in it. Otherwise the hotel was quite full. Fearing to be billeted in a twenty-two franc room, by mistake, I instantly confirmed my arrangements at the bureau. There was no mistake: I had ordered a twelve-franc room and had been given one. The very civil clerk hoped that I was satisfied with it, for otherwise there was nothing vacant. I hastened to say that I was more than satisfied, fearing the fate of Esau.

I arrived about three in the afternoon of a cloudless and glorious day, the last of the series. I hurried down to the rink, having had the prudence to put skates in the forefront of my luggage, and spent a divine but struggling hour or two, coming up to the hotel about sunset. I had letters to write, and after ordering tea to be sent up to my gorgeous apartment, No. 23, on the first floor, I went straight up there.

The door was ajar and — I feel certain I should not even remember this now except in the light of what followed — just as I got close to it, I heard some faint movement inside the room and instinctively knew that my servant was there unpacking. Next moment I was in the room myself, and it was empty. The unpacking had been finished, and everything was neat, orderly, and comfortable. My barometer was on the table, and I observed with dismay that it had gone down nearly half an inch. I did not give another thought to the movement I thought I had heard from outside.

Certainly I had a delightful room for my twelve francs a day. There were, as I have said, two beds in it, on one of which were already laid out my dress-clothes, while night-things were disposed on the other. There were two windows, between which stood a large washing-stand, with plenty of room on it; a sofa with its back to the light stood conveniently near the pipes of central heating, there were a couple of good arm-chairs, a writing table, and, rarest of luxuries, another table, so that every time one had breakfast it was not necessary to pile up a drift of books and papers to make room for the tray. My window looked east, and sunset still flamed on the western faces of the virgin snows, while above, in spite of the dejected barometer, the sky was bare of clouds, and a thin slip of pale crescent moon was swung high among the stars that still burned dimly in these first moments of their kindling. Tea came up for me without delay, and, as I ate, I regarded my surroundings with extreme complacency.

Then, quite suddenly and without cause, I saw that the disposition of the beds would never do; I could not possibly sleep in the bed that my servant had chosen for me, and without pause I jumped up, transferred my dress clothes to the other bed, and put my night things where they had been. It was done breathlessly almost, and not till then did I ask myself why I had done it. I found I had not the slightest idea. I had merely felt that I could not sleep in the other bed. But having made the change I felt perfectly content.

My letters took me an hour or so to finish, and I had yawned and blinked considerably over the last one or two, in part from their inherent dullness, in part from quite natural sleepiness. For I had been in the train for twenty-four hours, and was fresh to these bracing airs which so conduce to appetite, activity, and sleep, and as there was still an hour before I need dress, I lay down on my sofa with a book for excuse, but the intention to slumber as reason. And consciousness ceased as if a tap had been turned off.

Then — I dreamed. I dreamed that my servant came very quietly into the room, to tell me no doubt that it was time to dress. I supposed there were a few minutes to spare yet, and that he saw I was dozing, for, instead of rousing me, he moved quietly about the room, setting things in order. The light appeared to me to be very dim, for I could not see him with any distinctness, indeed, I only knew it was he because it could not be any body else. Then he paused by my washing-stand, which had a shelf for brushes and razors above it, and I saw him take a razor from its case and begin stropping it; the light was strongly reflected on the blade of the razor. He tried the edge once or twice on his thumb-nail, and then to my horror I saw him trying it on his throat. Instantaneously one of those deafening dream-crashes awoke me, and I saw the door half open, and my servant in the very act of coming in. No doubt the opening of the door had constituted the crash.

I had joined a previously-arrived party of five, all of us old friends, and accustomed to see each other often; and at dinner, and afterwards in intervals of bridge, the conversation roamed agreeably over a variety of topics, rocking-turns and the prospects of weather (a thing of vast importance in Switzerland, and not a commonplace subject) and the performances at the opera, and under what circumstances as revealed in dummy's hand, is it justifiable for a player to refuse to return his partner's original lead in no trumps. Then over whisky and soda and the repeated 'last cigarette,' it veered back via the Zantzigs to thought transference and the transference of emotion. Here one of the party, Harry Lambert, put forward the much discussed explanation of haunted houses based on this principle. He put it very concisely.

'Everything that happens,' he said, 'whether it is a step we take, or a thought that crosses our mind, makes some change in its immediate material world. Now the most violent and concentrated emotion we can imagine is the emotion that leads a man to take so extreme a step as killing himself or somebody else. I can easily imagine such a deed so eating into the material scene, the room or the haunted heath, where it happens, that its mark lasts an enormous time. The air rings with the cry of the slain and still drips with his blood. It is not everybody who will perceive it, but sensitives will. By the way, I am sure that man who waits on us at dinner is a sensitive.'

It was already late, and I rose.

'Let us hurry him to the scene of a crime,' I said. 'For myself I shall hurry to the scene of sleep.'

Outside the threatening promise of the barometer was already finding fulfilment, and a cold ugly wind was complaining among the pines, and hooting round the peaks, and snow had begun to fall. The night was thickly overcast, and it seemed as if uneasy presences were going to and fro in the darkness. But there was no use in ill augury, and certainly if we were to be house-bound for a few days I was lucky in having so commodious a lodging. I had plenty to occupy myself with indoors, though I should vastly have preferred to be engaged outside, and in the immediate present how good it was to lie free in a proper bed after a cramped night in the train.

I was half-undressed when there came a tap at my door, and the waiter who had served us at dinner came in carrying a bottle of whisky. He was a tall young fellow, and though I had not noticed him at dinner, I saw at once now, as he stood in the glare of the electric light, what Harry had meant when he said he was sure he was a sensitive. There is no mistaking that look: it is exhibited in a peculiar 'inlooking' of the eye. Those eyes, one knows, see further than the surface . . .

'The bottle of whisky for monsieur,' he said

putting it down on the table.

'But I ordered no whisky,' said I. He looked puzzled.

'Number twenty-three?' he said. Then he glanced at the other bed.

'Ah, for the other gentleman, without doubt,' he said.

'But there is no other gentleman,' said I.

'I am alone here.'

He took up the bottle again.

'Pardon, monsieur,' he said. 'There must be a mistake. I am new here; I only came today.'

'But I thought — '

'Yes?' said I.

'I thought that number twenty-three had ordered a bottle of whisky,' he repeated.

'Goodnight, monsieur, and pardon.'

I got into bed, extinguished the light, and feeling very sleepy and heavy with the oppression, no doubt, of the snow that was coming, expected to fall asleep at once. Instead my mind would not quite go to roost, but kept sleepily stumbling about among the little events of the day, as some tired pedestrian in the dark stumbles over stones instead of lifting his feet. And as I got sleepier it seemed to me that my mind kept moving in a tiny little circle. At one moment it drowsily recollected how I had thought I had heard movement inside my room, at the next it remembered my dream of some figure going stealthily about and stropping a razor, at a third it wondered why this Swiss waiter with the eyes of a 'sensitive' thought that number twenty-three had ordered a bottle of whisky. But at the time I made no guess as to any coherence between these little isolated facts; I only dwelt on them with drowsy persistence. Then a fourth fact came to join the sleepy circle, and I wondered why I had felt a repugnance against using the other bed.

But there was no explanation of this forthcoming, either, and the outlines of thought grew more blurred and hazy, until I lost consciousness altogether.

Next morning began the series of awful days, sleet and snow falling relentlessly with gusts of chilly wind, making any out-of-door amusement next to impossible. The snow was too soft for tobogganing, it balled on the skis, and as for the rink it was but a series of pools of slushy snow.

This in itself, of course, was quite enough to account for any ordinary depression and heaviness of spirit, but all the time I felt there was something more than that to which I owed the utter blackness that hung over those days. I was beset too by fear that at first was only vague, but which gradually became more definite, until it resolved itself into a fear of number twenty-three and in particular a terror of the other bed. I had no notion why or how I was afraid of it, the thing was perfectly causeless, but the shape and the outline of it grew slowly clearer, as detail after detail of ordinary life, each minute and trivial in itself, carved and moulded this fear, till it became definite. Yet the whole thing was so causeless and childish that I could speak to no one of it; I could but assure myself that it was all a figment of nerves disordered by this unseemly weather.

However, as to the details, there were plenty of them. Once I woke up from a strangling nightmare, unable at first to move, but in a panic of terror, believing that I was sleeping in the other bed. More than once, too, awaking before I was called, and getting out of bed to look at the aspect of the morning, I saw with a sense of dreadful misgiving that the bed-clothes on the other bed were strangely disarranged, as if some one had slept there, and smoothed them down afterwards, but not so well as not to give notice of the occupation. So one night I laid a trap, so to speak, for the intruder of which the real object was to calm my own nervousness (for I still told myself that I was frightened of nothing), and tucked in the sheet very carefully, laying the pillow on the top of it. But in the morning it seemed as if my interference had not been to the taste of the occupant, for there was more impatient disorder than usual in the bedclothes, and on the pillow was an indentation, round and rather deep, such as we may see any morning in our own beds. Yet by day these things did not frighten me, but it was when I went to bed at night that I quaked at the thought of further developments.

It happened also from time to time that I wanted something brought me, or wanted my servant. On three or four of these occasions my bell was answered by the 'Sensitive,' as we called him, but the Sensitive, I noticed, never came into the room. He would open the door a chink to receive my order and on returning would again open it a chink to say that my boots, or whatever it was, were at the door. Once I made him come in, but I saw him cross himself as, with a face of icy terror, he stepped into the room, and the sight somehow did not reassure me. Twice also he came up in the evening, when I had not rung at all, even as he came up the first night, and opened the door a chink to say that my bottle of whisky was outside. But the poor fellow was in a state of such bewilderment when I went out and told him that I had not ordered whisky, that I did not press for an explanation. He begged my pardon profusely; he thought a bottle of whisky had been ordered for number twenty-three. It was his mistake, entirely — I should not be charged for it; it must have been the other gentleman. Pardon again; he remembered there was no other gentleman, the other bed was unoccupied.

It was on the night when this happened for the second time that I definitely began to wish that I too was quite certain that the other bed was unoccupied. The ten days of snow and sleet were at an end, and to-night the moon once more, grown from a mere slip to a shining shield, swung serenely among the stars. But though at dinner everyone exhibited an extraordinary change of spirit, with the rising of the barometer and the discharge of this huge snow-fall, the intolerable gloom which had been mine so long but deepened and blackened. The fear was to me now like some statue, nearly finished, modelled by the carving hands of these details, and though it still stood below its moistened sheet, any moment, I felt, the sheet might be twitched away, and I be confronted with it. Twice that evening I had started to go to the bureau, to ask to have a bed made up for me, anywhere, in the billiard-room or the smoking-room, since the hotel was full, but the intolerable childishness of the proceeding revolted me. What was I afraid of? A dream of my own, a mere nightmare? Some fortuitous disarrangement of bed linen? The fact that a Swiss waiter made mistakes about bottles of whisky? It was an impossible cowardice.

But equally impossible that night were billiards or bridge, or any form of diversion. My only salvation seemed to lie in downright hard work, and soon after dinner I went to my room (in order to make my first real counter-move against fear) and sat down solidly to several hours of proof-correcting, a menial and monotonous employment, but one which is necessary, and engages the entire attention. But first I looked thoroughly round the room, to reassure myself, and found all modern and solid; a bright paper of daisies on the wall, a floor parquetted, the hot-water pipes chuckling to themselves in the corner, my bed-clothes turned down for the night, the other bed — The electric light was burning brightly, and there seemed to me to be a curious stain, as of a shadow, on the lower part of the pillow and the top of the sheet, definite and suggestive, and for a moment I stood there again throttled by a nameless terror. Then taking my courage in my hands I went closer and looked at it. Then

I touched it; the sheet, where the stain or shadow was, seemed damp to the hand, so also was the pillow. And then I remembered; I had thrown some wet clothes on the bed before dinner. No doubt that was the reason. And fortified by this extremely simple dissipation of my fear, I sat down and began on my proofs. But my fear had been this, that the stain had not in that first moment looked like the mere greyness of water-moistened linen.

From below, at first came the sound of music, for they were dancing to-night, but I grew absorbed in my work, and only recorded the fact that after a time there was no more music. Steps went along the passages, and I heard the buzz of conversation on landings, and the closing of doors till by degrees the silence became noticeable. The loneliness of night had come.

It was after the silence had become lonely that I made the first pause in my work, and by the watch on my table saw that it was already past midnight. But I had little more to do; another half-hour would see the end of the business, but there were certain notes I had to make for future reference, and my stock of paper was already exhausted. However, I had bought some in the village that afternoon, and it was in the bureau downstairs, where I had left it, when I came in and had subsequently forgotten to bring it upstairs. It would be the work of a minute only to get it.

The electric light had brightened considerably during the last hour, owing no doubt to many burners being put out in the hotel, and as I left the room I saw again the stain on the pillow and sheet of the other bed. I had really forgotten all about it for the last hour, and its presence there came as an unwelcome surprise. Then I remembered the explanation of it, which had struck me before, and for purposes of self-reassurement I again touched it. It was still damp, but — had I got chilly with my work? For it was warm to the hand. Warm, and surely rather sticky. It did not seem like the touch of the water-damp. And at the same moment I knew I was not alone in the room. There was something there, something silent as yet, and as yet invisible. But it was there.

Now for the consolation of persons who are inclined to be fearful, I may say at once that I am in no way brave, but that terror which, God knows, was real enough, was yet so interesting, that interest overruled it. I stood for a moment by the other bed, and, half-consciously only, wiped the hand that had felt the stain, for the touch of it, though all the time I told myself that it was but the touch of the melted snow on the coat I had put there, was unpleasant and unclean. More than that I did not feel, because in the presence of the unknown and the perhaps awful, the sense of curiosity, one of the strongest instincts we have, came to the fore. So, rather eager to get back to my room again, I ran downstairs to get the packet of paper. There was still a light in the bureau, and the Sensitive, on night-duty, I suppose, was sitting there dozing. My entrance did not disturb him, for I had on noiseless felt slippers, and seeing at once the package I was in search of, I took it, and left him still unawakened. That was somehow of a fortifying nature. The Sensitive anyhow could sleep in his hard chair; the occupant of the unoccupied bed was not calling to him to-night.

I closed my door quietly, as one does at night when the house is silent, and sat down at once to open my packet of paper and finish my work. It was wrapped up in an old news-sheet, and struggling with the last of the string that bound it, certain words caught my eye. Also the date at the top of the paper caught my eye, a date nearly a year old, or, to be quite accurate, a date fifty-one weeks old. It was an American paper and what it recorded was this:

'The body of Mr. Silas R. Hume, who committed suicide last week at the Hotel Beau Site, Moulin sur Chalons, is to be buried at his house in Boston, Mass. The inquest held in Switzerland showed that he cut his throat with a razor, in an attack of delirium tremens induced by drink. In the cupboard of his room were found three dozen empty bottles of Scotch whisky . . . '

So far I had read when without warning the electric light went out, and I was left in, what seemed for the moment, absolute darkness. And again I knew I was not alone, and I knew now who it was who was with me in the room.

Then the absolute paralysis of fear seized me. As if a wind had blown over my head, I felt the hair of it stir and rise a little. My eyes also, I suppose, became accustomed to the sudden darkness, for they could now perceive the shape of the furniture in the room from the light of the starlit sky outside. They saw more too than the mere furniture. There was standing by the wash-stand between the two windows a figure, clothed only in night-garments, and its hands moved among the objects on the shelf above the basin. Then with two steps it made a sort of dive for the other bed, which was in shadow. And then the sweat poured on to my forehead.

Though the other bed stood in shadow I could still see dimly, but sufficiently, what was there. The shape of a head lay on the pillow, the shape of an arm lifted its hand to the electric bell that was close by on the wall, and I fancied I could hear it distantly ringing. Then a moment later came hurrying feet up the stairs and along the passage outside, and a quick rapping at my door.

'Monsieur's whisky, monsieur's whisky,' said a voice just outside. 'Pardon, monsieur, I brought it as quickly as I could.'

The impotent paralysis of cold terror was still on me. Once I tried to speak and failed, and still the gentle tapping went on at the door, and the voice telling some one that his whisky was there. Then at a second attempt, I heard a voice which was mine saying hoarsely:

'For God's sake come in; I am alone with it.'

There was the click of a turned door-handle, and as suddenly as it had gone out a few seconds before, the electric light came back again, and the room was in full illumination. I saw a face peer round the corner of the door, but it was at another face I looked, the face of a man sallow and shrunken, who lay in the other bed, staring at me with glazed eyes. He lay high in bed, and his throat was cut from ear to ear; and the lower part of the pillow was soaked in blood, and the sheet streamed with it.

Then suddenly that hideous vision vanished, and there was only a sleepy-eyed waiter looking into the room. But below the sleepiness terror was awake, and his voice shook when he spoke.

'Monsieur rang?' he asked.

No, monsieur had not rung. But monsieur made himself a couch in the billiard-room.

The Thing in the Hall

The following pages are the account given me by Dr. Assheton of the Thing in the Hall. I took notes, as copious as my quickness of hand allowed me, from his dictation, and subsequently read to him this narrative in its transcribed and connected form. This was on the day before his death, which indeed probably occurred within an hour after I had left him, and, as readers of inquests and such atrocious literature may remember, I had to give evidence before the coroner's jury. Only a week before Dr. Assheton had to give similar evidence, but as a medical expert, with regard to the death of his friend, Louis Fielder, which occurred in a manner identical with his own. As a specialist, he said he believed that his friend had committed suicide while of unsound mind, and the verdict was brought in accordingly. But in the inquest held over Dr. Assheton's body, though the verdict eventually returned was the same, there was more room for doubt.

For I was bound to state that only shortly before his death, I read what follows to him; that he corrected me with extreme precision

353

on a few points of detail, that he seemed perfectly himself, and that at the end he used these words:

'I am quite certain as a brain specialist that I am completely sane, and that these things happened not merely in my imagination, but in the external world. If I had to give evidence again about poor Louis, I should be compelled to take a different line. Please put that down at the end of your account, or at the beginning, if it arranges itself better so.'

There will be a few words I must add at the end of this story, and a few words of explanation must precede it. Briefly, they are these.

Francis Assheton and Louis Fielder were up at Cambridge together, and there formed the friendship that lasted nearly till their death. In general attributes no two men could have been less alike, for while Dr. Assheton had become at the age of thirty-five the first and final authority on his subject, which was the functions and diseases of the brain, Louis Fielder at the same age was still on the threshold of achievement. Assheton, apparently without any brilliance at all, had by careful and incessant work arrived at the top of his profession, while Fielder, brilliant at school, brilliant at college and brilliant ever afterwards, had never done anything. He was too eager, so it seemed to his friends, to set about the dreary work of patient investigation and logical deductions; he was for ever guessing and prying, and striking out luminous ideas, which he left burning, so to speak, to illumine the work of others. But at bottom, the two men had this compelling interest in common, namely, an insatiable curiosity after the unknown, perhaps the most potent bond yet devised between the solitary units that make up the race of man. Both — till the end — were absolutely fearless, and Dr. Assheton would sit by the bedside of the man stricken with bubonic plague to note the gradual surge of the tide of disease to the reasoning faculty with the same absorption as Fielder would study X-rays one week, flying machines the next, and spiritualism the third. The rest of the story, I think, explains itself — or does not quite do so. This, anyhow, is what I read to Dr. Assheton, being the connected narrative of what he had himself told me. It is he, of course, who speaks.

'After I returned from Paris, where I had studied under Charcot, I set up practice at home. The general doctrine of hypnotism, suggestion, and cure by such means had been accepted even in London by this time, and, owing to a few papers I had written on the subject, together with my foreign diplomas, I found that I was a busy man almost as soon as I had arrived in town. Louis Fielder had his ideas about how I should make my debut (for he had ideas on every subject, and all of them original), and entreated me to come and live, not in the stronghold of doctors, 'Chloroform Square,' as he called it, but down in Chelsea, where there was a house vacant next his own.

'Who cares where a doctor lives,' he said, 'so long as he cures people? Besides you don't believe in old methods; why believe in old localities? Oh, there is an atmosphere of painless death in Chloroform Square! Come and make people live instead! And on most evenings I shall have so much to tell you; I can't 'drop in' across half London.'

Now if you have been abroad for five years, it is a great deal to know that you have any intimate friend at all still left in the metropolis, and, as Louis said, to have that intimate friend next door is an excellent reason for going next door. Above all, I remembered from Cambridge days, what Louis' 'dropping in' meant. Towards bed-time, when work was over, there would come a rapid step on the landing, and for an hour, or two hours, he would gush with ideas. He simply diffused life, which is ideas, wherever he went. He fed one's brain, which is the one thing which matters. Most people who are ill, are ill because their brain is starving, and the body rebels, and gets lumbago or cancer. That is the chief doctrine of my work such as it has been. All bodily disease springs from the brain. It is merely the brain that has to be fed and rested and exercised properly to make the body absolutely healthy, and immune from all disease. But when the brain is affected, it is as useful to pour medicines down the sink, as make your patient swallow them, unless — and this is a paramount limitation — unless he believes in them.

I said something of the kind to Louis one night, when, at the end of a busy day, I had dined with him. We were sitting over coffee in the hall, or so it is called, where he takes his meals. Outside, his house is just like mine, and ten thousand other small houses in London, but on entering, instead of finding a narrow passage with a door on one side, leading into the dining-room, which again communicates with a small back room called 'the study,' he has had the sense to eliminate all unnecessary walls, and consequently the whole ground floor of his house is one room, with stairs leading up to the first floor. Study, dining-room and passage have been knocked into one; you enter a big room from the front door. The only drawback is that the postman

357

makes loud noises close to you, as you dine, and just as I made these commonplace observations to him about the effect of the brain on the body and the senses, there came a loud rap, somewhere close to me, that was startling.

'You ought to muffle your knocker,' I said, 'anyhow during the time of meals.'

Louis leaned back and laughed.

'There isn't a knocker,' he said. 'You were startled a week ago, and said the same thing. So I took the knocker off. The letters slide in now. But you heard a knock, did you?'

'Didn't you?' said I.

'Why, certainly. But it wasn't the postman. It was the Thing. I don't know what it is. That makes it so interesting.'

Now if there is one thing that the hypnotist, the believer in unexplained influences, detests and despises, it is the whole root-notion of spiritualism. Drugs are not more opposed to his belief than the exploded, discredited idea of the influence of spirits on our lives. And both are discredited for the same reason; it is easy to understand how brain can act on brain, just as it is easy to understand how body can act on body, so that there is no more difficulty in the reception of the idea that the strong mind can direct the weak one, than there is in the fact of a wrestler of greater strength overcoming one of less. But that spirits should rap at furniture and divert the course of events is as absurd as administering phosphorus to strengthen the brain. That was what I thought then.

However, I felt sure it was the postman, and instantly rose and went to the door. There were no letters in the box, and I opened the door. The postman was just ascending the steps. He gave the letters into my hand.

Louis was sipping his coffee when I came back to the table.

'Have you ever tried table-turning?' he asked. 'It's rather odd.'

'No, and I have not tried violet-leaves as a cure for cancer,' I said.

'Oh, try everything,' he said. 'I know that that is your plan, just as it is mine. All these years that you have been away, you have tried all sorts of things, first with no faith, then with just a little faith, and finally with mountain-moving faith. Why, you didn't believe in hypnotism at all when you went to Paris.'

He rang the bell as he spoke, and his servant came up and cleared the table. While this was being done we strolled about the room, looking at prints, with applause for a Bartolozzi that Louis had bought in the New

Cut, and dead silence over a 'Perdita' which he had acquired at considerable cost. Then he sat down again at the table on which we had dined. It was round, and mahogany-heavy, with a central foot divided into claws.

'Try its weight,' he said; 'see if you can push it about.'

So I held the edge of it in my hands, and found that I could just move it. But that was all; it required the exercise of a good deal of strength to stir it.

'Now put your hands on the top of it,' he said, 'and see what you can do.'

I could not do anything, my fingers merely slipped about on it. But I protested at the idea of spending the evening thus.

'I would much sooner play chess or noughts and crosses with you,' I said, 'or even talk about politics, than turn tables. You won't mean to push, nor shall I, but we shall push without meaning to.'

Louis nodded.

'Just a minute,' he said, 'let us both put our fingers only on the top of the table and push for all we are worth, from right to left.'

We pushed. At least I pushed, and I observed his finger-nails. From pink they grew to white, because of the pressure he exercised. So I must assume that he pushed too. Once, as we tried this, the table creaked.

But it did not move.

Then there came a quick peremptory rap, not I thought on the front door, but somewhere in the room.

'It's the Thing,' said he.

To-day, as I speak to you, I suppose it was. But on that evening it seemed only like a challenge. I wanted to demonstrate its absurdity.

'For five years, on and off, I've been studying rank spiritualism,' he said. 'I haven't told you before, because I wanted to lay before you certain phenomena, which I can't explain, but which now seem to me to be at my command. You shall see and hear, and then decide if you will help me.'

'And in order to let me see better, you are proposing to put out the lights,' I said.

'Yes; you will see why.'

'I am here as a sceptic,' said I.

'Scep away,' said he.

Next moment the room was in darkness, except for a very faint glow of firelight. The window-curtains were thick, and no street-illumination penetrated them, and the familiar, cheerful sounds of pedestrians and wheeled traffic came in muffled. I was at the side of the table towards the door; Louis was opposite me, for I could see his figure dimly silhouetted against the glow from the smouldering fire.

'Put your hands on the table,' he said,

'quite lightly, and — how shall I say it — expect.'

Still protesting in spirit, I expected. I could hear his breathing rather quickened, and it seemed to me odd that anybody could find excitement in standing in the dark over a large mahogany table, expecting. Then — through my finger-tips, laid lightly on the table, there began to come a faint vibration, like nothing so much as the vibration through the handle of a kettle when water is beginning to boil inside it. This got gradually more pronounced and violent till it was like the throbbing of a motor-car. It seemed to give off a low humming note. Then quite suddenly the table seemed to slip from under my fingers and began very slowly to revolve.

'Keep your hands on it and move with it,' said Louis, and as he spoke I saw his silhouette pass away from in front of the fire, moving as the table moved.

For some moments there was silence, and we continued, rather absurdly, to circle round, keeping step, so to speak, with the table. Then Louis spoke again, and his voice was trembling with excitement.

'Are you there?' he said.

There was no reply, of course, and he asked it again. This time there came a rap like that which I had thought during dinner to be the

362

postman. But whether it was that the room was dark, or that despite myself I felt rather excited too, it seemed to me now to be far louder than before. Also it appeared to come neither from here nor there, but to be diffused through the room.

Then the curious revolving of the table ceased, but the intense, violent throbbing continued. My eyes were fixed on it, though owing to the darkness I could see nothing, when quite suddenly a little speck of light moved across it, so that for an instant I saw my own hands. Then came another and another, like the spark of matches struck in the dark, or like fire-flies crossing the dusk in southern gardens. Then came another knock of shattering loudness, and the throbbing of the table ceased, and the lights vanished.

Such were the phenomena at the first séance at which I was present, but Fielder, it must be remembered, had been studying, 'expecting,' he called it, for some years. To adopt spiritualistic language (which at that time I was very far from doing), he was the medium, I merely the observer, and all the phenomena I had seen that night were habitually produced or witnessed by him. I make this limitation since he told me that certain of them now appeared to be outside his own control altogether. The knockings

363

would come when his mind, as far as he knew, was entirely occupied in other matters, and sometimes he had even been awakened out of sleep by them. The lights were also independent of his volition.

Now my theory at the time was that all these things were purely subjective in him, and that what he expressed by saying that they were out of his control, meant that they had become fixed and rooted in the unconscious self, of which we know so little, but which, more and more, we see to play so enormous a part in the life of man. In fact, it is not too much to say that the vast majority of our deeds spring, apparently without volition, from this unconscious self. All hearing is the unconscious exercise of the aural nerve, all seeing of the optic, all walking, all ordinary movement seem to be done without the exercise of will on our part. Nay more, should we take to some new form of progression, skating, for instance, the beginner will learn with falls and difficulty the outside edge, but within a few hours of his having learned his balance on it, he will give no more thought to what he learned so short a time ago as an acrobatic feat, than he gives to the placing of one foot before the other.

But to the brain specialist all this was intensely interesting, and to the student of hypnotism, as I was, even more so, for (such was the conclusion I came to after this first séance), the fact that I saw and heard just what Louis saw and heard was an exhibition of thought-transference which in all my experience in the Charcot-schools I had never seen surpassed, if indeed rivalled. I knew that I was myself extremely sensitive to suggestion, and my part in it this evening I believed to be purely that of the receiver of suggestions so vivid that I visualised and heard these phenomena which existed only in the brain of my friend.

We talked over what had occurred upstairs. His view was that the Thing was trying to communicate with us. According to him it was the Thing that moved the table and tapped, and made us see streaks of light.

'Yes, but the Thing,' I interrupted, 'what do you mean? Is it a great-uncle — oh, I have seen so many relatives appear at seances, and heard so many of their dreadful platitudes — or what is it? A spirit? Whose spirit?'

Louis was sitting opposite to me, and on the little table before us there was an electric light. Looking at him I saw the pupil of his eye suddenly dilate. To the medical man — provided that some violent change in the light is not the cause of the dilation — that meant only one thing, terror. But it quickly resumed its normal proportion again.

Then he got up, and stood in front of the fire.

'No. I don't think it is great-uncle anybody,' he said. 'I don't know, as I told you, what the Thing is. But if you ask me what my conjecture is, it is that the Thing is an Elemental.'

'And pray explain further. What is an Elemental?'

Once again his eye dilated.

'It will take two minutes,' he said. 'But, listen. There are good things in this world, are there not, and bad things? Cancer, I take it is bad, and — and fresh air is good; honesty is good, lying is bad. Impulses of some sort direct both sides, and some power suggests the impulses. Well, I went into this spiritualistic business impartially. I learned to 'expect,' to throw open the door into the soul, and I said, 'Anyone may come in.' And I think Something has applied for admission, the Thing that tapped and turned the table and struck matches, as you saw, across it. Now the control of the evil principle in the world is in the hands of a power which entrusts its errands to the things which I call Elementals. Oh, they have been seen; I doubt not that they will be seen again. I did not, and do not ask good spirits to come in. I don't want 'The

Church's one foundation' played on a musical box. Nor do I want an Elemental. I only threw open the door. I believe the Thing has come into my house and is establishing communication with me. Oh, I want to go the whole hog. What is it? In the name of Satan, if necessary, what is it? I just want to know.'

What followed I thought then might easily be an invention of the imagination, but what I believed to have happened was this. A piano with music on it was standing at the far end of the room by the door, and a sudden draught entered the room, so strong that the leaves turned. Next the draught troubled a vase of daffodils, and the yellow heads nodded. Then it reached the candles that stood close to us, and they fluttered burning blue and low. Then it reached me, and the draught was cold, and stirred my hair. Then it eddied, so to speak, and went across to Louis, and his hair also moved, as I could see. Then it went downwards towards the fire, and flames suddenly started up in its path, blown upwards. The rug by the fireplace flapped also.

'Funny, wasn't it?' he asked.

'And has the Elemental gone up the chimney?' said I.

'Oh, no,' said he, 'the Thing only passed us.'

Then suddenly he pointed at the wall just behind my chair, and his voice cracked as he spoke.

'Look, what's that?' he said. 'There on the wall.'

Considerably startled I turned in the direction of his shaking finger. The wall was pale grey in tone, and sharp-cut against it was a shadow that, as I looked, moved. It was like the shadow of some enormous slug, legless and fat, some two feet high by about four feet long. Only at one end of it was a head shaped like the head of a seal, with open mouth and panting tongue.

Then even as I looked it faded, and from somewhere close at hand there sounded another of those shattering knocks.

For a moment after there was silence between us, and horror was thick as snow in the air. But, somehow, neither Louis nor I was frightened for more than one moment. The whole thing was so absorbingly interesting.

'That's what I mean by its being outside my control,' he said. 'I said I was ready for any — any visitor to come in, and by God, we've got a beauty.'

Now I was still, even in spite of the appearance of this shadow, quite convinced that I was only taking observations of a most curious case of disordered brain accompanied by the most vivid and remarkable thought-transference. I believed that I had not seen a slug-like shadow at all, but that Louis had visualised this dreadful creature so intensely that I saw what he saw. I found also that his spiritualistic trash-books, which I thought a truer nomenclature than textbooks, mentioned this as a common form for Elementals to take. He on the other hand was more firmly convinced than ever that we were dealing not with a subjective but an objective phenomenon.

For the next six months or so we sat constantly, but made no further progress, nor did the Thing or its shadow appear again, and I began to feel that we were really wasting time. Then it occurred to me, to get in a so-called medium, induce hypnotic sleep, and see if we could learn anything further. This we did, sitting as before round the dining-room table. The room was not quite dark, and I could see sufficiently clearly what happened.

The medium, a young man, sat between Louis and myself, and without the slightest difficulty I put him into a light hypnotic sleep. Instantly there came a series of the most terrific raps, and across the table there slid something more palpable than a shadow, with a faint luminance about it, as if the surface of it was smouldering. At the moment the medium's face became contorted to a mask of hellish terror; mouth and eyes were both open, and the eyes were focussed on something close to him. The Thing, waving its head, came closer and closer to him, and reached out towards his throat. Then with a yell of panic, and warding off this horror with his hands, the medium sprang up, but It had already caught hold, and for the moment he could not get free. Then simultaneously Louis and I went to his aid, and my hands touched something cold and slimy. But pull as we could we could not get it away. There was no firm hand-hold to be taken; it was as if one tried to grasp slimy fur, and the touch of it was horrible, unclean, like a leper. Then, in a sort of despair, though I still could not believe that the horror was real, for it must be a vision of diseased imagination, I remembered that the switch of the four electric lights was close to my hand. I turned them all on. There on the floor lay the medium, Louis was kneeling by him with a face of wet paper, but there was nothing else there. Only the collar of the medium was crumpled and torn, and on his throat were two scratches that bled.

The medium was still in hypnotic sleep, and I woke him. He felt at his collar, put his hand to his throat and found it bleeding, but, as I expected, knew nothing whatever of what had passed. We told him that there had been an unusual manifestation, and he had, while in sleep, wrestled with something. We had got the result we wished for, and were much obliged to him.

I never saw him again. A week after that he died of blood-poisoning.

From that evening dates the second stage of this adventure. The Thing had materialised (I use again spiritualistic language which I still did not use at the time). The huge slug, the Elemental, manifested itself no longer by knocks and waltzing tables, nor yet by shadows. It was there in a form that could be seen and felt. But it still — this was my strong point — was only a thing of twilight; the sudden kindling of the electric light had shown us that there was nothing there. In this struggle perhaps the medium had clutched his own throat, perhaps I had grasped Louis' sleeve, he mine. But though I said these things to myself, I am not sure that I believed them in the same way that I believe the sun will rise tomorrow.

Now, as a student of brain-functions and a student in hypnotic affairs, I ought perhaps to have steadily and unremittingly pursued this extraordinary series of phenomena, but I had my practice to attend to, and I found that with the best will in the world, I could think of nothing else except the occurrence in the hall next door. So I refused to take part in any further séance with Louis. I had another reason also. For the last four or five months he was becoming depraved. I have been no prude or Puritan in my own life, and I hope I have not turned a Pharisaical shoulder on sinners. But in all branches of life and morals, Louis had become infamous. He was turned out of a club for cheating at cards, and narrated the event to me with gusto. He had become cruel; he tortured his cat to death; he had become bestial. I used to shudder as I passed his house, expecting I knew not what fiendish thing to be looking at me from the window.

Then came a night only a week ago, when I was awakened by an awful cry, swelling and falling and rising again. It came from next door. I ran downstairs in my pyjamas, and out into the street. The policeman on the beat had heard it too, and it came from the hall of Louis' house, the window of which was open. Together we burst the door in. You know what we found. The screaming had ceased but a moment before, but he was dead already. Both jugulars were severed, torn open.

It was dawn, early and dusky when I got back to my house next door. Even as I went in something seemed to push by me, something soft and slimy. It could not be Louis' imagination this time. Since then I have seen glimpses of it every evening. I am awakened at night by tappings, and in the shadows in the corner of my room there sits something more substantial than a shadow.'

Within an hour of my leaving Dr. Assheton, the quiet street was once more aroused by cries of terror and agony. He was already dead, and in no other manner than his friend, when they got into the house.

The House with the Brick-Kiln

The hamlet of Trevor Major lies very lonely and sequestered in a hollow below the north side of the south downs that stretch westward from Lewes, and run parallel with the coast. It is a hamlet of some three or four dozen inconsiderable houses and cottages much girt about with trees, but the big Norman church and the manor house which stands a little outside the village are evidence of a more conspicuous past. This latter, except for a tenancy of rather less than three weeks, now four years ago, has stood unoccupied since the summer of 1896, and though it could be taken at a rent almost comically small, it is highly improbable that either of its last tenants, even if times were very bad, would think of passing a night in it again. For myself — I was one of the tenants — I would far prefer living in a workhouse to inhabiting those low-pitched oak-panelled rooms, and I would sooner look from my garret windows on to the squalor and grime of Whitechapel than from the diamond-shaped and leaded panes of the Manor of Trevor Major on to the boskage of its cool thickets, and the glimmering of its clear chalk streams where the quick trout glance among the waving water-weeds and over the chalk and gravel of its sliding rapids.

It was the news of these trout that led Jack Singleton and myself to take the house for the month between mid-May and mid-June, but as I have already mentioned a short three weeks was all the time we passed there, and we had more than a week of our tenancy yet unexpired when we left the place, though on the very last afternoon we enjoyed the finest dry-fly fishing that has ever fallen to my lot. Singleton had originally seen the advertisement of the house in a Sussex paper, with the statement that there was good dry-fly fishing belonging to it, but it was with but faint hopes of the reality of the dry-fly fishing that we went down to look at the place, since we had before this so often inspected depopulated ditches which were offered to the unwary under high-sounding titles. Yet after a half-hour's stroll by the stream, we went straight back to the agent, and before nightfall had taken it for a month with option of renewal.

We arrived accordingly from town at about five o'clock on a cloudless afternoon in May, and through the mists of horror that now stand between me and the remembrance of what occurred later, I cannot forget the exquisite loveliness of the impression then conveyed. The garden, it is true, appeared to have been for years untended; weeds half-choked the gravel paths, and the flower-beds were a congestion of mingled wild and cultivated vegetations. It was set in a wall of mellowed brick, in which snap-dragon and stone-crop had found an anchorage to their liking, and beyond that there stood sentinel a ring of ancient pines in which the breeze made music as of a distant sea. Outside that the ground sloped slightly downwards in a bank covered with a jungle of wild-rose to the stream that ran round three sides of the garden, and then followed a meandering course through the two big fields which lay towards the village. Over all this we had fishing-rights; above, the same rights extended for another quarter of a mile to the arched bridge over which there crossed the road which led to the house. In this field above the house on the fourth side, where the ground had been embanked to carry the road, stood a brick-kiln in a ruinous state. A shallow pit, long overgrown with tall grasses and wild field-flowers, showed where the clay had been digged.

The house itself was long and narrow; entering, you passed direct into a square panelled hall, on the left of which was the dining-room which communicated with the passage leading to the kitchen and offices. On the right of the hall were two excellent sitting-rooms looking out, the one on to the gravel in front of the house, the other on to the garden. From the first of these you could see, through the gap in the pines by which the road approached the house, the brick-kiln of which I have already spoken. An oak staircase went up from the hall, and round it ran a gallery on to which the three principal bedrooms opened. These were commensurate with the dining-room and the two sitting-rooms below. From this gallery there led a long narrow passage shut off from the rest of the house by a red-baize door, which led to a couple more guest-rooms and the servants' quarters.

Jack Singleton and I share the same flat in town, and we had sent down in the morning Franklyn and his wife, two old and valued servants, to get things ready at Trevor Major, and procure help from the village to look after the house, and Mrs. Franklyn, with her stout comfortable face all wreathed in smiles, opened the door to us. She had had some previous experience of the 'comfortable quarters' which go with fishing, and had come down prepared for the worst, but found it all of the best. The kitchen-boiler was not furred; hot and cold water was laid on in the most convenient fashion, and could be obtained from taps that neither stuck nor leaked. Her husband, it appeared, had gone into the village to buy a few necessaries, and she brought up tea for us, and then went upstairs to the two rooms over the dining-room and bigger sitting-room, which we had chosen for our bedrooms, to unpack. The doors of these were exactly opposite one another to right and left of the gallery, and Jack, who chose the bedroom above the sitting-room, had thus a smaller room, above the second sitting-room, unoccupied, next his and opening out from it.

We had a couple of hours' fishing before dinner, each of us catching three or four brace of trout, and came back in the dusk to the house. Franklyn had returned from the village from his errand, reported that he had got a woman to come in to do housework in the mornings, and mentioned that our arrival had seemed to arouse a good deal of interest. The reason for this was obscure; he could only tell us that he was questioned a dozen times as to whether we really intended to live in the house, and his assurance that we did produced silence and a shaking of heads. But the country-folk of Sussex are notable for their silence and chronic attitude of disapproval, and we put this down to local idiosyncrasy.

The evening was exquisitely warm, and after dinner we pulled out a couple of basket-chairs on to the gravel by the front door, and sat for an hour or so, while the night deepened in throbs of gathering darkness. The moon was not risen and the ring of pines cut off much of the pale starlight, so that when we went in, allured by the shining of the lamp in the sitting-room, it was curiously dark for a clear night in May. And at that moment of stepping from the darkness into the cheerfulness of the lighted house, I had a sudden sensation, to which, during the next fortnight, I became almost accustomed, of there being something unseen and unheard and dreadful near me. In spite of the warmth, I felt myself shiver, and concluded instantly that I had sat out-of-doors long enough, and without mentioning it to Jack, followed him into the smaller sitting-room in which we had scarcely yet set foot. It, like the hall, was oak-panelled, and in the panels hung some half-dozen of water-colour sketches, which we examined, idly at first, and then with growing interest, for they were executed with extraordinary finish and delicacy, and each represented some aspect of the house or garden. Here you looked up the gap in the fir-trees into a crimson sunset; here the garden, trim and carefully tended, dozed beneath some languid summer noon; here an angry wreath of storm-cloud brooded over the meadow where the trout-stream ran grey and leaden below a threatening sky, while another, the most careful and arresting of all, was a study of the brick-kiln. In this, alone of them all, was there a human figure; a man, dressed in grey, peered into the open door from which issued a fierce red glow. The figure was painted with miniature-like elaboration; the face was in profile, and represented a youngish man, clean-shaven, with a long aquiline nose and singularly square chin. The sketch was long and narrow in shape, and the chimney of the kiln appeared against a dark sky. From it there issued a thin stream of grey smoke.

Jack looked at this with attention.

'What a horrible picture!' he said, 'and how beautifully painted! I feel as if it meant something, as if it was a representation of something that happened, not a mere sketch. By Jove! — '

He broke off suddenly and went in turn to each of the other pictures.

'That's a queer thing,' he said. 'See if you notice what I mean.'

With the brick-kiln rather vividly impressed on my mind, it was not difficult to see what he had noticed. In each of the pictures appeared the brick-kiln, chimney and all, now seen faintly between trees, now in full view, and in each the chimney was smoking.

'And the odd part is that from the garden side, you can't really see the kiln at all,' observed Jack, 'it's hidden by the house, and yet the artist F.A., as I see by his signature, puts it in just the same.'

'What do you make of that?' I asked.

'Nothing. I suppose he had a fancy for brick-kilns. Let's have a game of picquet.'

A fortnight of our three weeks passed without incident, except that again and again the curious feeling of something dreadful being close at hand was present in my mind. In a way, as I said, I got used to it, but on the other hand the feeling itself seemed to gain in poignancy. Once just at the end of the fortnight I mentioned it to Jack.

'Odd you should speak of it,' he said, 'because I've felt the same. When do you feel it? Do you feel it now, for instance?'

We were again sitting out after dinner, and as he spoke I felt it with far greater intensity than ever before. And at the same moment the house-door which had been closed, though probably not latched, swung gently open, letting out a shaft of light from the hall, and as gently swung to again, as if something had stealthily entered.

'Yes,' I said. 'I felt it then. I only feel it in the evening. It was rather bad that time.'

Jack was silent a moment.

'Funny thing the door opening and shutting like that,' he said. 'Let's go indoors.'

We got up and I remember seeing at that moment that the windows of my bedroom were lit; Mrs. Franklyn probably was making things ready for the night. Simultaneously, as we crossed the gravel, there came from just inside the house the sound of a hurried footstep on the stairs, and entering we found Mrs. Franklyn in the hall, looking rather white and startled.

'Anything wrong?' I asked.

She took two or three quick breaths before she answered:

'No, sir,' she said, 'at least nothing that I can give an account of. I was tidying up in your room, and I thought you came in. But there was nobody, and it gave me a turn. I left my candle there; I must go up for it.'

I waited in the hall a moment, while she again ascended the stairs, and passed along the gallery to my room. At the door, which I could see was open, she paused, not entering.

'What is the matter?' I asked from below.

'I left the candle alight,' she said, 'and it's gone out.' Jack laughed.

'And you left the door and window open,' said he.

'Yes, sir, but not a breath of wind is stirring,' said Mrs. Franklyn, rather faintly.

This was true, and yet a few moments ago the heavy hall-door had swung open and back again. Jack ran upstairs.

'We'll brave the dark together, Mrs. Franklyn,' he said.

He went into my room, and I heard the sound of a match struck. Then through the open door came the light of the rekindled candle and simultaneously I heard a bell ring in the servants' quarters. In a moment came steps, and Franklyn appeared.

'What bell was that?' I asked.

'Mr. Jack's bedroom, sir,' he said.

I felt there was a marked atmosphere of nerves about for which there was really no adequate cause. All that had happened of a disturbing nature was that Mrs. Franklyn had thought I had come into my bedroom, and had been startled by finding I had not. She had then left the candle in a draught, and it had been blown out. As for a bell ringing, that, even if it had happened, was a very innocuous proceeding.

'Mouse on a wire,' I said. 'Mr. Jack is in my room this moment lighting Mrs. Franklyn's candle for her.'

386

Jack came down at this juncture, and we went into the sitting-room. But Franklyn apparently was not satisfied, for we heard him in the room above us, which was Jack's bedroom, moving about with his slow and rather ponderous tread. Then his steps seemed to pass into the bedroom adjoining and we heard no more.

I remember feeling hugely sleepy that night, and went to bed earlier than usual, to pass rather a broken night with stretches of dreamless sleep interspersed with startled awakenings, in which I passed very suddenly into complete consciousness. Sometimes the house was absolutely still, and the only sound to be heard was the sighing of the night breeze outside in the pines, but sometimes the place seemed full of muffled movements and once I could have sworn that the handle of my door turned. That required verification, and I lit my candle, but found that my ears must have played me false. Yet even as I stood there, I thought I heard steps just outside, and with a considerable qualm, I must confess, I opened the door and looked out. But the gallery was quite empty, and the house quite still. Then from Jack's room opposite I heard a sound that was somehow comforting, the snorts of the snorer, and I went back to bed and slept again, and when next I woke, morning was already breaking in red lines on the horizon, and the sense of trouble that had been with me ever since last evening had gone.

Heavy rain set in after lunch next day, and as I had arrears of letter-writing to do, and the water was soon both muddy and rising, I came home alone about five, leaving Jack still sanguine by the stream, and worked for a couple of hours sitting at a writing-table in the room overlooking the gravel at the front of the house, where hung the water-colours. By seven I had finished, and just as I got up to light candles, since it was already dusk, I saw, as I thought, Jack's figure emerge from the bushes that bordered the path to the stream, on to the space in front of the house. Then instantaneously and with a sudden queer sinking of the heart quite unaccountable, I saw that it was not Jack at all, but a stranger. He was only some six yards from the window, and after pausing there a moment he came close up to the window, so that his face nearly touched the glass, looking intently at me. In the light from the freshly-kindled candles I could distinguish his features with great clearness, but though, as far as I knew, I had never seen him before, there was something familiar about both his face and figure. He appeared to smile at me, but the

388

smile was one of inscrutable evil and malevolence, and immediately he walked on, straight towards the house door opposite him, and out of sight of the sitting-room window.

Now, little though I liked the look of the man, he was, as I have said, familiar to my eye, and I went out into the hall, since he was clearly coming to the front door, to open it to him and learn his business. So without waiting for him to ring, I opened it, feeling sure I should find him on the step. Instead, I looked out into the empty gravel-sweep, the heavy-falling rain, the thick dusk.

And even as I looked, I felt something that I could not see push by me through the half-opened door and pass into the house. Then the stairs creaked, and a moment after a bell rang.

Franklyn is the quickest man to answer a bell I have ever seen, and next instant he passed me going upstairs. He tapped at Jack's door, entered and then came down again.

'Mr. Jack still out, sir?' he asked.

'Yes. His bell ringing again?'

'Yes, sir,' said Franklyn, quite imperturbably.

I went back into the sitting-room, and soon Franklyn brought a lamp. He put it on the table above which hung the careful and curious picture of the brick-kiln, and then with a sudden horror I saw why the stranger on the gravel outside had been so familiar to me. In all respects he resembled the figure that peered into the kiln; it was more than a resemblance, it was an identity.

And what had happened to this man who had inscrutably and evilly smiled at me? And what had pushed in through the half-closed door?

At that moment I saw the face of Fear; my mouth went dry, and I heard my heart leaping and cracking in my throat. That face was only turned on me for a moment, and then away again, but I knew it to be the genuine thing; not apprehension, not foreboding, not a feeling of being startled, but Fear, cold Fear. And then though nothing had occurred to assuage the Fear, it passed, and a certain sort of reason usurped — for so I must say — its place. I had certainly seen somebody on the gravel outside the house; I had supposed he was going to the front door. I had opened it, and found he had not come to the front door. Or — and once again the terror resurged — had the invisible pushing thing been that which I had seen outside? And if so, what was it? And how came it that the face and figure of the man I had seen were the same as those which were so scrupulously painted in the picture of the brick-kiln?

I set myself to argue down the Fear for which there was no more foundation than this, this and the repetition of the ringing bell, and my belief is that I did so. I told myself, till I believed it, that a man — a human man — had been walking across the gravel outside, and that he had not come to the front door but had gone, as he might easily have done, up the drive into the high-road.

I told myself that it was mere fancy that was the cause of the belief that Something had pushed in by me, and as for the ringing of the bell, I said to myself, as was true, that this had happened before. And I must ask the reader to believe also that I argued these things away, and looked no longer on the face of Fear itself. I was not comfortable, but I fell short of being terrified.

I sat down again by the window looking on to the gravel in front of the house, and finding another letter that asked, though it did not demand, an answer, proceeded to occupy myself with it. Straight in front led the drive through the gap in the pines, and passed through the field where lay the brick-kiln. In a pause of page-turning I looked up and saw something unusual about it; at the same moment an unusual smell came to my nostril. What I saw was smoke coming out of the chimney of the kiln, what I smelt was the odour of roasting meat. The wind — such as there was — set from the kiln to the house. But as far as I knew the smell of roast meat probably came from the kitchen where dinner, so I supposed, was cooking. I had to tell myself this: I wanted reassurance, lest the face of Fear should look whitely on me again.

Then there came a crisp step on the gravel, a rattle at the front door, and Jack came in.

'Good sport,' he said, 'you gave up too soon.'

And he went straight to the table above which hung the picture of the man at the brick-kiln, and looked at it. Then there was silence; and eventually I spoke, for I wanted to know one thing.

'Seen anybody?' I asked.

'Yes. Why do you ask?'

'Because I have also; the man in that picture.'

Jack came and sat down near me.

'It's a ghost, you know,' he said. 'He came down to the river about dusk and stood near me for an hour. At first I thought he was real — was real, and I warned him that he had better stand further off if he didn't want to be hooked. And then it struck me he wasn't real, and I cast, well, right through him, and about seven he walked up towards the house.'

'Were you frightened?'

'No. It was so tremendously interesting. So you saw him here too. Whereabouts?'

'Just outside. I think he is in the house now.'

Jack looked round.

'Did you see him come in?' he asked.

'No, but I felt him. There's another queer thing too; the chimney of the brick-kiln is smoking.'

Jack looked out of the window. It was nearly dark, but the wreathing smoke could just be seen.

'So it is,' he said, 'fat, greasy smoke. I think I'll go up and see what's on. Come too?'

'I think not,' I said.

'Are you frightened? It isn't worth while. Besides, it is so tremendously interesting.'

Jack came back from his little expedition still interested. He had found nothing stirring at the kiln, but though it was then nearly dark the interior was faintly luminous, and against the black of the sky he could see a wisp of thick white smoke floating northwards. But for the rest of the evening we neither heard nor saw anything of abnormal import, and the next day ran a course of undisturbed hours. Then suddenly a hellish activity was manifested.

That night, while I was undressing for bed, I heard a bell ring furiously, and I thought I heard a shout also. I guessed where the ring came from, since Franklyn and his wife had long ago gone to bed, and went straight to Jack's room. But as I tapped at the door I heard his voice from inside calling loud to me. 'Take care,' it said, 'he's close to the door.'

A sudden qualm of blank fear took hold of me, but mastering it as best I could, I opened the door to enter, and once again something pushed softly by me, though I saw nothing.

Jack was standing by his bed, half-undressed — I saw him wipe his forehead with the back of his hand.

'He's been here again,' he said. 'I was standing just here, a minute ago, when I found him close by me. He came out of the inner room, I think. Did you see what he had in his hand?'

'I saw nothing.'

'It was a knife; a great long carving knife. Do you mind my sleeping on the sofa in your room to-night? I got an awful turn then. There was another thing too. All round the edge of his clothes, at his collar and at his wrists, there were little flames playing, little white licking flames.' But next day, again, we neither heard nor saw anything, nor that night did the sense of that dreadful presence in the house come to us. And then came the last day. We had been out till it was dark, and as I said, had a wonderful day among the fish. On reaching home we sat together in the sitting-room, when suddenly from overhead came a tread of feet, a violent pealing of the bell, and the moment after yell after yell as of someone in mortal agony. The thought occurred to both of us that this might be Mrs. Franklyn in terror of some fearful sight, and together we rushed up and sprang into Jack's bedroom.

The doorway into the room beyond was open, and just inside it we saw the man bending over some dark huddled object. Though the room was dark we could see him perfectly, for a light stale and impure seemed to come from him. He had again a long knife in his hand, and as we entered he was wiping it on the mass that lay at his feet. Then he took it up, and we saw what it was, a woman with head nearly severed. But it was not Mrs. Franklyn.

And then the whole thing vanished, and we were standing looking into a dark and empty room. We went downstairs without a word, and it was not till we were both in the sitting-room below that Jack spoke.

'And he takes her to the brick-kiln,' he said rather unsteadily.

'I say, have you had enough of this house? I

have. There is hell in it.'

About a week later Jack put into my hand a guide-book to Sussex open at the description of Trevor Major, and I read:

'Just outside the village stands the picturesque manor house, once the home of the artist and notorious murderer, Francis Adam. It was here he killed his wife, in a fit, it is believed, of groundless jealousy, cutting her throat and disposing of her remains by burning them in a brick-kiln.'

'Certain charred fragments found six months afterwards led to his arrest and execution.'

So I prefer to leave the house with the brick-kiln and the pictures signed F. A. to others.

The Terror by Night

The transference of emotion is a phenomenon so common, so constantly witnessed,
that mankind in general have long ceased
to be conscious of its existence, as a thing
worth our wonder or consideration, regarding
it as being as natural and commonplace as
the transference of things that act by the
ascertained laws of matter. Nobody, for
instance, is surprised, if when the room is too
hot, the opening of a window causes the cold
fresh air of outside to be transferred into the
room, and in the same way no one is
surprised when into the same room, perhaps,
which we will imagine as being peopled with
dull and gloomy persons, there enters some
one of fresh and sunny mind, who instantly
brings into the stuffy mental atmosphere a
change analogous to that of the opened
windows. Exactly how this infection is
conveyed we do not know; considering the
wireless wonders (that act by material laws)
which are already beginning to lose their
wonder now that we have our newspaper
brought as a matter of course every morning
in mid-Atlantic, it would not perhaps be rash

to conjecture that in some subtle and occult way the transference of emotion is in reality material too. Certainly (to take another instance) the sight of definitely material things, like writing on a page, conveys emotion apparently direct to our minds, as when our pleasure or pity is stirred by a book, and it is therefore possible that mind may act on mind by means as material as that.

Occasionally, however, we come across phenomena which, though they may easily be as material as any of these things, are rarer, and therefore more astounding. Some people call them ghosts, some conjuring tricks, and some nonsense. It seems simpler to group them under the head of transferred emotions, and they may appeal to any of the senses. Some ghosts are seen, some heard, some felt, and though I know of no instance of a ghost being tasted, yet it will seem in the following pages that these occult phenomena may appeal at any rate to the senses that perceive heat, cold, or smell. For, to take the analogy of wireless telegraphy, we are all of us probably 'receivers' to some extent, and catch now and then a message or part of a message that the eternal waves of emotion are ceaselessly shouting aloud to those who have ears to hear, and materialising themselves for those who have eyes to see. Not being, as a rule, perfectly tuned, we grasp but pieces and fragments of such messages, a few coherent words it may be, or a few words which seem to have no sense. The following story, however, to my mind, is interesting, because it shows how different pieces of what no doubt was one message were received and recorded by several different people simultaneously. Ten years have elapsed since the events recorded took place, but they were written down at the time.

Jack Lorimer and I were very old friends before he married, and his marriage to a first cousin of mine did not make, as so often happens, a slackening in our intimacy. Within a few months after, it was found out that his wife had consumption, and, without any loss of time, she was sent off to Davos, with her sister to look after her. The disease had evidently been detected at a very early stage, and there was excellent ground for hoping that with proper care and strict regime she would be cured by the life-giving frosts of that wonderful valley.

The two had gone out in the November of which I am speaking, and Jack and I joined them for a month at Christmas, and found that week after week she was steadily and quickly gaining ground. We had to be back in town by the end of January, but it was settled that Ida should remain out with her sister for a week or two more. They both, I remember, came down to the station to see us off, and I am not likely to forget the last words that passed:

'Oh, don't look so woebegone, Jack,' his wife had said; 'you'll see me again before long.'

Then the fussy little mountain engine squeaked, as a puppy squeaks when its toe is trodden on, and we puffed our way up the pass.

London was in its usual desperate February plight when we got back, full of fogs and still-born frosts that seemed to produce a cold far more bitter than the piercing temperature of those sunny altitudes from which we had come. We both, I think, felt rather lonely, and even before we had got to our journey's end we had settled that for the present it was ridiculous that we should keep open two houses when one would suffice, and would also be far more cheerful for us both.

So, as we both lived in almost identical houses in the same street in Chelsea, we decided to 'toss,' live in the house which the coin indicated (heads mine, tails his), share expenses, attempt to let the other house, and, if successful, share the proceeds. A French five-franc piece of the Second Empire told us it was 'heads.'

We had been back some ten days, receiving

402

every day the most excellent accounts from Davos, when, first on him, then on me, there descended, like some tropical storm, a feeling of indefinable fear. Very possibly this sense of apprehension (for there is nothing in the world so virulently infectious) reached me through him: on the other hand both these attacks of vague foreboding may have come from the same source. But it is true that it did not attack me till he spoke of it, so the possibility perhaps inclines to my having caught it from him. He spoke of it first, I remember, one evening when we had met for a good-night talk, after having come back from separate houses where we had dined.

'I have felt most awfully down all day,' he said; 'and just after receiving this splendid account from Daisy, I can't think what is the matter.'

He poured himself out some whisky and soda as he spoke.

'Oh, touch of liver,' I said. 'I shouldn't drink that if I were you. Give it me instead.'

'I was never better in my life,' he said.

I was opening letters, as we talked, and came across one from the house agent, which, with trembling eagerness, I read.

'Hurrah,' I cried, 'offer of five gu as — why can't he write it in proper English — five guineas a week till Easter for number 31. We shall roll in guineas!'

'Oh, but I can't stop here till Easter,' he said.

'I don't see why not. Nor by the way does Daisy. I heard from her this morning, and she told me to persuade you to stop. That's to say, if you like. It really is more cheerful for you here. I forgot, you were telling me something.'

The glorious news about the weekly guineas did not cheer him up in the least.

'Thanks awfully. Of course I'll stop.'

He moved up and down the room once or twice.

'No, it's not me that is wrong,' he said, 'it's It, whatever It is. The terror by night.'

'Which you are commanded not to be afraid of,' I remarked.

'I know; it's easy commanding. I'm frightened: something's coming.'

'Five guineas a week are coming,' I said. 'I shan't sit up and be infected by your fears. All that matters, Davos, is going as well as it can. What was the last report? Incredibly better. Take that to bed with you.'

The infection — if infection it was — did not take hold of me then, for I remember going to sleep feeling quite cheerful, but I awoke in some dark still house and It, the terror by night, had come while I slept. Fear and misgiving, blind, unreasonable, and paralysing, had taken and gripped me. What was it? Just as by an aneroid we can foretell the approach of storm, so by this sinking of the spirit, unlike anything I had ever felt before, I felt sure that disaster of some sort was presaged.

Jack saw it at once when we met at breakfast next morning, in the brown haggard light of a foggy day, not dark enough for candles, but dismal beyond all telling.

'So it has come to you too,' he said.

And I had not even the fighting-power left to tell him that I was merely slightly unwell.

Besides, never in my life had I felt better.

All next day, all the day after that fear lay like a black cloak over my mind; I did not know what I dreaded, but it was something very acute, something that was very near. It was coming nearer every moment, spreading like a pall of clouds over the sky; but on the third day, after miserably cowering under it, I suppose some sort of courage came back to me: either this was pure imagination, some trick of disordered nerves or what not, in which case we were both 'disquieting ourselves in vain,' or from the immeasurable waves of emotion that beat upon the minds of men, something within both of us had caught a current, a pressure. In either case it was infinitely better to try, however ineffectively, to stand up against it. For these two days I had neither worked nor played; I had only shrunk and shuddered; I planned for myself a busy day, with diversion for us both in the evening.

'We will dine early,' I said, 'and go to the 'Man from Blankley's.' I have already asked Philip to come, and he is coming, and I have telephoned for tickets. Dinner at seven.'

Philip, I may remark, is an old friend of ours, neighbour in this street, and by profession a much-respected doctor.

Jack laid down his paper.

'Yes, I expect you're right,' he said. 'It's no use doing nothing, it doesn't help things. Did you sleep well?'

'Yes, beautifully,' I said rather snappishly, for I was all on edge with the added burden of an almost sleepless night.

'I wish I had,' said he.

This would not do at all.

'We have got to play up!' I said. 'Here are we two strong and stalwart persons, with as much cause for satisfaction with life as any you can mention, letting ourselves behave like worms. Our fear may be over things imaginary or over things that are real, but it is the fact of being afraid that is so despicable. There is nothing in the world to fear except fear. You know that as well as I do. Now let's read our papers with interest. Which do you back, Mr. Druce, or the Duke of Portland, or the Times Book Club?'

That day, therefore, passed very busily for me; and there were enough events moving in front of that black background, which I was conscious was there all the time, to enable me to keep my eyes away from it, and I was detained rather late at the office, and had to drive back to Chelsea, in order to be in time to dress for dinner instead of walking back as I had intended.

Then the message, which for these three days had been twittering in our minds, the receivers, just making them quiver and rattle, came through.

I found Jack already dressed, since it was within a minute or two of seven when I got in, and sitting in the drawing-room. The day had been warm and muggy, but when I looked in on the way up to my room, it seemed to me to have grown suddenly and bitterly cold, not with the dampness of English frost, but with the clear and stinging exhilaration of such days as we had recently spent in Switzerland. Fire was laid in the grate but not lit, and I went down on my knees on the hearth-rug to light it.

'Why, it's freezing in here,' I said. 'What

donkeys servants are! It never occurs to them that you want fires in cold weather, and no fires in hot weather.'

'Oh, for heaven's sake don't light the fire,' said he, 'it's the warmest muggiest evening I ever remember.'

I stared at him in astonishment. My hands were shaking with the cold. He saw this.

'Why, you are shivering!' he said. 'Have you caught a chill? But as to the room being cold let us look at the thermometer.'

There was one on the writing-table.

'Sixty-five,' he said.

There was no disputing that, nor did I want to, for at that moment it suddenly struck us, dimly and distantly, that It was 'coming through.' I felt it like some curious internal vibration.

'Hot or cold, I must go and dress,' I said.

Still shivering, but feeling as if I was breathing some rarefied exhilarating air, I went up to my room. My clothes were already laid out, but, by an oversight, no hot water had been brought up, and I rang for my man. He came up almost at once, but he looked scared, or, to my already-startled senses, he appeared so.

'What's the matter?' I said.

'Nothing, sir,' he said, and he could hardly articulate the words. 'I thought you rang.'

'Yes. Hot water. But what's the matter?'

He shifted from one foot to the other.

'I thought I saw a lady on the stairs,' he said, 'coming up close behind me. And the front-door bell hadn't rung that I heard.'

'Where did you think you saw her?' I asked.

'On the stairs. Then on the landing outside the drawing-room door, sir,' he said. 'She stood there as if she didn't know whether to go in or not.'

'One — one of the servants,' I said. But again I felt that It was coming through.

'No, sir. It was none of the servants,' he said.

'Who was it then?'

'Couldn't see distinctly, sir, it was dim-like. But I thought it was Mrs. Lorimer.'

'Oh, go and get me some hot water,' I said.

But he lingered; he was quite clearly frightened.

At this moment the front door bell rang. It was just seven, and already Philip had come with brutal punctuality while I was not yet half dressed.

'That's Dr. Enderly,' I said. 'Perhaps if he is on the stairs you may be able to pass the place where you saw the lady.'

Then quite suddenly there rang through the house a scream, so terrible, so appalling in its agony and supreme terror, that I simply stood still and shuddered, unable to move. Then by an effort so violent that I felt as if something must break, I recalled the power of motion, and ran downstairs, my man at my heels, to meet Philip who was running up from the ground floor. He had heard it too.

'What's the matter?' he said. 'What was that?'

Together we went into the drawing-room. Jack was lying in front of the fireplace, with the chair in which he had been sitting a few minutes before overturned. Philip went straight to him and bent over him, tearing open his white shirt.

'Open all the windows,' he said, 'the place reeks.'

We flung open the windows, and there poured in so it seemed to me, a stream of hot air into the bitter cold. Eventually Philip got up.

'He is dead,' he said. 'Keep the windows open. The place is still thick with chloroform.'

Gradually to my sense the room got warmer, to Philip's the drug-laden atmosphere dispersed.

But neither my servant nor I had smelt anything at all.

A couple of hours later there came a telegram from Davos for me. It was to tell me to break the news of Daisy's death to Jack, and was sent by her sister. She supposed he would. come out immediately. But he had been gone two hours now.

I left for Davos next day, and learned what had happened. Daisy had been suffering for three days from a little abscess which had to be opened, and, though the operation was of the slightest, she had been so nervous about it that the doctor gave her chloroform. She made a good recovery from the anaesthetic, but an hour later had a sudden attack of syncope, and had died that night at a few minutes before eight, by Central European time, corresponding to seven in English time. She had insisted that Jack should be told nothing about this little operation till it was over, since the matter was quite unconnected with her general health, and she did not wish to cause him needless anxiety.

And there the story ends. To my servant there came the sight of a woman outside the drawing-room door, where Jack was, hesitating about her entrance, at the moment when Daisy's soul hovered between the two worlds; to me there came — I do not think it is fanciful to suppose this — the keen exhilarating cold of Davos; to Philip there came the fumes of chloroform. And to Jack, I must suppose, came his wife. So he joined her.